PRAISE FOR

'*A Loyal Traitor* is a thoroughly gripping spy thriller. Tim Glister puts the reader at the heart of the Cold War and captures the high stakes paranoia of the era brilliantly.'

Adam Hamdy, author of *Black 13*

'There is a ruthless female killer at large, sightings of a Soviet submarine and ambitious KGB officers fomenting audacious coups. All this and references to Harry Palmer and *The Day of the Jackal*, cram the stage with scenery before a climax at the Royal Opera House.'

The Times, thriller of the month

'*A Loyal Traitor* is an accomplished and atmospheric spy novel with an original protagonist and a burning question at its heart. Considered and entertaining, I was drawn in from page one.'

Charlotte Philby, author of *A Double Life*

'Stunningly authentic, masterfully plotted and brilliantly composed, this is historical thriller writing at its very best.'

Matthew Richardson, author of *The Insider*

'Original, gritty and compelling, *A Loyal Traitor* cements Glister's reputation as a master storyteller. Fans of John le Carré will love this!'

Awais Khan, author of *No Honour*

'Intelligent, involving and gripping… The jigsaw pieces of the complex plot are picture-perfect.'

Choice Magazine, hardback of the month

'The plot is fast-paced, with plenty of tension and action.'

Mystery People

'It is incredibly satisfying reading a follow-up that not only matches but surpasses the original… This is superior stuff. A lean, intelligent espionage thriller skilfully rendering not just the messy truth of Cold War operations, but the intimate emotional toll of such work.' Dominic Nolan, author of *Vine Street*

'Tim Glister is creating such an elegant and vivid style of his own. This is another pitch-perfect portrayal of a Cold War crisis. A distinctive and fascinating thriller, which I hugely enjoyed.'
Holly Watt, author of *To the Lions*

'A brilliantly convoluted plot with layer on layer of subplot at every turn.' *Shots* Magazine

PRAISE FOR *RED CORONA*

'Relentless and sleek. This pitch-perfect debut – a gripping espionage thriller in the vein of Charles Cumming, Tom Rob Smith and Mick Herron – signals the arrival of a remarkable talent.'
A.J. Finn, author of *The Woman in the Window*

'Catchy title! Actually, *Red Corona* has nothing to do with viruses, but the space race in 1961… An entertaining, not to say nostalgic, espionage thriller.' *The Times* and *Sunday Times* Crime Club

'A thoroughly engaging spy thriller that had me gripped from start to finish and left me desperate for more!'
S.J. Watson, author of *Before I Go to Sleep*

'Thrills by the bucket… An entertaining blend of Le Carré-like in-house establishment rivalries and sheer propulsive action reminiscent of Len Deighton.' Maxim Jakubowski

A LOYAL TRAITOR

TIM GLISTER

A Point Blank Book

First published in Great Britain, Australia and the Republic of Ireland by Point Blank,
an imprint of Oneworld Publications, 2022
This mass market paperback edition published 2022

Copyright © Tim Glister, 2022

The moral right of Tim Glister to be identified as the Author of this work has been
asserted by him in accordance with the Copyright, Designs, and Patents Act 1988

All rights reserved
Copyright under Berne Convention
A CIP record for this title is available from the British Library

ISBN 978-0-86154-168-3
ISBN 978-0-86154-167-6 (ebook)

Typeset in Janson MT 12/15pt by Geethik Technologies
Printed and bound in Great Britain by Clays Ltd, Elcograf S.p.A.

This book is a work of fiction. Names, characters, businesses,
organizations, places, and events are either the product of the author's
imagination or are used fictitiously. Any resemblance to actual
persons, living or dead, events, or locales is entirely coincidental.

Oneworld Publications
10 Bloomsbury Street
London WC1B 3SR
England

Stay up to date with the latest books,
special offers, and exclusive content from
Oneworld with our newsletter

Sign up on our website
oneworld-publications.com/point-blank

PROLOGUE

Stalin was dead, and Khrushchev was gone.

It was thirteen years since the great man who was both the one true son and father of the Soviet Union had been found on the bedroom floor of his dacha, semi-conscious and slowly dying from a brain haemorrhage. And it was five months since his liberal-minded but increasingly erratic successor had been forced into retirement by the ambitious troika of Aleksei Kosygin, Leonid Brezhnev, and Nikolai Podgorny.

The three new leaders were still struggling to calm a skittish nation and cement their grip on the vast power they'd claimed. Their preferred technique was taking every opportunity they could find to borrow from the collective memory of Stalin's ultimate authority, which was why an unofficial week of mourning had been declared to mark the anniversary of his death.

It was a time of sombre, private reflection and the occasional public outburst. Cities, towns and villages across Russia had fallen near silent, and Moscow was no exception. Its streets were quiet. Its children were suddenly neither seen nor heard, forced to stay inside and watch the drifts of snow that had filled their parks and playgrounds all winter finally start to melt. And its adults shuffled soundlessly to the buses, trams, and trains that would take them to work and bring them home again. No one lingered outside after sunset as the temperature dropped back below freezing, not even the city's sizeable but officially non-existent homeless population. Even they were off somewhere quietly drinking or crying to the memory of Stalin.

So, the resident of Zavodskoy Poyezd, 6, was entirely alone as they stepped out of the five-storey tenement at 8 p.m., gently closed the door behind them and made their way the short distance to Izmaylovskaya metro station.

Zavodskoy Poyezd, 6, with its flaking yellow plaster and scattered, unused balconies, was one of a hundred identical buildings all over Moscow. And its latest inhabitant, who had moved into one of its ground-floor apartments a week ago, looked like one of the thousands of workers who crossed the city every day, with their heavy coat wrapped round their body, thick gloves covering their hands, and a rabbit-fur hat pulled down low over their brow.

The metro rumbled along the edge of the vast, dark forest that separated Izmaylovo and Ivanovskoye districts, before plunging underground into the tunnel that took the M3 line into the heart of the Soviet capital.

The train only had one passenger, and only one pair of boots stepped down onto the tiled platform at Arbatskaya station and walked through its long, vaulted concourse hung with bronze chandeliers.

The streets around Arbatskaya were as deserted as everywhere else. It took the lone traveller ten minutes to reach their destination: a small mansion set back behind the Tchaikovsky Conservatory. And just another five to kill everyone inside.

A light knock brought the father of the house to the front door, and a quick flash of the blade hidden in the arm of the assassin's coat sliced his throat and severed his vocal cords. Leather-wrapped hands grabbed the man by his shoulders, silently lowering him onto the rug that ran the length of the hallway as blood seeped from the thick red line across his neck and trickled down his trachea and into his lungs. The man was still alive as the assassin left him on the floor and moved deeper into the house, but he wouldn't be for long.

The mansion was warm and elegantly appointed – the kind of place reserved for a member of the nomenklatura who preferred to walk to their office in the State Kremlin Palace rather than drive in from one of the city's outer suburbs every morning.

The assassin followed the lingering aroma of stewed meat and warm bread through the dining room into the kitchen.

The wife of the dying man turned from the sink at the sound of unfamiliar feet behind her. Unlike her husband, she managed to let out a deep, loud and terrified scream before the bloody blade plunged into her stomach and the china plate she'd been washing smashed on the floor. She stared at the assassin as the knife was pulled from her soft, fleshy belly and then, to spare her a long and agonising death, stabbed into the side of her neck, severing her carotid artery. Her body slumped down onto the floor, a spray of red smearing the grey marble of the counter.

The assassin held the long blade under the tap that was still running with scalding water, watching the blood of two people swirl into the suds and down the drain, before leaving it to dry with the rest of the cutlery and going upstairs.

In the first bedroom was a large bed and an empty crib. In the next one, the assassin found the crib's occupant, a six-month-old girl, held in the arms of her eight-year-old brother. The baby was silent, contentedly wriggling in her sibling's arms, unaware of the tragedy that was befalling her family. The boy was doing his best to hide how scared he was, but the assassin could see the tears on his cheeks and the damp stain that ran down the leg of his pyjamas.

There was nowhere the boy and his sister could run, no nook or cupboard they could hide in. The assassin stepped into the room, causing the floorboards to creak and the boy to whimper. He was paralysed with fear, and did nothing to stop the assassin gently lifting the baby out of his arms and delicately placing her on the blanket that covered her brother's small, narrow bed. He also didn't move when his own head was cradled for a moment before the sharp, swift twist that snapped his neck.

The baby could have been left to live, but those weren't the assassin's orders. So the gloved fingers tucked the girl under her brother's blanket, and held the edge of it over her mouth and nose until she stopped wriggling.

Then the heavy boots walked downstairs, past the body of the father, whose blood had started to stain the hall rug, and back out into the cold night.

By 10 p.m. the assassin was back in the empty bedroom of the ground-floor apartment at Zavodskoy Poyezd, 6, lying on a thin mattress, eyes staring at the ceiling and focusing on nothing. Sleep rarely came easily after a murder. But it wasn't guilt or pride that kept the assassin awake, it was just simple adrenaline.

They didn't know what the man in the house had done to deserve the annihilation of his whole family, or that the orders to kill them all had been sent direct from a member of the troika itself. These minor details were irrelevant, and soon enough there'd be a new mission that would require the assassin's full attention.

MARCH 1966

CHAPTER 1

It took a full minute of polite hammering to rouse Richard Knox from his deep, dead sleep.

He had no clue who wanted him so urgently, or where he was. But, as he slowly let the increasingly loud knocking wake him up, he started to remember.

He recalled the long journey back to London a week ago from the joint intelligence conference with the Americans and Australians about the Venona Project in Sydney. Then the three rushed days in Leconfield House, MI5's headquarters on Curzon Street in Mayfair. A flight across the Atlantic to Ottawa. His meetings with the Canadian Directorate of Security and Intelligence. And two more flights that took him first to Vancouver and then to Victoria, the tiny capital of British Columbia nestled on the southern tip of Vancouver Island.

'Okay, I'm coming,' he shouted at the door as he rolled across the expansive bed he'd been lying on, face down and fully clothed.

He looked at his watch – a 1956 Omega with a silver body and tan leather strap – and his disorientation immediately turned to anger.

Knox had arrived at The Empress, the grand chateau-esque hotel that dominated Victoria Harbour next to the British Columbia Parliament building, after 1 a.m. He'd asked the night manager for a wake-up call at 4 p.m. His body was exhausted from all his recent travelling and he needed to give it some time to recover. But he also had an appointment to keep. His watch said it was ten past seven. Could his jet lag really have made him sleep for almost eighteen hours?

He threw open a set of heavy brocade curtains, wincing as light flooded through the windows and lit up the room. Knox hadn't paid much attention to the small suite when he'd checked in – he'd been too tired to notice anything but the bed – but he now saw that whoever had decorated The Empress's bedchambers had seen fit to cover every surface in them with rich patterns and clashing embroidery. He didn't like it.

He straightened his jumper and ran his hands through his thick mop of black hair as he walked over to the door and prepared to hurl some very strong words at whoever was on the other side of it.

'I asked for a wake-up call at four,' he told the teenage bellboy he found waiting for him in the corridor in a stiff, maroon uniform.

'Yes, sir,' the starched young man replied. 'The manager sent me up when no one answered.'

'Well, you took your time.'

'Excuse me?' The bellboy was too young to mask his confusion. 'The manager tried for ten minutes, then I came straight up.'

That didn't make sense to Knox, until his still half-asleep brain reminded him that it was March, he was in Canada, and it was still light outside.

'What's the time difference between here and Ottawa?' he asked.

'Three hours,' the young man replied without having to think about it.

'That sounds about right,' Knox said. 'Sorry for being short with you. And thank you for checking on me.'

'No problem at all, sir,' the bellboy replied, both his voice and shoulders noticeably relieved by the abrupt change in Knox's tone.

Knox felt a pang in his stomach. If it was just after four o'clock then he'd still slept for fourteen hours. He was hungry.

'Where can I get some food?' he asked.

'The lobby lounge is open. Or I could arrange room service.'

'The lounge will be fine.' Knox had never enjoyed eating in the same room he slept in.

'If that's everything, sir?' the bellboy asked.

'Yes, and thank you again,' Knox replied.

They stared at each other in silence for an awkward moment before Knox realised the teenager was probably waiting for a tip for being his human alarm clock – and for putting up with his short temper. But by the time he retrieved his wallet from the coat he'd flung across the desk next to his bed the bellboy had disappeared.

Twenty minutes and a cold shower later, Knox walked into the lobby lounge in a fresh pair of dark trousers and a muted olive green jumper, with his wool coat over his arm.

The hotel's designer had exercised considerably more restraint here. The large space was bright, light, and calm. The polished wood floor was bathed in late-afternoon sun and dotted with white columns, tall plants, and small tables occupied almost exclusively by couples devouring miniature sandwiches. Knox had arrived in the middle of afternoon tea.

He picked an empty spot that looked out over the hotel's front lawn and across the harbour. A moment later a waitress appeared. Her uniform looked as rigid as the bellboy's, and her face as young.

'Will you be joining us for afternoon tea?' she asked.

Knox nodded.

'And what would you like today?' she continued. 'We have twenty-one varieties at The Empress. Earl Grey, Darjeeling, Assam, Lapsang Souchong, Ceylon Orange Pekoe, Rose Pouchong—'

Knox held up his hand to stop her. 'Coffee will be fine.'

The waitress departed, and Knox turned his attention to the window and the water beyond it. A large ferry was pulling up to its moorings as smaller ones, each no larger than a delivery van, criss-crossed the harbour. Occasionally, the boats were joined by a sight that couldn't be witnessed anywhere else on the planet: planes. Victoria Harbour wasn't just a seaport, it was also an international airport – the only one in the world whose runway was made of water.

Seaplanes arrived and left from the docks just a few yards in front of The Empress. Some made the short hop over to Vancouver and back, others the slightly longer one over the border with America to Seattle. And a few privately owned ones did both, whenever they wanted. Knox had been sent all the way from London to find one particular plane that fell into that last category.

He'd taken the half-hour trip from Vancouver to Victoria himself the night before. His recent travels around the world had mostly cured his old fears of flying – a result of living in London through the Blitz, then being shuttled between combat zones in military transports in the last days of World War Two. But, seeing how small and flimsy the seaplanes looked in the light of day, he was glad his first experience in one had been under cover of darkness.

Knox's selection of sandwiches, which were delivered on a three-tiered gold and china plate stand, were delicious. The coffee, unfortunately, was not. It was too weak, and there was far too much of it – a subtle sign, Knox thought, that betrayed how popular Vancouver Island had become with American holidaymakers.

The couple at the next table got up to leave and, keeping an eye on the harbour, Knox reached over and picked up the papers they'd left behind.

The local taste in coffee might have owed more to Canada's closest neighbour than her European heritage, but her news definitely didn't. The front-page headlines were split between two stories. First, the continued reeling about the snap election Harold Wilson, the British Labour Prime Minister, had called last month in a desperate – or sensible, depending on which editorial you read – attempt to increase his single-figure majority in the Commons. And second, the latest problems Ian Smith was stirring up in Rhodesia, which had recently declared independence, severed ties with Britain and – again, depending on the paper – seemed to be trying its best to derail the polite and orderly decline of the Empire.

Knox frowned. This didn't feel like the time for one of MI5's most senior officers to be plane-spotting over cucumber sandwiches at the edge of the world. But, if Knox was entirely honest with himself, he didn't mind as much as he should. He was tired. More tired than he should be. And it wasn't the kind of tiredness that fourteen hours of sleep could fix. It was the kind that meant something fundamental in his life might have to change soon.

Knox had been sent all this way 'for a chat'. Those had been the exact words James Holland, the director general of MI5 and Knox's patron and friend of twenty years, had used during his brief London stopover.

'A chat with whom?' Knox had asked, sitting in Holland's office, next to his own on the fifth floor of Leconfield House.

'Sir Guy Northcott,' Holland replied.

'I recognise the name. The textile magnate.'

'Whose advancements in industrial fabric design earned him a knighthood.'

'Industrial fabric design?'

'Uniforms,' Holland said. 'Fire-retardant, quick-drying, thermal. If you work for the armed forces, the police or the NHS you've worn something dreamed up by Northcott.'

'Are we putting in an order for the Watchers?' Knox asked.

The Watchers were MI5's leg men, a combination of courier and street spy the Service used to monitor low-level targets. For years, Knox had been trying to stop them wearing their unofficial and highly recognisable livery of dark grey suits and beige mackintoshes, with little success.

Holland ignored his deputy's joke and continued. 'It's a rather delicate matter, actually. Ever since Golitsyn defected and spilled the beans about the Cambridge traitors, the Americans have been getting increasingly paranoid about undocumented people sneaking around the place.'

Knox could sense the irritation starting to slip through Holland's words. The DG had more than enough to deal with at home and, unusually for MI5, abroad, without jittery allies adding to it – he needed someone to take whatever this problem was off his plate, and that someone was Knox.

'What's that got to do with Northcott?' Knox asked.

'He officially retired five years ago. Fancied travelling the world on a quest for global peace and understanding, according to an article the *Telegraph* wrote about it. He settled on Vancouver Island, spending his days hiking in the woods or flying around in his seaplane. The problem is, he never files a flight plan and almost always has a young male passenger with him, a different one each trip who apparently is never seen again.'

'So the Americans think he's up to no good?'

'The Americans don't trust anyone interested in universal brotherhood. Concerns have been quietly raised. They've never been happy about the Soviet Union being so close to them over there, or about how open their border with Canada is.'

'But they're not sure enough to take matters into their own hands and work out exactly what he's doing,' Knox said.

'Just enough to ask us to do it for them,' Holland replied with a sigh.

And that was why Knox was now in Victoria, waiting for a seaplane to turn up, so he could ask a knight of the realm if he was smuggling Soviet agents through America's back door.

CHAPTER 2

Knox buttoned up his coat as he stepped out of The Empress's ivy-clad entrance. It was a sunny afternoon, but spring was taking its time to arrive on Canada's Pacific coast. He could have stayed at his window table, watching the harbour, for the rest of the day, but he didn't want to run the risk of Northcott arriving at the dock and leaving again before he had the chance to introduce himself. He also didn't fancy drinking any more of the lounge's coffee.

To Knox's left, across two manicured lawns bordered with stunted bulbs, was the Parliament building. It was even more grandiose than The Empress, with imposing domes rather than faux turrets on its roof. The harbour stretched round to his right, curving widely through the heart of Victoria before eventually carving a narrow path up deep into the island.

He crossed over the road that separated the hotel from the dock and took up a position at the top of the steps that led down to the row of floating jetties. Thanks to Northcott's lack of flight plan Knox had no idea when he'd appear, but according to the Canadian Directorate of Security and Intelligence he always returned to Victoria before sunset. That was in two and a half hours. Already feeling the cold start to seep through his boots, Knox hoped it would be sooner.

Normally a job like this one would fall to the security liaison officer stationed in Ottawa – one of the ranks of junior MI5 agents assigned to assist Britain's former colonies with their internal security. Unfortunately, Canada's SLO had been recalled to London two weeks ago after falling prey to a KGB provocation.

According to the brief and rather gruff precis Holland had given Knox, the SLO – who had only been in Ottawa for six months – had been tricked into believing the Ralliement National, a right-wing political party campaigning for independence in Quebec, was secretly being funded by the Soviets. When he escalated it, the KGB claimed innocence, and the Ralliement National exclaimed their offence at British interference in their affairs both officially and loudly. Political tensions across Canada increased, and MI5 had egg on its face, which was exactly what the KGB had intended.

Knox watched the small ferries dance their way across the calm of the harbour. Every ten minutes or so a seaplane momentarily interrupted their ballet. He watched six come and go, cutting direct lines between the dock and the outer harbour where they had a long enough stretch of water to take off and land. None of them were Northcott's.

Knox had been given the make and registration of his seaplane in Ottawa and, when he'd pointed out that he wasn't an aviation expert, a description too. He was looking for a yellow fuselage with a pair of vivid turquoise wings strapped across the top of it. Northcott, he was told, was hard to miss.

Finally, just as Knox was beginning to consider retreating back into The Empress he spotted a flash of bright blue turn into the inner harbour.

He walked down to the floating jetty as the seaplane pulled alongside it, cut its engines and stopped its twin rotor blades spinning. The door of the cockpit opened and Knox got his first proper look at Sir Guy Northcott. His file photo in Leconfield House had shown a fairly unremarkable businessman in his late sixties with neat hair, clean-shaven, wearing a sombre, expensive-looking suit. The man climbing down the steps cut into the side of his plane looked the complete opposite. His long, grey hair was slicked back from his heavily bearded face, and he wore a thick, roll-neck jumper. He looked like he should be crewing a fishing trawler somewhere in the North Sea.

Another man followed him out of the plane. He was another opposite. Where the older man looked relaxed, confident in his own skin and world, his younger companion seemed utterly terrified. He was thin, almost frail, his hair roughly cut short against his skull. He couldn't have been a day over twenty, and his wide eyes darted round, looking for signs of danger in everything they saw. He wore frayed slacks and a thin leather jacket, and held a canvas duffle bag to his chest.

'Sir Guy?' Knox said, pulling his hand out of his coat pocket and extending it towards Northcott.

'It's a while since anyone called me that,' Northcott replied, shaking Knox's hand as an easy smile creased the skin at the edges of his mouth and eyes.

He turned to the young man, who was instinctively backing away from Knox. 'It's okay, Jimmy. This fellow's a Brit. Nothing for you to worry about. Jimmy Furlock, meet...?'

'Richard Knox,' Knox said, nodding at Furlock and then turning back to Northcott. 'And I'm sorry to interrupt your afternoon, but I was wondering if you had a few moments to talk.'

Northcott's eyes narrowed a fraction, and he glanced at Furlock again. He looked a little less anxious, but he was also starting to shiver.

'Why not,' Northcott said to Knox, still grinning. 'But let's find somewhere a bit warmer.'

He pointed past Knox at a large Lincoln Continental that was idling at the kerbside where Knox had been moments before.

Twenty minutes later Knox, Northcott and Furlock were in the drawing room of Northcott's house. It sat high up on a private, fence-ringed bluff overlooking the Haro Strait, and was surprisingly modest – two storeys in the North American style that blended huge panels of smooth glass with consciously rough blocks of wood and stone.

'That rock over there is Sidney Island, which is in Canada,' Northcott said, pointing through the large windows that faced the strait. 'And that one on the right is San Juan, which is in America. The Sunday sailors can never keep it right in their heads and are always accidentally crossing the border. More coffee, Richard?'

'Thank you,' Knox replied, offering up his cup.

Northcott shared Knox's appreciation for rich beans, served short and strong.

'So,' Northcott said. 'Who have I upset now?'

'Would you prefer to discuss this in private?' Knox asked, subtly tilting his head towards Furlock, who was sitting hunched at the end of a leather chesterfield across from Knox's high-backed chair, eyes still wide and scared. His cup sat untouched on the low coffee table in front of him.

'No need,' Northcott replied. 'We're all friends here, aren't we?'

Knox nodded as he took a sip of his coffee. 'Some questions have been asked about your recent flights, and your passengers,' he said.

Furlock's eyes grew even wider and he pushed himself further into the corner of the sofa.

'I was wondering when people were going to notice. But I thought it would be someone a little more local.' Northcott gave Furlock a reassuring look. 'Tell me, Richard, did you fight in the war?'

'I did,' he replied. 'In France.'

'I didn't,' Northcott said. 'I wasn't allowed. I was deemed too valuable. It was more important for me to make outfits for people like you to die in than get my own hands dirty. But I did my part, and it was a righteous war, wasn't it?'

'I think so,' Knox replied, wary of the direction Northcott was suddenly steering the conversation.

'Of course you do. We won. Righteousness is our prerogative.' Northcott took a deep gulp of his coffee. 'And what do you think about Vietnam?'

'It's not my war,' Knox said.

'It's not America's either, really. It's certainly not Jimmy's. But it's still scarred him for life. Have you ever been injured for the causes you believe in, Richard?'

It was another surprisingly direct question, and one Knox had been asked before. The first time had been over a bottle of wine in a restaurant on the Île Saint-Louis in Paris twenty-two years ago by another high-born Brit. A man who wasn't all that dissimilar from Northcott, and who had become one of Knox's closest friends – a friend Knox thought about every day even though he'd been dead for seven years.

'A couple of times.' Knox thought about the old gash across the top of his head a delirious, half-starved German soldier had given him during the war, and the more recent scar on his chest, put there by a kidnapped Russian scientist who had almost shot him through the heart five years ago.

'Jimmy,' Northcott said, 'take your jacket off.'

Reluctantly, Furlock pulled his arms out of his jacket sleeves and shrugged it off his shoulders. He looked even more gaunt in just the white T-shirt he was wearing underneath. Knox noticed first that the T-shirt was stained with sweat and dirt, and second that Furlock's arms were both covered in the raised welts of knife cuts and what he guessed were cigarette burns.

'Jimmy shouldn't be here. He should be face down in the jungle somewhere outside Saigon. But the will to live is strong, especially when there's no bloody reason for you to die. Jimmy wouldn't mind me saying he's not a fighter. Violence isn't in his soul. But he's strong. His will carried him all the way from Dallas to the west coast. He hitched rides with people who hadn't really wanted to help him, slept in doorways and woke up to boots in his stomach.'

Northcott sat down next to Furlock as he shifted awkwardly under Knox's gaze.

'His family had disowned him when he wouldn't volunteer to be thrown on his country's rubbish heap of a war,' Northcott continued, smiling again at the young man. 'But he didn't give up. And I think it's only fair that someone doesn't give up on him. You might not be able to see it, Richard, but Jimmy's damn brave.'

'I think I do,' Knox replied, as he quickly processed Northcott's revelation.

The old knight wasn't spending his retirement sneaking Russians agents over the border into America after all. He was running a secret airborne railroad to get young draft dodgers out of it.

CHAPTER 3

Abey Bennett pulled her right foot out of the invisible patch of thick mud it had been slowly sinking into for the last five minutes and frowned as she tried to make out her boot's newly distorted and clumped outline in the dark.

'This doesn't smell right,' she said, her voice barely above a whisper.

'It's a prisoner exchange in the jungle in the middle of the night,' Tripp Warren replied, his voice low too. 'How right is it supposed to smell?'

The two junior CIA field agents scanned the thick vegetation in front of them before turning back to the mouth of the cave behind them. Theoretically they were supposed to be guarding it, but with only one pistol and one torch between them they wouldn't be able to do much if what was about to happen went sour.

Inside the cave were more CIA agents, with more torches and more guns, and a bruised and drugged Haitian man.

It was a heavy, sweltering night, and the only thing that stopped Bennett from feeling entirely bitter about being left out in the open, and being the one holding the torch and not the gun, was that it was a fraction of a degree cooler in the clearing.

The cave was just north of the town of Banica, and just on the right-hand side of the border that divided the island of Hispaniola between Haiti to the west and the Dominican Republic to the east. It was a sacred place, the Cerro de San Francisco, where Christians from all over the Caribbean pilgrimaged to stand under the water that dripped from its roof and smear their faces with the limestone dust from its walls. But this evening it was being used for purposes far less holy.

Bennett flashed light at a sudden movement in the trees, but dropped the beam when nothing emerged into the open. In fact, they hadn't seen a single startled boar or curious bat since they'd arrived over an hour ago. Nature, it seemed, was giving the Cerro de San Francisco a wide berth this evening.

The two junior agents looked like inverts of each other. Bennett's tanned skin and dark hair revealed her part Kiowa Native American heritage, while Warren's ice blond hair and alabaster complexion betrayed his Northern European ancestry. The only feature they shared was piercing blue eyes. Bennett was also about a decade older than Warren, but her diminutive stature and short, pixie haircut went some way to obscuring the age difference.

'We shouldn't be doing this,' Bennett said.

Warren shrugged. 'Sometimes the enemy of our enemy is our friend.'

'But we're friends with the Dominicans, and Papa Doc hates both of us.'

François 'Papa Doc' Duvalier, the leader of Haiti, who had made himself President For Life two years ago, had never had a good relationship with the Dominican Republic or the United States, who he thought lavished an unfair amount of attention – and financial aid – on his next-door neighbour.

'I meant Castro. We still owe Papa Doc for supporting the trade embargo,' Warren said, adding 'even if he is a nutjob tinpot' under his breath.

There was another rustle in the trees. This time Bennett's torch lit up a string of hard faces stepping out of the jungle. Six men, all in the green khaki uniforms of the Tonton Macoute – Duvalier's secret police and personal death squad. Five of the men carried Kalashnikovs, their hands tight round the grips and barrels of their rifles. The sixth man held a thick rope that pulled another prisoner behind him. This man was white, covered in roughly twice as many bruises as Bennett had seen on the Haitian being guarded in the cave, and filthy with dirt. He looked like he'd been dragged all the way from Port-au-Prince.

The Macoutes walked straight past Bennett and Warren, not even bothering to give them the most cursory of glances.

Inside the cave the atmosphere immediately changed from hot and anxious to hot and tense. The CIA agents kept their eyes on the Macoutes, and they kept theirs on the man kneeling on the floor. Even in his drugged state he seemed to sense the men around him stiffen, and recognised the new arrivals as they came to a halt in the glow of the torches. His eyes bulged with fear and he tried to scrabble away from them, but his body was too weak.

Bennett wasn't supposed to know who the CIA's prisoner was, but she did. He was Guillaume Asselin, a minor deputy of Clément Barbot, the ex-head of the Tonton Macoute. Barbot had briefly assumed power in Haiti after Duvalier suffered a massive heart attack in 1959. When Duvalier had recovered and reclaimed the presidency, he accused Barbot of plotting to overthrow him, and had the Macoutes execute their leader. Duvalier's memory was long and murderous, and seven years later he was still hunting down Barbot's associates.

One of the Americans broke from the semicircle that had formed around Asselin and stepped forward towards the Macoutes. He was Jay Gibson, currently the most senior US intelligence officer on Hispaniola. Like the other agents, he was struggling with the heat the cave had trapped from the day, but he refused to wipe the sweat off his forehead or pull at the shirt that was stuck to his chest and back.

Gibson was a thick man, a college quarterback once upon a time who now seemed to carry most of his weight in his chest and shoulders by sheer stubbornness. He was about twice the size of the Haitian who broke from their line to square up to him. This Macoute looked the same as the others – his uniform shirt was unbuttoned halfway, revealing his lean, muscled chest. But unlike the others he now let his gun hang on its strap across his shoulder, and had a pistol clipped to his belt. He didn't need to be ready to defend himself against the Americans; his men would do that for him.

'We were told he wouldn't be harmed,' Gibson said, gesturing at the battered man with the rope digging into his wrists.

From her position at the mouth of the cave, Bennett could see that the Macoutes' prisoner wasn't as terrified as Asselin, but not by much. She also had no idea who he was, and she didn't like that.

The Macoute leader just stared at Gibson.

'Give him to us,' he said eventually.

His accent was a mix of French and Haitian Creole, and his mouth glinted in the torchlight – both of his rows of teeth were completely gold.

Gibson looked at him for a long, silent moment. Then he blinked first.

'Let's get on with this,' he said, seemingly to everyone in the cave.

Two CIA agents pulled Asselin off the ground, holding him up as his legs refused to carry his weight.

'This isn't right,' Bennett said to Warren. 'We have to stop this.'

'That isn't our job,' Warren replied.

Bennett and Warren's orders had been to keep watch in case more Macoutes were waiting for their friends out in the night. They shouldn't even have been watching what was going on in the cave, but neither of them had been able to keep their eyes off the Haitians since they'd arrived. And now Bennett couldn't just keep watching, or stop her legs from carrying her into the Cerro de San Francisco.

The sound of her boots added another echo to the Macoutes's, who were already turning away from the other CIA agents, two of them dragging Asselin between them. The others gripped their Kalashnikovs tighter as Bennett got closer.

'Stop,' she said, her voice reverberating around the two groups of men.

The Macoutes kept walking.

'Stand down, agent,' Gibson said. His voice was as loud as hers, and as angry.

Bennett stood her ground, but the mouth of the cave was too wide for her to block the Macoutes. They just snaked around her. Their leader was the last to leave the cave. He gave Bennett a wide, golden grin as he passed her, and made a show of pulling his pistol from his belt.

She watched as the Haitians reached the treeline. Three of them immediately disappeared into the dark, but the two carrying Asselin paused at the edge of the jungle, waiting for their leader. When he reached them, he raised his pistol.

Bennett started after him. But she felt a hand on her shoulder holding her back. It was Warren. All she could do was watch as Asselin was shot point-blank through the head. The sound of the single bullet smashing through skull filled the air. Then the two Macoutes pulled Asselin's lifeless body into the trees, and their leader gave the Americans one last vicious grin before he vanished after them.

CHAPTER 4

Knox wasn't scheduled to leave Victoria until the next afternoon, in case he'd needed more than one chat with Northcott. He hadn't.

He spent less than an hour at the errant knight's house on the bluff, much to Furlock's relief, then was driven back to The Empress in the Lincoln. He had an early dinner of steak and a Chilean Malbec in the hotel's ostentatious restaurant, then retired to his room. Unfortunately, even though his body was still shattered, and he'd polished off the whole bottle of wine in under an hour, his sleep was brief and fitful.

In the morning, Knox wandered Victoria's streets looking for something to fill his time. A few blocks from the hotel he stumbled on a cinema that was showing an early screening of the recent adaptation of John le Carré's *The Spy Who Came in from the Cold.* Given the outside temperature was still hovering around freezing, he took the hint.

The auditorium was narrow, sloped, and empty. Knox had his pick of seats. He chose one in the middle of a row near the back and settled in.

The film was slow, meditative, and depressingly realistic. James Bond had been running round a technicolour world entertaining moviegoers for the last five years, but Richard Burton's black and white Alec Leamas and le Carré's story full of schemes and machinations that cost too many people their lives and achieved vanishingly little felt far more familiar to Knox.

On his short hop to Vancouver, Knox thought about Burton, slumped on the floor of a prison cell staring up at the man who had betrayed him and trying to work out exactly whose web he'd been caught in. Then on his Air Canada flight to Toronto he let his mind work through his long trip and brief encounter with Northcott.

A younger Knox would have been disgusted by Furlock, branded him a coward and told him to go back to America and accept his duty, like he'd done in 1944. But, as Northcott had said, that had been a just war. Everyone Knox fought side by side with understood why they were there: to protect freedom and defend the world against tyranny. But it was hard to say the same thing about America's decade-long conflict in Vietnam.

For ten bloody years, thousands of young lives and millions of dollars had been spent failing to drive communism out of South East Asia. If anything it had spread, establishing footholds in Laos and Cambodia as well. The longer the war dragged on, the less people were sure why America was there in the first place. Some people even morbidly joked that it was only because their troop carriers had gone the wrong way when they'd left Korea in 1953. Public opinion was starting to turn.

So was Knox's, and not just about Vietnam.

When Holland had asked him to become a soldier in the new Cold War, Knox had jumped at the chance to continue serving his country. But that was twenty years ago, and now he couldn't escape the feeling that he'd ended up caught in a perpetual stalemate, a war of paranoid attrition and meaningless skirmishes.

Northcott might not have been smuggling Soviet agents into America, but someone, somewhere would be, or pretending to to keep the CIA and FBI on edge and chasing phantoms. America would be doing exactly the same, turning disgruntled Soviet military attachés or low-level members of KGB *residenturas* wherever they could. And both would be gleefully sneaking people over the Berlin Wall while complaining it had been the other side's belligerence that had somehow willed almost a hundred miles of concrete, barbed wire, and no-man's-land into existence between Germany's Federal and Democratic Republics.

Britain would be doing its part too, keeping extremely close tabs on the secret forces at work in the hearts of her allies and enemies.

Knox was still a soldier, still doing his duty. But his conviction no longer felt entirely total or unquestioning. As his plane started its descent outside Toronto, his mind went again to Burton raging behind the wheel of a car at Claire Bloom about the dirty work he'd been unknowingly forced to do. He thought too about Northcott's refusal to tell him where Furlock and all the men before him went after they landed in Victoria, and his own to press for the information. Maybe they were all holed up somewhere in Vancouver, waiting for fake Canadian passports. Maybe they headed east as soon as they could, and tried their luck on the ranches and farms of the vast prairies that stretched across the country. Wherever they disappeared to, Knox didn't want to be the one responsible for hunting them down.

His visit to Canada had been both fruitless and pointless. And so, really, had his trip to Australia.

The Venona Project had been decrypting old Soviet communications for twenty years, hunting for traitors long hidden and often long gone. It had been instrumental in identifying Russian assets working in the West, like Klaus Fuchs, the German physicist who had been stealing classified information from the Manhattan Project, and Guy Burgess and Donald Maclean, the Cambridge students-turned-diplomats who had suddenly defected to Moscow in 1951, followed twelve years later by their comrade, MI6 officer Kim Philby. But its successes were always historic, retroactive, and Knox still couldn't really see the point in flying all the way to Canberra to spend four days locked in a conference room with the Australians and Americans while everyone congratulated each other for uncovering yet another nefarious but minor plot years after it had done its damage.

Canada, Australia, and how many other of his trips around the Commonwealth had meant nothing and delivered less?

Knox had a couple of hours in Toronto Airport before his BOAC flight to London, so he found a bar and ordered a whisky. He hoped the spirit might do what last night's Malbec had failed to and help him sleep on the overnight flight.

Shortly before he was called to board the man at the bar next to him got up, leaving behind the paper he'd been reading. Out of habit, Knox reached over and scanned the front page. More rumours about the election, more criticism of Smith and what was happening in the Empire's latest ex-colony. He didn't bother reading beyond the headlines, and instead just folded the paper in half, dropped it on the bar in front of the empty seat next to him, and cradled the last of his whisky as he waited for his flight number to be announced.

CHAPTER 5

Knox's Boeing 707 landed at London Airport early the next morning. He didn't go straight to MI5 headquarters after he'd gone through passport control and collected his luggage. Instead, he picked up his gunmetal-grey E-type Jaguar from the car park, skirted the edge of the capital and headed north.

Knox had never seen the need for a car living in London, but for the last two years he'd been dividing what little time he spent in Britain between the city and the country, so one had become a necessity.

Rabley Heath was an old manor house nestled in a forest on a hill in Hertfordshire. It wasn't as significant as nearby Knebworth House, or Hatfield, but it had still made an impact on the local geography as the catalyst for a village to spread along the wooded lanes that led to its gates.

It was a mongrel of a house. Originally a Jacobean hall dating back to 1605, its tall, ornate red brick facade had become flanked by two Georgian wings of columned York stone in the early 1800s. The most recent addition to it – a low-slung modernist extension that ran the entire length of the rear of the house – had been built in the late thirties, just before the outbreak of the war. The cream box had wide sash windows that gave visitors uninterrupted views of the impressive grounds, and an enormous parquet floor that was sprung for dancing. But it had been a long time since anyone had thrown a party at Rabley Heath.

It was always a strange homecoming for Knox, returning to a place where he lived but that wasn't really his.

Rabley Heath belonged to the family of Jack Williams. Williams was the man Northcott had reminded Knox of. The man who had been Knox's closest friend for fifteen years. The man who had joined Knox in MI5 after they met over wine and war stories during the strange days after the liberation of Paris. And the man Knox had sent to his death seven years ago.

Williams's parents, who'd sired their only child late in life, had both died shortly after the war. Williams had been the last scion of his line, but he was also not legally dead. Officially he was missing in action, which meant that Rabley Heath had been left standing empty and slowly turning to rack and ruin until the family's septuagenarian solicitor, unable to sell the house as it fell further into decay, wrote to Knox begging for his help.

Williams had used to joke that Rabley Heath wasn't so special.

'I'm from where the trains going places are still speeding up,' he'd say.

But he and Knox had spent years of happy, hungover weekend afternoons in its cavernous rooms and overgrown gardens, Williams slowly teaching Knox how to relax and Knox indoctrinating Williams into the orphan club he'd been a member of since his own parents had died when he was a child. Yet, Knox ignored the letter from the solicitor for months. Seven years after losing his best friend, he still wasn't ready to return to Rabley Heath. He told himself he was too busy with work, and his life in the city. But that wasn't true, and eventually one afternoon when he was sitting bored in his office on the fifth floor of Leconfield House he found himself writing a reply.

Now he had two homes to match his double life as a spy: his flat at the top of Kemp House, a tower block in the heart of Soho, and the gatehouse that stood guard at the entrance to Rabley Heath.

The gatehouse was small, with whitewashed walls and a grey tiled roof spotted with moss. There was one bedroom with a narrow bed up in the eaves, and the ground floor was a single room with a short couch, dining table, and kitchen counter, all also painted white. It was serene and peaceful – Knox's own monk's cell.

Knox's handwritten draft reports on Victoria and Australia were currently sitting on the dining table, filled with as much detail as he'd decided they deserved. And he was standing in front of the window above the kitchen counter. The radio was on but he wasn't listening to it. His ears were searching for another sound.

Eventually he heard the quiet thud that heralded the return of his one regular visitor.

He poured some milk he'd bought in the village an hour earlier into a saucer, then opened the window to let in the mottled caramel and white cat that was perched on its outside sill.

'Hello, Stinky,' Knox said. 'Been keeping an eye on the place?'

The cat paced up and down the counter, flicking his tail from side to side and pointedly ignoring both Knox and the milk.

'I'm sorry,' Knox said. 'I had to go away for work again.'

Stinky sat down, curled his tail round his feet, let out a single meow, then started lapping at the milk.

'Good boy,' Knox said, stroking Stinky's head and eliciting a series of faint purrs.

Knox had no idea who the cat belonged to, or what his actual name was. It was probably more sensible and noble than Stinky, but that's what Knox had christened the cat when he'd found him a few months ago in the depths of winter when he was walking the grounds after a heavy storm. The poor animal was caked in cold mud and mewling weakly after some misadventure in the rain. Knox had taken him to the gatehouse, cleaned and dried him off, and ever since he'd come to say hello and enjoy a saucer of milk whenever Knox was at Rabley Heath.

As soon as Stinky finished the milk he butted his head against Knox's arm, demanding one last stroke, then jumped back through the window. Knox watched him disappear into the hedge that lined the lane that led away from Rabley Heath wondering, as ever, where his real home was. Then he turned the radio off, pulled on a thin windbreaker, and set out to stroll the grounds.

Knox never went into the big house, but he would peer through its windows as he circled the estate, checking everything was as it should be. By now he knew every piece of fallen ceiling plaster, torn wallpaper and worn fabric.

While Hatfield House had been used as a hospital during the war thanks to its proximity to the de Havilland aerodrome, Rabley Heath had been used as a training base for the Special Operations Executive. The SOE was a paramilitary organisation of agitators and provocateurs, dreamed up by Churchill, who were used to stir up trouble and mischief behind enemy lines. The reason for the government's borrowing of the house had been kept secret, but once Knox and Williams had joined MI5 after the end of the war it hadn't taken them long to find it out.

The SOE hadn't left the place as they'd found it. Fireplaces were stained with soot marks, thick strips of wallpaper hung from walls, some rooms on the upper floor had been left stacked high with crates, and the ballroom floor had lost its bounce. But none of that seemed to bother Williams when he was finally given the keys to his home back.

Knox looked through the smudged window of one of the drawing rooms in the east wing and let his mind wander back through the countless hours he'd spent lying on its dust-caked sofa in a past life that felt simultaneously maddeningly distant and painfully close. After a few minutes of bitter-sweet reverie, he forced himself back into the present and moved on.

He completed his lap of the house and checked as much of the gardens as he could before they became impenetrable with knotty weeds and old bushes left to overgrow.

As he took the windbreaker off in the doorway of the gatehouse the telephone started to ring. He hadn't wanted his peaceful country retreat disturbed by having one installed, but Holland had insisted on it when Knox had announced he was taking over Rabley Heath. The price of his isolation was that it could be shattered at any moment.

He picked up the receiver and listened to the female voice on the other end.

'This is Avalon Logistics,' she said. 'Your delivery is due tomorrow morning.' Then she hung up.

It was a message from Holland. It was time to go back to London.

CHAPTER 6

'What the hell was that?' Jay Gibson asked Bennett from behind his desk in his small oven of an office.

Two fans were blowing full at him, but thick beads of sweat were still running down his temples. It was the middle of the afternoon the day after the exchange in Cerro de San Francisco, and it was hot.

'I was trying to stop someone being killed,' she replied.

She wasn't sweating, but it took all her willpower not to put her hand up to her short fringe, which kept fluttering, caught on the edge of the twin blasts from Gibson's fans.

'And how exactly were you going to do that? They were highly trained, ruthless murderers, and you had a torch.'

'The numbers were even,' Bennett said.

'Let me make this clear,' Gibson said, finally wiping his brow. 'As far as I'm concerned you're the most disposable American on this entire island. I'm not putting anyone's life at risk for you.'

A year ago thousands of US military and government personnel had flooded into the Dominican Republic as part of Operation Power Pack – the rapid incursion that put a swift end to the country's sudden and violent civil war, which had threatened to destabilise the already precarious political balance of the Caribbean. Then, a month later, the troops and ships had started to withdraw. But the US never left completely.

The CIA held on to the secure compound it had established at the port of Haina in the south of the capital, Santo Domingo. The complex, surrounded by high concrete walls and almost entirely roofed – to provide some respite from the harsh Caribbean sun and also block any attempts at airborne or orbital surveillance – was purposefully far away from the US embassy. It acted independently of it, and of Dominican law.

'Asselin was in our custody,' Bennett said, revealing to Gibson that she knew exactly who they'd handed over to the Tonton Macoute and sentenced to death. 'He was our responsibility.'

'He was never in our custody,' Gibson replied. 'We were never there.'

Bennett was shocked by the bluntness of his lies. 'That's not how we work,' she said.

Gibson let out a short snort. 'They tell you that at The Farm? Sorry to disappoint, but if you want honour and glory, you're in the wrong job.'

Bennett felt anger building inside her. She couldn't believe how casually he was dismissing what had happened last night, or the beliefs that had kept her going through countless battles before the one that was rapidly erupting between the two of them.

'Who did they give us?' she asked. 'Was he worth it at least?'

Gibson leaned back in his chair, brushed his hand over his damp hair, and stared at his insubordinate agent who was refusing to take her dressing-down quietly.

'For one thing, that's several levels above your security clearance. And for another, what makes you think you've earned the right to ask me to justify my orders?'

'But—' Bennett started before Gibson held up his hand to stop her.

'I'll tell you what,' he said. 'You can have as many last words as you want, once you get out of my office.'

'Sir—'

'Go!'

Bennett clenched her jaw, spun on her feet, and walked out of the room. She flung the door behind her, but caught it just before it hit the frame. Then she stalked across the compound, impotent rage burning inside her, and out into the docks.

She marched the three miles along the coastal road to Miramar, the area of Santo Domingo where most of the Haina CIA staff lived in a single apartment block, letting the sea breeze slowly cool her anger.

The United States had a chequered recent history with the Dominican Republic. The country had been under full-scale American occupation for eight years between 1916 and 1924 during the Banana Wars. Then, forty-one years later, the Yanks had returned. Much of Santo Domingo's population were grateful for America's help quelling the civil war. But some weren't, which was why all but the most senior CIA personnel lived in the same, high-fenced, pastel blue building in Miramar, and were ferried to and from Haina every day in a short convoy of discreetly armoured buses.

Bennett had realised over the months she'd been in the country, however, that she wasn't treated the same as the other Americans. She didn't know if it was because she was the only woman working at Haina, or because in the Caribbean's melting pot of genes and skin tones, hers meant that the Dominicans could tell that she wasn't one of them but weren't exactly sure what she was. Either way it gave her a strange kind of freedom. For once being the outsider made her more accepted, and able to freely walk the streets of Santo Domingo without worrying about getting lynched.

By the time Bennett reached Miramar the sun had started to fall, but this close to the equator that meant evening was just beginning. She didn't want to go straight to the little, one-room studio she'd been given at the bottom of the CIA block, and lie on her bed, staring at her ceiling fan for hours before she fell asleep. She wanted a drink.

Doralis's Bar was a squat, yellow box that sat between two empty plots of land a street over from the apartment building. Its walls were pockmarked with bullet holes and missing chunks of plaster from the running battles that had spread through Santo Domingo the previous spring, but it had survived the fighting mostly intact. Whatever had once stood on either side of it hadn't been so lucky.

Doralis, the owner, was an ancient Dominican woman who made everyone welcome and turned no one away, as long as they paid their bill. Anyone was free to order a beer or rum and pull up a plastic chair under a strip-light or an overturned crate beneath the stars. Doralis also had a knack for knowing when people needed someone to talk to, or when they needed to be left alone. And she liked Bennett.

Unfortunately, someone else in the bar also liked her. Tripp Warren was in a corner with a group of CIA men, and he looked like he was a good couple of rums down. As Bennett made her way over to the chipboard counter that Doralis permanently sat behind on a stool that was perfectly positioned to let her reach anything her customers might want, Warren detached himself from his drinking buddies and sidled up next to Bennett.

'How was Gibson?' he asked.

Warren, like everyone on the mission, had known Bennett was going to be dragged over the coals when they'd got back to Haina.

'A teddy bear, Tripp,' Bennett replied. 'A real teddy bear.'

Warren seemed wounded by Bennett's sarcasm. The outer edge of his eyebrows drooped, giving him a sad, puppy-dog look. But she didn't apologise, she just nodded at Doralis, saying hello, ordering a drink and asking for help in a single motion.

'It was a hell of a night,' he said. 'I'm just glad we all got through it okay.'

'Yeah, everyone except the guy who got shot in the head.' Bennett hadn't wanted to get into an argument, she'd just wanted to finish cooling off in peace, but she couldn't stop herself. 'Good thing he doesn't matter, right?'

'Look,' Warren said, taking a slow sip of his rum. 'All you can do now is shake it off and move on.' He swallowed again, but not because he'd had another swig of his drink. 'Maybe I could help.'

Bennett had been waiting weeks for Warren to say something like that, ever since they'd got too drunk with each other one night and ended up stumbling from the bar to Bennett's bed. It had been a mistake, but after months on the island Bennett had certain needs, and after so long spent in close quarters mistakes were bound to happen. She'd figured her subconscious had chosen Warren because he seemed like a fundamentally decent guy, and he was about as far down the pecking order as she was – no one could accuse her of trying to sleep her way to the top with Tripp Warren.

'Not tonight, Tripp,' she said.

'Oh,' he said, failing to hide the disappointment in his voice. 'You sure?'

'The lady's sure,' Doralis replied, sliding a rum and ice over the counter to Bennett as she tucked a long, loose strand of wiry grey hair behind her ear.

'Okay,' Warren said. 'Well, you know where to find me if you change your mind.'

'I'll let you know if I do,' Bennett said, throwing him a little smile to take away with him. Then she picked up her drink and turned back to the bar.

'He means well,' she said to Doralis.

'Those are the ones you got to watch out for,' the old woman replied.

Bennett laughed and drained her rum in a single gulp.

CHAPTER 7

The attention of every single person crammed into the dark basement was fixed on the man slouching in the centre of the makeshift stage. Thirty pairs of eyes and ears were all waiting for what he was going to say next.

His hair was messy and matted, his beard thick. He wore two jackets over his shirt, and held his glass of vodka in hands wrapped in fingerless gloves. The man looked like a homeless streetwalker. But he wasn't.

He took a breath and downed his drink. His audience mirrored him, tipping their heads back as one and letting their eighth glass of cheap alcohol slide down their throats.

'I ride the lines,' he said, finally breaking the silence. His voice was as rough as the vodka. 'I am the city's but it is not mine. I am everywhere and nowhere. Everyone but no one. A great emblem and a terrible shame. Your warning. The fear that sustains you, and the balm that you crave.'

He gestured at one of the young women kneeling at his feet at the edge of the stacked pallets he was raised up on, and the acolyte magicked a bottle out of air to refill his glass.

'You feed me your scraps,' he continued. 'But your plates stay full. You quench my thirst but your glass never empties. You share your bed, but you don't feel me lie next to you.'

He raised his vodka, ready for his finale.

'We are comrades!'

The crowd scrambled to fill their own glasses so they could all salute together and cheer the man's latest, scathing commentary on the Russian condition.

Vadim Rykov stood at the back of the room, leaning against a wooden pillar. The room was warm, but the earth that surrounded it was still cool and its walls were damp with condensation from all the breathing bodies.

Rykov looked like he didn't belong in the basement. He looked like a poster boy for the modern Soviet Union. And that's precisely what he was.

His hair was short and neat, held in place with pomade. His face was made up of the kind of angles sculptors cut into granite – a strong, aquiline nose and a sharp, beardless jaw. And his suit was immaculately tailored, cut perfectly to his body without looking like it had been fitted at all.

He'd enjoyed the performance. It wasn't one of the poet's best pieces, and its metaphors were a little forced, but the audience had lapped it up, like they always did. And Rykov couldn't fault the man's commitment to his act. He really did spend days and nights on the Moscow metro, bundled under thick layers of clothes and stinking of vodka and filth, glaring back at all the people who stared at him. Rykov knew that because he'd had him followed on several occasions.

There were a few similarities between Rykov and the rest of the poet's audience. He was young, and well fed enough to know that some people in communist Russia were more equal than others. But he didn't share the shame they felt over their relatively comfortable lives, because he knew better than most how the Soviet system really worked – including the crucial role clandestine midnight events like this one played.

Officially Russia didn't have a bourgeoisie, but Rykov was currently looking out over its heads. For as long as civilisation had existed, those who wanted power had spent their lives fretting and pandering to the people at the top and bottom of society. But Rykov understood that every political system was built, sustained, or crippled by the middle classes. They also needed pandering to, but in a different, more subtle way. They wanted to feel that they had a part to play. They needed to believe their opinions, thoughts, and feelings meant something. But they never wanted to actually act on them. They wanted to rebel, but only a little, and without ever putting themselves in any real danger.

This gathering was literally and figuratively underground. It could be raided at any moment, and everyone carted off for a night in a cell or a slap on the wrist. But it wouldn't be. Because the more intelligent minds in the Party understood that while Russia's diffident middle classes were huddling in scattered basements congratulating each other about the illicit thrill of listening to an old drunk's musings, they weren't doing something more dangerous. It was better to keep them in the dark than drive them out into the open where they might realise just how many of them there were.

And, if for some stupid reason someone did decide to storm the cellar, at least one person in the crowd wouldn't be arrested. That person was Vadim Rykov, because he was a KGB officer. But he wasn't just any officer, he was a major and the head of Line Z, one of the Russian security service's most secret and feared divisions.

CHAPTER 8

Bennett sat drinking for hours until Doralis decided she'd had enough.

'You've done your wallowing, girl,' she said as she took Bennett's empty glass from her. 'Now go get some sleep.'

'Sure,' Bennett replied, her voice a little slurred from the steady stream of rum she'd been given. 'G'night, Doralis.'

She left some peso notes on the counter to cover her tab and left the bar, scratching her short hair as she stepped back out into the night, as if that would help dislodge all the thoughts clogging up her brain.

Bennett had spent her evening going over not just the events of the last twenty-four hours but the whole of the last five years.

When she'd been accepted into CIA field training she'd thought she'd finally be able to stop constantly fighting to prove herself with at least one hand always tied behind her back. At last, she'd be among people who wanted to serve their country as much as she did, and they'd all be competing for a prize they could share in the end. But it hadn't turned out that way.

Her time at The Farm, the nickname for the CIA training facility at Camp Peary in Virginia, had been tough. There were few women on the entire base, let alone in the training corps, and she was the only one who was part Native American. No one wanted anything to do with her. Bennett was disappointed but, just like so many times before, not completely surprised. Yet she hadn't thrown in the towel, decided life might be easier in the

FBI or going private at Pinkerton or another independent outfit. She'd worked harder than anyone else to prove she deserved to be there.

After she left The Farm with a performance record that should have put her at the top of her class but didn't, Bennett waited for her first posting. And she kept waiting, while all her fellow graduates were sent off somewhere to protect America and her interests. Eventually she received a string of short-lived, menial assignments that demanded less of her than the years she'd spent as a file clerk for the agency before going to Virginia. Then one afternoon, completely out of the blue and with only a few hours' notice, she was sent to Santo Domingo.

She'd been caught up in the rushing wave of the American occupation, and it had been exhilarating. All clichés aside, she'd felt like she was making a difference, protecting the Dominican Republic from tumbling into chaos or, worse, communism. But in the last year things had become murkier, less clear-cut, and she wasn't sure who she was helping any more.

The operation in Cerro de San Francisco was wrong. A foreign national had been killed in CIA custody, or as near as dammit to it, and Bennett wanted to know how much blood she had on her hands. But Gibson had shot her down. Maybe he was right and his identity was above her pay grade, but something felt off about the whole thing. There'd been no whispers around Haina about a rescue, no quiet pats on backs for bringing in one of their own. It really was like the mission hadn't happened – a true black op.

A great deal of trouble had been gone to for one man. He was clearly valuable. But to who? And why?

As she walked away from Doralis's, feeling the night-time breeze come in off the sea – the bitter salt mingling with the heady, pungent scents of orchids and nicotianas – Bennett decided she was going to find out the answers to those questions.

Gibson might not want to tell her, but he wasn't her only option. She wondered if Warren might know, or be able to find out. She also wondered if he was still awake. His overnight stay had been a mistake, but the sex had also been pretty good.

However, at the corner in front of the CIA apartment block her burgeoning lust abruptly evaporated at the sight of a man standing in the middle of the road.

Seeing someone else on Santo Domingo's quiet streets this late at night wasn't that strange. But this man was. He was white, so white it looked like his skin hadn't seen the sun in months, and his hair was long, greasy and knotted. His clothes were dark, heavy wool, completely out of place in the Caribbean. And he was staring at Bennett.

The small, still sober bit of Bennett's mind wanted her to turn round and walk away. But the larger rum-soaked part wanted to go home.

'Can I do something for you?' she asked, matching the stranger's stare.

'You are Abey Bennett,' the man replied.

His voice was hoarse, and quiet, but his accent was unmistakable – he was British.

Bennett tried to cover her surprise at hearing her name. 'Who wants to know?'

'I need your help,' he said. He hugged his arms to his chest, as if he was shivering against a cold only he could feel.

'And I need to know who you are.'

The man paused for a moment, then he said three words that made Bennett freeze – 'I'm the Wolf.'

The Wolf was a legend. A Soviet super-agent who could strike anywhere and any time without leaving a trace. No one in any Western intelligence agency knew who the Wolf was, or if they even really existed. For some, that made them the most terrifying enemy in the whole Cold War, more dangerous than Castro or Mao, or whoever would win the latest battle for supremacy that had taken over the Kremlin. They were the personification of the never-ending threat of communism, spreading undetected around the world like the worst, most vicious cancer. For others, the Wolf was just a fantasy. They were nothing more than a convenient excuse to explain operations gone wrong, and a bogeyman used to inflame paranoia.

Bennett was a believer. She kept it quiet, and she'd tried to resist it, but the myth of the Wolf had been too compelling. For years, she'd quietly trawled through the mission reports and vague snatches of intelligence she'd been tasked with archiving into oblivion, and filed away in her head the odd stories she'd overhear or see in the middle pages of newspapers – the unexplained deaths or curious events that, with a little imagination, could be connected to other equally strange things that might have happened months ago and thousands of miles apart.

The sceptics said there was no way one person could be responsible for everything that had been pinned on the Wolf. So much death and violence was attributed to them it was almost impossible for one man – and any discussion on the subject always assumed they were a man – to be behind it all. But, the way Bennett saw it, every Western intelligence agency should pray it was all the work of one man, because if it wasn't that meant there was a whole pack of wolves out there.

The man standing in front of Bennett didn't look like a killer but, in the second she had to process his sudden appearance and sober herself up, she decided that if he really was a Soviet superagent he probably wouldn't look like one.

'How do you know who I am?' she asked.

The man's eyes were still on Bennett, but she realised they were glazed, milky and unfocused.

'I-I don't know,' he said.

'How did you find me?'

His hands gripped his arms tighter. 'I don't remember.'

'Do you know where you are?'

Another pause. 'No.'

'Jesus,' Bennett said to herself.

Her shoulders, which had been up somewhere close to her ears, started to drop. There was no way this man was the Wolf. He was some drunk or addict who had been kicked off a cargo ship and given a couple of pesos to trick her.

The only person she'd talked to about the Wolf in Santo Domingo was Warren, in a brief post-coital attempt at conversation when the combination of alcohol and orgasm had made her lower her guard. He must have been waiting for a chance to throw it in her face, and she'd given him one tonight. The whole block was probably at their windows waiting to laugh at her.

'Okay,' she said to the man. 'Well, you tell Tripp that you're both real funny, but I've had a long day and I'm going to bed.'

'Please,' the man said, the milkiness starting to clear from his eyes. 'I need your help.'

'You need someone's, but not mine.'

Bennett stepped past him and walked to the gate that led to the apartment complex. She noticed there were no lights in any of the windows. No one was watching. There wasn't even anyone in the small guardhouse that stood next to the gate. There was just her, and the man, who had followed her over the road without making a sound and was now grabbing her shoulders and spinning her back round to face him.

'You are Abey Bennett,' he said again. His voice was stronger, the British accent more pronounced, and his eyes were suddenly urgent with focus. 'You are from Lakin, Kansas. Your mother died three years ago. You miss her. You feel guilty for not being there when it happened, and for how much you hate that she didn't see you become a CIA agent. Your brothers still live in Lakin. You don't miss them. And you're the only person who can help me.'

Bennett was stunned. There was no way some crazy vagrant could know all that about her – or anyone in Haina. She'd never talked to her colleagues about her family or where she was from.

She pulled his hands off her. They came away easily, as if his outburst had drained all the energy from him.

'Help you with what?' she asked.

'I don't know,' he said, his voice feeble again, and his eyes now begging.

'Okay,' she replied slowly, glancing again at the dark, silent apartment block and making a quick calculation. 'Tell you what, let's start with getting you some rest. Just don't try and pull anything funny.'

This man might not be the Wolf, but he knew more than he should about Bennett, and she was curious about how he'd come by so much personal information. She wanted to get him somewhere she could contain him, and question him. But that wasn't going to happen for at least a few hours, because as soon as she opened the door to her studio, the man collapsed on her bed and fell into a deep, unwakeable sleep.

CHAPTER 9

Knox had all of five minutes to consider the stack of papers that had been left for him to review in his office on the fifth floor of Leconfield House before he was summoned next door to see Holland.

Holland kept his own desk fastidiously neat, clear of everything except what he was dealing with at that precise moment, and, sitting in the single chair across from the director general of MI5, Knox noticed two manila folders on the vast slab of mahogany between them.

'Rested from your break?' Holland asked, as he pulled a chamois from a drawer and polished the lenses of his metal-rimmed glasses.

It was a rhetorical question, and a rebuke for Knox not coming straight back to headquarters after his long journey from Vancouver Island.

'So, what was Northcott up to?'

This time Knox answered. 'Not what we thought.'

'How reassuring,' Holland replied, returning the chamois to its home. 'Care to elaborate?'

Knox explained what he'd discovered in Victoria, going into a little more detail than had made it into his official report.

'I trust you told him to put a stop to it,' Holland said, when he was done.

'Should I have?'

'The Americans will certainly think so.'

'They were scared Northcott was working for the Russians. He isn't. I don't think whatever else he gets up to is any of our business.'

'They'll disagree,' Holland said.

'I'm sure,' Knox replied. 'But with respect to the Americans, if they're that concerned about losing a few unwilling conscripts then they can revoke his landing permit.'

Holland huffed in response, acknowledging that the Northcott affair had been a waste of time, and so would any further discussion about it. Time, Knox thought a little bitterly, that Holland might not have to spare.

Leconfield House was a palace of secrets, and rumours. The most recent one was that Holland was thinking about retiring. The idea had seemed ludicrous to Knox when he'd overheard it, muttered between two junior agents who hadn't realised he was in earshot. Holland had been in charge of the Service for less than a decade, and he was still relatively young. There was also plenty going on at home and across the Commonwealth that meant it wasn't time for him to take his hands off MI5's reins. And, on top of all that, Holland hadn't said anything about it to Knox himself. But the weary second-guessing that the Cold War had drilled into so much of Knox's life had left him wondering more and more if there wasn't some truth in the gossip; and, if there was, why hadn't Holland discussed it with the man who was supposed to be one of his closest and most trusted advisers?

The possibility of a Leconfield House without Holland irritated Knox. It also made him question his own shelf life as a spy. Maybe their joint future was the second thing the director general wanted to discuss. Knox doubted it. The first folder on Holland's desk was for Knox's mission to Canada. The second would be for his next one. Knox was loyal to his mentor. He would always do what Holland told him to and go wherever he was sent, no matter what or where. But he could feel a prick of nerves as he glanced at the desk again. He had no desire to get straight back on another plane. However, after an uncharacteristic moment of silence, he bit the bullet.

'How are things in Harare?' he asked.

'A mess,' Holland replied.

'Any sign that Moscow's involved?'

Holland shook his head. 'This is entirely our own problem. Though that doesn't mean there isn't a chance it'll turn into another Zanzibar, and Smith will end up getting into bed with the Soviets or Chinese.'

'Imagine kicking up all this stink to avoid giving half your country the vote only to end up a communist vassal.'

'Stranger things have happened.'

'Anything I can do to help?' Knox asked, pre-empting the order he guessed Holland was about to give him.

There was a long, torturous pause before Holland replied.

'No, I need you on something here.'

Knox hoped the relief that flooded through him didn't show on his face.

Holland put his hand on the second folder, but he didn't open it or push it over to Knox yet.

'The Kosygin summit is going ahead,' he said.

That was not what Knox had expected Holland to say.

'Really? I assumed it had been cancelled as soon as the election was called.'

'As far as anyone outside Leconfield House and a few offices in Whitehall is concerned, it was. Wilson doesn't want to be seen cosying up to the chairman of the Council of Ministers of the Soviet Union while his majority hangs in the balance, but apparently the trade deal he's dangling in front of us is too valuable to dismiss.'

'Valuable, or necessary?' Knox asked.

Both men knew that the country's economy was on the slide, squeezed by decreasing productivity, increasing globalisation, and a hefty deficit inherited from Macmillan's Conservative government. They also knew that the last Labour prime minister, Clement Attlee, had been forced to devalue the pound in order to stabilise the country's post-war recovery, and Wilson was desperate to avoid doing so again.

'De Gaulle is still blocking our attempts at closer economic ties with Europe, and President Johnson still hates Wilson. Our options are limited.'

'Stranger things,' Knox repeated.

'We simply can't afford for the summit to go badly.' It was clear that by 'we' Holland meant both the country and MI5.

'It's going to be a very discreet visit,' he continued. 'A few meetings, some private dinners and the like. Laing is managing our part of the proceedings and has all the details.'

Simon Laing was the SLO who had been recalled from Ottawa – the reason Knox had been sent to Canada. Clearly Holland was giving the junior officer a chance to redeem himself.

'Do you want me to babysit him?' Knox asked.

'Actually,' Holland replied. 'I want him to babysit you.'

'Sir?'

'Would you rather I sent you to Rhodesia?'

'What I want isn't relevant,' Knox said, after another short silence that finally betrayed his true feelings on the matter.

Holland huffed again, at last sliding the folder across his desk. 'Read through this, then go find Laing.'

CHAPTER 10

Rykov's office wasn't in the Lubyanka or the Kremlin. Befitting his department's unusual status, Line Z was based in an anonymous four-storey white stucco building sandwiched between a hotel and a power plant on the northern edge of the island that hugged the sweeping curve of the Moskva River as it passed through the centre of Moscow. According to the row of signs that lined the arch leading from the street to a small courtyard, the building was home to the Moscow offices of several small Soviet industrial communes. But these were all covers. Line Z occupied the entire place.

Rykov had started his KGB career in its imposing headquarters on Lubyanka Square as the assistant to General Grigor Medev, the head of the scientific directorate. Rykov was just twenty-two when Medev had been killed in Stockholm five years ago as he tried to stop a Russian physicist called Irina Valera from defecting to the West. Rykov had kept the directorate running smoothly in the immediate aftermath of Medev's death – so smoothly in fact that a number of its staff and scientists hadn't realised that their chief was no longer issuing their orders. Some considered this a presumption of power that should have seen Rykov packed off to a gulag, but others saw something different. They saw potential. Rykov was transferred to Line Z.

The KGB was a multi-tentacled beast of directorates, departments, services and lines. The first chief directorate was so large it had been split into multiple numbered and lettered sections that covered every aspect of Soviet intelligence and security, from research and domestic surveillance to international operations. Each section was supposed to have a clear responsibility and remit. Directorate S dealt with illegals – the Soviet agents who operated around the globe without official cover or diplomatic protection – Directorate K oversaw counter-intelligence, and the scientific directorate's official designation was Directorate T.

Line Z, however, was an anomaly. Originally founded as an experiment in free rein, it had quietly but relentlessly evolved, combining elements from other sections to create a miniature, fully formed intelligence agency within the KGB. After Khrushchev's retirement, it had caught Brezhnev's eye and his blessing and backing had given Rykov protection, influence, and power.

Line Z worked globally, combined research, human and signals intelligence, and was rumoured to employ tactics even more violent than the KGB's feared active measures and wet work units. All to achieve the section's – and Rykov's – singular aim of causing chaos in the West.

Rykov believed that for communism to claim final, total victory, it wouldn't be enough for it to just defeat the West. The West would have to fail itself as well, and he knew that those were two subtly different things. He wasn't interested in the small battles and tiny victories that obsessed the other directorate chiefs. It was his job to keep the Soviet Union's enemies chasing their tails. And he was very good at it, which meant that though he had several high-ranking supporters he also had many enemies.

As he stood at one of the high windows in his office that looked out across the Moskva to Zaryadye Park and the high walls and domes of the Kremlin, he could see one of those enemies on their way to pay him a visit.

He watched as a familiar black Gaz-22 Volga drove over the Bolshoi Moskvoretsky Bridge and through the archway directly beneath him.

The building was a warren of offices, corridors, and dead ends. But the Volga's passenger knew exactly where they were going. After a few minutes, Rykov's door opened.

'Comrade,' Major Natalya Yegerova said, announcing herself.

Yegerova was a slight woman, made even thinner by the boxy dress uniform she seemed to wear every hour of the day. Her skin was pale and her long hair was twisted in an intricate plait that hung at the nape of her neck. She was only a few years older than Rykov, but she looked like she was from a bygone Russia.

They were both majors, but Rykov technically outranked Yegerova. She was a senior member of the much larger Directorate S, but Rykov was head of his section. This was a distinction that he knew she both suspected and resented.

'I have a quandary,' she said, coming to a rigid halt in front of Rykov's desk.

He stayed at the window.

'And that would be?' he asked.

'We have received word that an asset has been captured by the Americans in the Caribbean.'

'That does sound unfortunate,' he replied. 'Do you require Line Z's assistance retrieving them?'

Rykov's voice and mouth remained casually neutral, but inside he was smiling. As a section devoted to clandestine operations, Directorate S felt its toes stepped on by Line Z more than most, and he enjoyed goading its members whenever he had the opportunity.

'He wasn't one of ours. So I must assume he belongs to you.'

'I don't believe so,' Rykov said, pushing himself away from the window and sitting behind his desk. 'But operational security would obviously require me to say that.'

'And what of our operational security?' Yegerova asked. 'Our agents put their lives in danger all over the world every day. Your directorate's undeclared activities are an unacceptable risk to them.'

It was the standard, posturing refrain that was parroted whenever someone felt Line Z encroaching on their territory. And it never worked.

'Are we not all simply soldiers in the same great fight?' Rykov countered. 'None of our lives are worth more than any others.'

'Of course not,' she snapped. 'But you must share your plans with Directorate S so we can work together and all triumph.'

Rykov was being facetious, but Yegerova was not. He'd heard her spout similar rhetoric before, and it always seemed to him that she truly believed what she was saying, and that she spoke like she was being recorded – as if she was constantly preparing her defence for when whatever she said might be used against her. It was probably very prudent, but it was also the kind of thing that put a low ceiling on a career in the KGB. Propaganda was for the people, not spies.

'No,' he said, finally adding a little edge to his voice. 'I must not. But you are free, as ever, to take your concerns about this directorate and its methods to as many of our fellow comrades as you may wish. Perhaps the general secretary would be interested in them.'

This was Rykov's usual response to complaints like Yegerova's, and his ultimate defence: Brezhnev – the higher power he could invoke and no one could question.

'Perhaps he would,' Yegerova replied, hollowly, knowing that he wouldn't.

As she stalked back through the maze of corridors to her waiting Volga, Rykov returned to his window and thought about what he'd learned in the last five minutes.

Her visit had been as much a warning as a fishing trip. Rykov was used to attracting the attention of other forces within the KGB who were desperate to take his place in Brezhnev's good books or just wanted to see the shine of his rising star dulled a little. And now it was clear that Yegerova was watching him very closely – but also that she had no idea of what he and Line Z were up to.

CHAPTER 11

Knox found Simon Laing in the School Hall on the third floor of Leconfield House. With its evenly spaced rows of identical laminate desks, it was easy to see how the wide open-plan space had earned its nickname. The School Hall was where MI5's newest recruits proved themselves.

It was the middle of the afternoon but the third floor was deserted and dim. Its overhead lamps had been turned off by some budget-conscious custodian, and only a few of the desks had their anglepoises switched on.

Knox recognised Laing from afar, hunched over a stack of papers in one of the small pools of light. Laing was short and wiry. He looked like he'd never eaten a square meal in his life. The impression was compounded by his slim-cut grey suit, and his helmet of black hair, slicked to his scalp with Brylcreem. He reminded Knox of a broken pencil.

Knox had spent an hour clearing the files that had been piled up for him, and trying to decide if Holland was punishing him with his new assignment or not. Then he'd asked for the report on Laing's truncated posting in Ottawa. It took him another hour to digest Laing's debriefing and the subsequent investigation into the Ralliement National honeytrap. Knox concluded that Laing had made a logical call, he'd just bet on the wrong horse. Good agents were driven by one of two things, process or intuition, and the best agents understood how to balance the two. But Knox knew knowledge like that could take a whole career to learn.

Knox reached Laing's desk and stood next to it, waiting for the younger man to register his presence. He didn't.

'Busy, Laing?' Knox said, eventually.

'Yes,' Laing replied, still absorbed by the document in his hands. When, after a moment's silence, he looked up and realised who had said his name, he added, 'sir.'

'Fancy a walk round the garden?' Knox asked.

The garden was the rose garden in the south-east corner of Hyde Park, a few streets away from Leconfield House. It was a favoured spot for MI5 officers to have delicate conversations they wanted to keep private.

'Of course, sir,' Laing replied, quickly squaring away his files and returning them to the clerk, who would ferry them to secure storage.

Five minutes later they were on the other side of the Park Lane underpass. Knox had set a leisurely pace, and could tell Laing was struggling to walk so slowly. He also noticed that the younger officer's arms didn't swing as he moved – they were held rigid at his side.

They'd just passed the fountain of Diana, goddess of hunting, in the middle of the garden when Laing turned to Knox and asked why they were there.

'I'd say I wanted to smell the roses, but we're a few weeks early,' Knox replied.

It wasn't a very good joke, but he expected at least some reaction from Laing, even merely as a professional courtesy. But he just looked at his superior and nodded, as if he'd taken his statement completely literally.

Knox decided to get to the point. 'Holland thought I might be able to help you with the Kosygin summit.'

'Thank you, sir,' Laing replied. 'But I think I have everything under control.'

'I'm sure you do, but I don't think it was a suggestion.'

Laing tensed, then gave the slightest nod.

'You're more than welcome to review my plans, and the contingencies I've put in place with the Met,' he said. 'I'm also liaising with Six, and have spoken to White in case Pipistrelle has picked up anything that could impact security.'

Pipistrelle was MI5's top-secret, highly advanced, and almost entirely undetectable bugging system. After six years of rapaciously competitive development by the planet's spy agencies, it was still one of the most effective pieces of surveillance technology in the world. It was the jewel in MI5's crown, and knowledge of its existence had not been shared with the other Venona countries, or the rest of Britain's allies – even MI6 only received the occasional, sparing precis of the secret conversations it overheard in embassies, offices, and living rooms.

Knox started to realise why Holland had wanted him to meet Laing. He sounded just like he had when he was starting out: earnest, and dedicated to the point of obsession. He was also, Knox imagined, still stewing over what had happened in Canada.

'That sounds fairly comprehensive,' Knox said. 'But perhaps there's something I can add. A second pair of eyes is always useful.'

Laing slowed to a stop, and Knox could sense him stiffening even more. They'd looped round the garden and were now back at the other side of the fountain.

'May I speak freely, sir?'

'Of course.'

'I appreciate what you're doing. I know I made a mistake in Ottawa, and I know I have to serve my penance. But this is a waste of your time. This is a simple job and I'm on top of it.'

Knox was silent for a second, both surprised and impressed by Laing's sudden burst of directness.

'Send me what you have, and I'll decide that,' he said.

Laing gave another acquiescent nod. 'If you'll excuse me, I'll see to it right away.'

Knox let him go.

CHAPTER 12

'Where on Earth have you been?' Malcolm White asked as Knox stepped into the cavernous research and development department deep in the bowels of Leconfield House.

White was the head of the department, and the man almost solely responsible for the innovations like Pipistrelle that let British intelligence keep some kind of pace with its immeasurably better funded and resourced American and Russian counterparts.

Knox had decided to see if there was anything else happening in MI5 headquarters that he could help with while he waited for Laing's files. His first stop was White, who he found exactly where he expected him to be, inspecting his latest contraption that straddled the divide between science and wizardry – a perfectly smooth black box suspended on wires that connected it to a series of bronze coils.

Knox looked at the mechanism, conscious that he had no idea what it could possibly be used for, or what mysteries it might contain.

'Had to take a little trip,' he replied. He pointed at the box. 'What's this?'

'Nothing yet,' White replied. 'I assumed you'd been packed off to Africa like the rest of the bloody Service.'

Knox peeled his eyes away from White's box and looked around him, registering how calm the department was. Normally it was busy with people in lab coats or rolled-up sleeves buzzing between control panels, but now it was as quiet as the School Hall. There were just a few technicians working at the huge Atlas computer that was the beating metal heart of Pipistrelle. And White, tinkering with his newest invention, which, now Knox looked at it again, he saw was surrounded on White's desk by sea charts.

'I've been spared that joy,' Knox said. 'Holland's asked me to keep an eye on Laing and the Kosygin visit.'

'Ah, passing on your knowledge to the next generation?' White said as he gave up on the box and switched his attention to the charts.

Knox guessed White knew all about Laing's inglorious return from Ottawa, and the bone he'd been thrown by Holland.

'Something like that,' Knox replied. 'What do you think of him?'

'Laing? I like him. He always files his requisitions correctly.'

'He's very young.'

'Not compared to you when you signed up.'

Knox had still been a teenager, just, when Holland had persuaded him to join MI5 in 1945. But the world was different then – the war made everyone feel older than they were. Laing was twenty-five and had already been an SLO. It might not have gone perfectly, but it was still an impressive achievement at his age.

'True,' Knox conceded.

'He also does what I tell him,' White added, the usual clipped edges of his voice getting a little sharper.

'Are you still upset about the tracker?' Knox replied.

'We agreed every Service car should have one installed. You were in the room when it was decided. So why are you the only officer who hasn't had it done?'

'Because my car doesn't belong to the Service. It's mine.'

For a professional spy, Knox was extremely protective of his own privacy. He'd accepted the need for a telephone in Rabley Heath, but he drew the line at someone being able to know where he was any time of day or night.

'I'm in the phone book,' he said. 'And I promise I'll use a pool car for anything serious.'

White shook his head and turned back to the sea charts.

'What do you want, Richard?' he asked.

'Can't I just have a chat with a fellow old-timer?'

'No, because I'm busy and you're moping.'

'I'm not.'

'Yes you are.'

Knox gestured at the desk.

'Planning a sailing trip?' he asked.

'My latest headache,' White replied. 'The navy is convinced there's a Russian submarine playing silly buggers in the Channel shipping lanes.'

'Silly buggers?'

'Slipping in and out of the wakes of cargo ships, suddenly registering in front of ferries and forcing them to change course before vanishing again. Basically being a nuisance. But the navy can only catch shadows of it. They think it's got some kind of new technology that's stopping them finding it, so they've come to me to solve their problem for them.'

'Well, you are a magician,' Knox said.

'I fear this might be outside the realms of even my skills.'

Knox looked at the nooks and crannies of the British and French coasts laid out between them. 'Sounds like you need something to lure it out into the open.'

'Maybe,' White said. 'But I can't shake the feeling that that's exactly what it's doing to us.'

CHAPTER 13

Simon Laing wasn't happy. He didn't like having his solitude disturbed, and he didn't like that the man who had been sent to Canada to clean up his mess was now going to be hovering over him as he sat out his purgatory.

'It's a mark,' he'd been told after he'd returned from Ottawa and gone through a week of debriefing that had felt like a month. 'But one that will fade in time.'

All Laing wanted was to be left alone to get on with his job, but Knox's sudden attention felt like the stain on his service record was already having fresh ink poured on it. Managing MI5's security for Kosygin's secret conference with Wilson was Laing's responsibility and he knew he could handle it. He didn't need his hand holding, but he hadn't been given a choice.

After Laing had made his excuses and left Knox in the rose garden, he'd gone straight back to Leconfield House and requested the same files he'd handed over to the records clerk twenty minutes earlier, which detailed all the recent Pipistrelle intelligence about known Soviet agents in London that he had the security clearance to read.

Then, once he'd committed to memory the latest reports he hadn't managed to read before Knox had interrupted him, he gave them all back to the clerk again, told him which files to send up to the fifth floor, and made his way home to the small set of rooms he rented in a terraced street just north of Kentish Town tube station.

Laing didn't know any of the other residents of the three-storey house he'd found and taken between his debriefing sessions on an optimistically short let. And he didn't want to, because getting to know them would mean giving in to a fate he'd tried so hard to avoid and still hoped wasn't completely sealed.

Most people who became spies did it for one of three reasons: ideology, ego, or excitement. Laing was different. He'd become a spy for the chance to escape. This made Britain's domestic intelligence agency an odd choice of employer, but MI5 had approached him precisely with the intention of sending him far away.

Laing was an only child, born in the middle of the war. He was the product of a rapid love affair and a quick marriage. His father was a Canadian fighter pilot stationed at RAF Hornchurch, who was an ace at picking Luftwaffe bombers out of the sky in the first few months of the war until the Germans got their revenge on him in the Battle of Britain.

Laing's mother kept his father's memory alive with second-hand stories of the beautiful wilds of Canada. But these tales just made the young boy fixate on the idea of leaving the small Essex town where he was regularly stared at in the street. He hated the haunted looks he got from strangers who recognised him as part of that odd in-between generation that were too old to be children of peace but young enough to remind people of the innocence the war had stolen from them.

On top of that, the genes that had made his father the perfect size for a Spitfire cockpit had conspired to make Laing a very slow and late developer. He was a small, frail-looking child and a short, scrawny teenager, and it didn't take long for children five years his junior to spurt up taller and stronger than him. No one wanted to be his friend. So, he focused on his studies at school, where he was often literally in a class of his own; distanced himself from everyone around him, including his mother; and did his best not to attract attention from anyone. However, he couldn't resist MI5's interest in him.

The Service's quest to replenish its ranks after losing so many of its best men to the war had eventually led it to the son of a dead Canadian pilot. The officers sent to recruit Laing wooed him with the possibility of building a new life for himself abroad, and he jumped at the chance. He was groomed, trained to become a security liaison officer, and promised that his first posting would be in Canada. A brief visit to meet his paternal grandparents in Toronto had even been arranged before he took up his position in Ottawa.

Somehow Laing had been given everything he'd ever wanted, and he'd ruined it. But he was determined to get it all back, so if that meant putting up with Knox's unwanted and unnecessary supervision then that's what he'd do. He'd jump through every hoop the Service put in front of him to get away from Britain again.

CHAPTER 14

Bennett's time off the sidelines lasted all of six hours – and for five of them nothing happened.

She'd spent the night curled up in the small wicker chair she kept next to the door of her studio, her eyes fixed on the unconscious body of the man who she was increasingly convinced was not a Soviet super-soldier, and her body wired from the mystery and several cups of instant Folgers coffee. It was a long way from the best she'd ever drunk, but it did the job, and no one seemed to notice or care when she liberated the occasional jar from the Haina stores.

The stranger's sleep had been so deep and still there were a few moments when Bennett thought he might actually be dead. But he'd woken up as the sun rose and the small room started to swelter again after its brief midnight reprieve from the island heat.

'Do you know where you are?' Bennett asked as he turned over, pulled himself onto his elbows, and rubbed his eyes at her.

'No.' His accent still sounded British, but now Bennett could hear an inflection in it she couldn't place – like he'd lived in a foreign country for years and it had rubbed off on him.

'Do you know who you are?'

Another 'No'.

'Do you know me?'

His brow furrowed for a moment as he concentrated on her. Then he said, 'Abey Bennett.'

Bennett wasn't sure if she should be relieved or worried that the only thing he seemed sure of was who she was. But at least he was calmer now, and agreed to let her take him to Haina for a medical examination and some food.

And that was when she found herself benched again.

As soon as they got out of the car that had taken them to the port the stranger was put in handcuffs by two of the young soldiers who acted as the CIA's security guards and dragged away. He didn't struggle.

Bennett went straight to Gibson.

'He was my walk in,' she said, as soon as she was inside his office, just over twelve hours since she'd stormed out of it.

'So?' Gibson replied.

'That makes him my asset.'

'The hell it does.' It was still early but the underarms of Gibson's shirt were already stained dark, and his forehead was slick with sweat. 'You're lucky I'm not slapping you with a reprimand for not bringing him in immediately.'

That would have been proper procedure, but Bennett knew that if she'd followed it Gibson would only have complained about being disturbed in the middle of the night.

'Worker bees don't get the honey,' Gibson said.

Bennett ignored the clunky metaphor.

'There's a connection between us,' she said. 'We should leverage it.'

'I'm not interested in you getting deep and meaningful. I want to know where he came from and what he's doing here. If he's smart he'll cooperate.'

'And if he doesn't?' Bennett asked.

'Then that's his problem.'

If Gibson wanted information extracted as quickly as possible, there was only one place in Haina the man would be taken. The whole Haina complex didn't officially exist, but there was one building in the compound that even most of the CIA staff pretended wasn't there – the MKULTRA interrogation block.

MKULTRA had started life in the 1950s as an experimental psychological warfare unit, which generally meant tricking unsuspecting civilians into taking LSD to see how they'd behave under the drug's influence. Unfortunately, the people they experimented on had a tendency to throw themselves out of high windows.

By the early 1960s most of its operations were shutting down, but parts of the unit lived on in compounds around the globe like Haina, where the CIA protected US interests in ways that would be considered highly illegal on American soil. Techniques included extreme isolation, starvation, sensory deprivation or overload, or hooking people on opioids to then force withdrawal on them. MKULTRA specialised in fast and violent information extraction, but it wasn't foolproof – people who survived invariably confessed to whatever they were told to.

When Bennett had first learned of MKULTRA, it had horrified her. The justification given by those who were less uncomfortable about its existence than her was that there were some truly evil people in the world who meant to do the United States unspeakable harm and needed to be dealt with by any means necessary – that one life was worth it if it stopped another Pearl Harbor. That always felt like a hollow excuse to her. She understood that the line of acceptability was often deeper, thinner, or more blurred than people thought when it came to national security, but MKULTRA definitely seemed to be on the wrong side of it.

However, her qualms didn't stop it from continuing its dark work, so most of the time she settled, like the rest of Haina, for just ignoring it. And the feeling seemed mutual. The MKULTRA interrogators didn't mix with their fellow Americans. They didn't live in the same apartment block in Miramar, and they didn't joke about who got caught in the latest tropical downpour over rums at Doralis's.

Now, Bennett wanted to march across the compound and demand to see her stranger. But she knew she couldn't. She had to wait.

During the day the MKULTRA block was permanently staffed, but at night it was left well alone and even avoided by the patrolling guards, in large part because they figured whoever might be inside would be in no condition to try to escape.

No one imagined anyone would want to break into the building, but that's what Bennett did after everyone else in Haina had called it a day and the sun was starting to set again.

Its brushed steel outer door was unlocked – testament to the power of fear in keeping people at bay – but Bennett slipped through it slowly and silently, just in case there was anyone other than prisoners still inside.

She found herself in what looked like an empty hospital corridor. The floor was rubberised, the walls were perfectly smooth, painted green up to waist height and white above, and the air stank of bleach.

She passed a series of heavy doors that faced each other. They all had a letter stencilled precisely in black next to their handles, but there were no windows to reveal what was on the other side of them.

At the end of the corridor was another door. This one was wood, its top half frosted glass. Bennett listened at it for a moment, then gently tried the handle, opening it as quietly as she could.

Inside was some kind of laboratory office. It was large, and three of its walls were lined with tall filing cabinets and glass cases filled with small phials of garishly coloured liquids. The fourth wall was dominated by a huge two-way mirror that looked into another room.

This one's floor, walls, and ceiling were all clad in shiny black tiles, and in the centre was a polished chrome chair, raised up off the ground on a podium. It had a high back and stirrups, and dark leather straps were attached all over it to keep whatever poor soul had to sit in it firmly in place. Two large television screens and what looked like several speakers were suspended from the ceiling above the chair on a chrome rig.

A shiver crept up Bennett's back as she peered through the mirror. The set-up looked like some kind of modern medieval torture chamber.

She turned away and looked at the two desks that stood next to each other in the middle of the lab. They both had an ashtray piled high with cigarette butts on them, along with a single folder and a small television set. The screens were marked A and B and were broadcasting live feeds of two small, bare cells.

The man who had been exchanged for Asselin sat in the corner of one of them, his knees tucked under his chin, his hands over his ears, and his face twisted in a rictus scream. There was a switch on the side of the small television. Bennett flicked it and the lab was suddenly filled with a deafening, discordant cacophony of grinding, pounding, and scraping coming from some hidden speaker. She turned it off after barely a second.

Her stranger was on the second screen. He was also sitting in the corner of his cell, but his legs were crossed, his arms were in his lap, and his face was completely still, his eyes locked on the camera. Bennett was sure he couldn't know she was watching him, but it felt like he did, and he was staring straight back at her. She flicked the switch on his television – he was being subjected to the same constant assault of noise as the other man, but he didn't seem to hear it.

Bennett turned the speaker off and picked up the file that had been left on the desk next to the screen. It was marked 'classified' but, after coming this far, Bennett chose to ignore that small detail. Inside were a series of transcripts of the man's apparent confessions. Each one seemed more confused, disjointed, and shorter, but all of them had words underlined or asterisked in red. The same words appeared more and more as the MKULTRA interrogators zeroed in on a succession of different subjects.

Bennett skimmed through the pages. The more she read the less she took in what had been forced out of the man, until the last page. The interrogators had pushed him to reveal his identity – his true identity. She could tell from the fractured notes that he'd struggled not only to tell them his name, but to know what it was. But then he had and, as Bennett read it, she realised she knew him.

CHAPTER 15

Bennett should have put the folder back on the desk, left the block, and forgotten about both men.

But she didn't. She couldn't bury what she'd just witnessed or banish it from her mind. The two men weren't being interrogated, they were being tortured, and she'd played a direct part in putting both of them in those cells, and in the hands of MKULTRA.

As she ran across the compound and out through the main gates, a tiny part of her brain registered that she hadn't even looked at the file of the man from Cerro de San Francisco. She'd been too astonished by what she'd discovered about her stranger. He wasn't the Wolf, but who he was made no sense. She knew him, but there was no way he could know her, because he was dead. At least he was supposed to be.

Bennett sprinted up to the highway and hailed a taxi that was making its way back to the centre of the capital from the barrios on the other side of the small estuary that Haina sprawled over. It was late, she was alone, and the car was old and rickety – it couldn't have more than a few hundred miles left in it – but the driver stopped for her, and didn't question the address she gave him.

They didn't drive to the CIA apartment block in Miramar. They headed into the middle of the city, to an area of bigger buildings and grander houses that had become Santo Domingo's diplomatic district after the civil war. There were still some signs of the fighting that had raged through the streets here, but more of them had been paved or painted over.

Even if the base he commanded was mostly a secret, Gibson was still the highest-ranking American intelligence officer in the Dominican Republic, and that meant he got to live among the other senior diplomats and spies in the capital. Bennett wasn't supposed to know which house was Gibson's but, of course, she did.

She got out of the cab, gave the driver more notes than she needed to, stalked up the stairs to the front door of Gibson's two-storey colonial home and banged on it. And she kept banging until it was flung open by a very angry-looking Dominican woman in a thin cotton nightdress. She glared at Bennett for a second before Gibson appeared behind her in a vest and trousers he'd clearly just pulled on. The woman wasn't Gibson's wife, because Gibson's wife lived in Bloomington, Indiana – another thing Bennett wasn't supposed to know.

'We have to hand him over to the British,' Bennett said past the woman to Gibson.

Gibson didn't need to ask who 'he' was. And the woman apparently decided she couldn't be bothered dealing with someone who was clearly Gibson's problem – she disappeared up the stairs that climbed up the side of the large living room and left Gibson and Bennett to fight out whatever they needed to.

'We don't have to do anything,' Gibson said, gesturing for Bennett to come inside out of view of any prying neighbours. 'No one knows he's here and no one's missing him.'

'I know someone who is,' Bennett replied.

Gibson crossed the living room into the kitchen. A moment later he reappeared with a single glass containing three ice cubes that were already wet and translucent after a few seconds in the un-frigid evening air.

He poured himself a Scotch from a bottle that had been left on a side table and asked, 'How is that possible?'

'Because I know who he is. He's not the Wolf.'

'Of course he isn't.' Gibson swirled the Scotch around the ice cubes.

'He's an ally, and we can't subject him to—'

'We know,' he said, cutting off Bennett's tirade before it could really get going, and then taking a sip of his Scotch. 'And we've got everything we can from him, so I don't really care what happens to the guy now.'

Gibson's dismissal of the man was cruel, but it also took the wind out of Bennett's sails. She'd come to his house ready for a fight, but the battle was over before it had begun. They stood looking at each other for a long moment, before Bennett said something that surprised them both.

'Can I take him back?' It was the first question she'd asked Gibson in almost a year that had been a genuine request instead of a thinly veiled accusation, and the first time her tone with him had been anything other than combative. 'I'm the one who brought him in. He's my responsibility. And I'd like to be the one who sees him home safe.'

Gibson was silent for almost a full minute, during which Bennett imagined how he might process her sudden, desperate request.

He had every right to haul her in front of a disciplinary board just for going into the MKULTRA building and reading their files. Adding in her insubordination in Cerro de San Francisco and general attitude problems, he might even get her thrown out of the agency. But, pushing the issue too far could cause problems for him – he was ultimately responsible for all security and staff at Haina, and Bennett's actions wouldn't reflect well on him. She also now had something she could hold over him – the woman upstairs waiting for him to come back to bed who wasn't his wife. If he gave Bennett what she wanted, he'd get what she guessed he wanted too: her out of his hair.

'Fine,' he said, putting his glass down next to the Scotch bottle. The ice had now completely melted, and diluted the amber liquid too much to be worth drinking.

Bennett couldn't believe she'd got the answer she'd wanted, but she also didn't dare say anything else out of fear Gibson would change his mind.

'Now,' he said, jutting his chin at the door. 'Hopefully for the last time, get out.'

CHAPTER 16

Captain Konon Tokorev stood alone on the tiny turret deck of the *Yorsh*. The night was dark and dull. Clouds covered the sky and misty rain filled the air, yet none of it seemed to touch the captain in his thick jacket and hat, or the large cigar wedged between his lips.

Tokorev was one of the Russian navy's longest-serving and most decorated submarine captains, which was why he'd been given command of the Soviet Union's latest nuclear-powered submarine on its very first shakedown cruise. The sub was so new it hadn't even been named. *Yorsh* was the unofficial moniker for its new class – the official one was Project 671. Launching a boat without a name was the worst bad luck if you were a superstitious sailor. Tokorev was not, and anyone on his skeleton crew of thirty who was could comfort themselves that Project 671 hadn't technically launched yet because it didn't technically exist.

If the *Yorsh* passed its sea trials it would be the first of a new fleet of nuclear-powered attack subs. At ninety metres long, with four decks and a pair of VM-4P pressurised water nuclear reactors that could push it to a cruising speed of thirty-two knots, it was larger and faster than the US Permit-class nuclear submarines that had been in service since 1961. And, equipped with both Type-53 torpedoes and cruise missiles, it was better armed than the next generation of Sturgeon-class boats the Russians knew were currently being built in shipyards on both American coasts. It could also stay underwater for eighty days without resurfacing, and was sheathed in a new generation of anechoic anti-sonar tiles that rendered it practically invisible at depth.

The *Yorsh* also had another trick up its sleeve: an experimental extremely-low-frequency communications system that was designed to let it stay in contact with its home base in Murmansk without needing to surface. The system, codenamed ZEVS, used two long ground dipoles buried in the Arctic tundra outside Murmansk to transmit ELF waves that could be received by submarines in deep water. Because ZEVS worked at just 82Hz it could only send rudimentary signals, and the submarines it talked to still had to use traditional surface communications to confirm or query the orders they received. But if the system's initial tests with the *Yorsh* proved effective, it could provide a huge advantage for the Russian navy in its endless game of underwater cat and mouse with the Americans.

Tokorev had been told by a member of the Party a good twenty years his junior before the *Yorsh* had left its wet dock that it was imperative that everything went right on its maiden cruise. Tokorev had bluntly told the man that every captain of every boat on the planet knew full well that they were responsible for making sure their mission was a success and their crew came home safe and alive.

The *Yorsh* had surfaced fifteen minutes ago, as per its pre-arranged schedule, ten nautical miles south of Weymouth. It had taken five minutes to send a short radio blast requesting clarification of their last ZEVS message, and five more to receive a coded confirmation of them. The sub's communication window was a strict twenty minutes. It might be able to hide from sonar underwater thanks to its anechoic tiles, but it had no protection against radar sweeps when its turret poked above the water. This meant Tokorev had only a few more minutes to quietly enjoy his cigar – until a voice behind him interrupted his peace.

'Are you planning on following our orders?' Lieutenant Maksim Starikov asked.

Every boat in the Russian navy was assigned a KGB officer, and Starikov was the *Yorsh*'s. Tokorev had dealt with a lot of KGB, and Starikov was the worst kind of representative of the Soviet security agency. He was young, arrogant, inexperienced, and generally didn't have a clue what was going on. Tokorev also didn't like the implication that he needed constant observation to check he was doing his job properly. He would happily have left Starikov on the dockside in Murmansk, or not minded much if he'd accidentally been tossed overboard somewhere along the Norwegian coast or in the North Sea as the *Yorsh* made its way to the English Channel.

'I am following our orders,' Tokorev replied, not turning round to face Starikov and keeping his eyes focused on the point where he'd bet with himself that the sea turned into sky.

He was irritated that he'd been disturbed, but he smiled to himself knowing Starikov would hate being outside in the rain. In this kind of weather, the stiff KGB-issue wool coat the young man had arrived at Murmansk in would already be soaked through.

'We are to surface for twenty minutes every four days unless in exceptional circumstances to give our status and confirm our orders,' Tokorev said, reciting the instructions that had been repeated to him over and over again.

'Which we have done,' Starikov replied.

'And what do you think they mean?'

Tokorev had questioned the orders they'd received barely a few hours ago over the ZEVS array because they fundamentally changed his mission parameters, which up until then had essentially been to see how much of a nuisance they could be in the Channel without getting caught. Now he was being asked to do something that would almost guarantee they'd be spotted and tracked.

'That is not our concern,' Starikov said, the usual answer given by junior KGB officers keen to conceal their own ignorance. 'Only following them is.'

'Ours is not to reason why,' Tokorev replied, sighing as he paraphrased 'The Charge of the Light Brigade' by the English poet Alfred Lord Tennyson. 'Ours is but to do and die.'

If the lieutenant had been smart enough to recognise Tokorev's half-quoting one of the greatest poetic works about the futility of war then he might have been in trouble – there were things even the Soviet Union's most decorated submarine captains couldn't get away with saying – but he wasn't.

'Exactly,' Starikov said, stiffening in his increasingly sodden uniform in a gesture of earnest, patriotic sincerity.

That elicited another smile from Tokorev as he peeled back the waxed sleeve of his heavy coat and checked his watch. The twenty minutes were up. He flicked the butt of his cigar out into the murky black sea and, without saying anything else, finally turned round to face Starikov, walked past him and started to climb down through the turret access hatch.

Thirty seconds later the submarine slipped back below the surface.

CHAPTER 17

White, of course, was right. Knox was moping. When he called it a day after sitting in his office reviewing Laing's extremely comprehensive reports and then absently staring across the roofs of Mayfair for a couple of hours, he left his Jaguar in the basement car park of Leconfield House, in its spot next to Holland's dark green Bentley S2, and decided to walk into Soho.

He took a circuitous route, heading east along Curzon Street, then dropping down onto Piccadilly, which would take him to Shaftesbury Avenue and then Rupert Street, which led up to Kemp House, the tower block his flat was perched on the top of.

It was the same walk he took every time he came back to London after being sent abroad. His reintroduction to the sights, sounds, and smells of the place that had been his home for most of his life. But today he didn't feel any echo of the heady glee that used to rush through him when he spent his childhood nights sneaking out of his grandmother's house in Bethnal Green and pounding the pavements of the city. Or the happy memories of summer days spent working and evenings spent drinking with Williams. Or even the dark thrill of noticing a lingering car or recognising a stranger's face in the crowd during the short years before the Cold War started heating up and the idea of the city being swamped with foreign intelligence agents became an assumed fact of life.

Knox barely registered the cabs and buses racing each other towards Piccadilly Circus. Or the crowds of office workers jostling with tourists under the endlessly flashing lights of its billboards. Or the market traders on Berwick Street who seemed intent on barricading the entrance to Kemp House.

It all washed past him in a slow, grey blur. It was like his senses had been dulled. And that was a problem. Because a spy without keen senses was a dangerous thing.

When Knox reached the top floor of Kemp House he poured himself a large gin from the drinks trolley he kept permanently stocked in his living room and looked out over a different set of roofs.

As he watched afternoon fade into evening across the city he wondered what was wrong with him. He'd yearned to come back to London when he'd been away, but now he was home he felt almost nothing. Maybe he was just shattered from his travels, but the flatness seemed more pervasive, and more alluring, than just simple exhaustion. He needed to do something before it swallowed him, and turned this cold warrior completely numb.

He used to look down on the city like a king watching over his ancient domain. Now, every time he came back to Kemp House he'd discover his view had changed. Old buildings would have vanished and new ones risen in their place. Kemp House wasn't even the tallest structure in the heart of the city any more. The slim, teetering column of Post Office Tower, with its cluster of aerials reaching up into the sky above Fitzrovia, had taken that crown, while, closer to Knox, the tessellated oblong of Centre Point was climbing higher and higher above Tottenham Court Road tube station. And the streets were different too: on the corners at the bottom of all these buildings the old Teddy boys had turned into mods, rockers, and hippies.

It felt like the city was evolving, and leaving him behind.

He thought about what Holland would say. He'd tell Knox to pull himself together and get on with his job. But he knew he wasn't going to whet his edges by checking Laing's dots and crosses. He needed a real reason. He just had no idea where or how to find one. Then he heard another voice. An American voice that belonged to an old friend. It was Abey Bennett's, and it was telling him to pull his head out of his ass.

The phrase lodged in his mind, and stayed there. In fact, Bennett's Midwestern accent only started to fade as he walked back into the R&D department in Leconfield House the following morning and found it completely transformed.

'You better bloody well be here to help,' White shouted at Knox over the sea of lab coats and uniforms that were crammed between desks and computer towers.

'Whatever I can do,' Knox shouted back as he fought his way over to White's desk.

Knox had decided he'd dismissed their brief conversation the previous afternoon about the Russian submarine too quickly. And judging from the hive of activity he'd just walked into, he was right.

'What's happening?' he asked when he finally reached White.

'A breakthrough, I hope,' he replied.

Overnight, the sightings of the ghost submarine had increased dramatically. No one knew if this was because of White's tinkering with the navy's sonar and radar systems or some sloppiness by whoever was messing about in the Channel, but everyone wanted to take advantage of the opportunity they'd been gifted.

'Has anyone else noticed?' Knox asked.

White shook his head. 'Nothing from the French, Dutch, or Belgians. At least nothing we've picked up. It feels like the ghost is putting on a show specifically for us. I've got every engineer in the place trying to work out why.'

'Is anyone looking at the other why?' Knox asked.

White frowned.

'If there's a pattern to the appearances it might reveal their mission,' Knox said. 'Give me the coordinates of the sightings and maybe I can help predict where they're going to show up next.'

'That's actually a very good idea,' White replied.

Then he told one of his assistants to clear some space and get Knox a map of the Channel.

Knox settled into the melee, thinking he might just have found what he needed to shake him out of his foggy mood – if the submarine was Russian, piercing whatever invisible armour they'd wrapped it in would be a major coup.

Unfortunately it turned out that this particular chink was a false start.

Knox studied the movements of the ghost, from its very first sighting to the new data he was being handed almost constantly. He tried to discern some logic to what the Russians were doing, but there wasn't any. He sifted through his limited knowledge of the history of the Channel – and borrowed some of the navy's – in case the Soviets were trying to send some kind of coded message, but if they were he couldn't find it.

There were a few points on the map the submarine kept its distance from, but it wasn't hard to work out why – they were all naval bases. There was one spot on the south coast of England that Knox avoided too: the inverted Y of water that cut the Isle of Wight off from the mainland and stretched up to Southampton. This was where de Gaulle had arrived to see Macmillan after crossing the Channel on the *Surcouf*, the French navy's latest T 47-class destroyer seven years ago. It was also where Jack Williams had died, the only member of a dive team sent on Knox's orders to take a closer look at the new French destroyer who hadn't returned from the mission.

White's attempts to come up with a technological solution to tracking the submarine also failed to bear fruit. More echoes were being caught, but they were still just echoes.

And then the submarine vanished. Three distinct radar pings were registered in a line heading out of the Channel into the Atlantic just after 4 p.m. Then, west of the Scilly Isles, it disappeared for good.

'It looks like you were right after all, they've just been toying with us,' Knox said to White as they watched the uniforms and lab coats start to trickle out of the R&D department an hour later.

'I know,' White replied, his voice the same mix of frustration and resignation as Knox's.

CHAPTER 18

The next day, heavy clouds filled the sky over Soho. The grey was back, and it felt like it was going to consume Knox and the whole city.

He found a near-empty bag of coffee beans from the Algerian Stores on Old Compton Street in one of his kitchen cupboards. And, as he ground just enough to make himself a very small and very strong coffee, he briefly wondered about walking up to King's Cross and taking a train back to Hertfordshire. At least at Rabley Heath it was normal for him to feel out of sync with his surroundings, watching the feral garden creep closer and closer to the big house that was his yet also wasn't. But he decided it was too soon to beat a retreat, or tell Holland that between the two of them he was the one who should be put out to pasture.

Knox's kitchen-cum-living room was less spartan than it had once been, though it was still fairly minimalist – a reflection of both Knox's tastes and the amount of time he spent in London. There was a Mies van der Rohe sofa, which he had to continually tell himself was more comfortable than it really was, with two abstract Hilma af Klint paintings hung above it. A small Ercol teak table that he'd bought to replace a much larger marble one he'd rarely used stood next to his kitchen counter. And, beyond that, there was only a well-stocked drinks trolley and a Magnusson-Grossman lounge chair.

After an icy shower he put on a light shirt, dark trousers and checked blazer from Henry Poole. He might have felt disconnected from the city, but his native's sixth sense told him the clouds hanging over London wouldn't break on him.

As he steeled himself for the walk to Mayfair, at first he didn't see the envelope that had been slipped under his door. Then he spotted it, lying tantalisingly on his hallway's dark floorboards. It was too early for the post, which would have been left in his pigeonhole on the ground floor anyway, and he didn't know any of his neighbours well enough for one of them to be leaving him morning notes. Someone was making a very direct approach.

Knox reached down, pinched the corner of the thick, off-white paper and turned it over. His name was written on the front and, from the weight of it, there was a letter inside.

He walked back to the kitchen counter, gently deposited the envelope on it, and thought about what to do. What he should do was cover it in something airtight, douse his hands, and call Leconfield House. But his instincts told him he wasn't under attack. He didn't think the envelope had been dipped in cyanide or filled with anthrax spores. Whoever the letter's author was, they wanted to make contact with him, not kill him.

Still, he needed to be cautious, so he used a knife to prise open the glued-down flap and tip out what was inside. Not a letter, but a card. It was marked in the same ink and handwriting as the envelope, and spelled out a simple message: Regent's Park Broad Walk, Midday, Old friends.

Adrenaline rushed through Knox. It was exhilarating, but it was also so long since he'd felt it that for a moment he wasn't sure what it was. He had no idea who these 'old friends' could be, but he wanted to know.

He put the card back into the envelope, slipped it into his jacket, and rushed out of the flat.

After yesterday's excitement, Leconfield House seemed even quieter than usual when Knox arrived twenty minutes later. He thought about checking in on Laing, but decided he should probably see if the younger officer had sent anything new about the Kosygin summit up to his office before he bothered him again. He also considered taking his note to White and getting him to check for any invisible messages or clues about who had sent it, but realised he wanted to keep his mystery to himself.

He found a fresh pile of folders on his desk. Laing was continuing to be as thorough as he'd claimed, and was making a point of letting Knox know. It took him most of the morning to read through the files Laing had compiled, followed by the latest communications on how poorly things were going in Rhodesia.

By all accounts events in Africa were moving quickly, and with total disregard for MI5's attempts to slow them down. Ian Smith had been branded a 'raw colonial' by Whitehall. Knox was fairly sure he was actually a despot in training. However, he couldn't help but be a little impressed by this farmer-turned-prime-minister's gall. Smith hadn't liked the caveats his old imperial overlord had attached to the freedom it wanted to hand down, so he'd gone ahead and claimed his own. He was determined to maintain white minority rule, and had refused to back down in the face of economic sanctions and international condemnation. Of course, Knox was also convinced the whole thing would end badly. Nation-building took more than sheer force of will, it needed patience, an ability to compromise, and powerful allies, none of which Smith had.

At eleven thirty, just as Knox had finally run out of distractions and was getting ready to head to Regent's Park, there was a knock at his door.

'Come in,' he said, trying not to sound too short as he glanced at his watch.

Laing stepped into the room, looking more anxious than Knox thought a human could.

'Sir,' he said. 'There's a serious problem with the summit.'

Knox looked at his watch again. He could spare five minutes. 'What is it?'

'He wants to go to the ballet.'

It took all of Knox's professional composure not to burst out laughing.

'Who?' he asked, struggling to keep his own voice level.

'Kosygin. He's found out Nureyev is dancing with the Royal Ballet and he wants to see it.'

'That doesn't sound so terrible,' Knox said, stepping out from behind his desk.

'I've spoken to the Opera House,' Laing replied. The performance is being broadcast live on the BBC.'

Laing's concerns now made a little more sense to Knox, but he still thought he was overreacting.

'I imagine they'll be filming the dancers rather than the audience,' Knox said as he slipped on his jacket.

'But what if someone makes an attempt on him and it ends up on national television?'

'No one wants to assassinate Kosygin except maybe Brezhnev,' Knox replied. 'And there's nothing we can do about that. He's the first Soviet leader whose been anything like close to open with the West. London is probably the safest place he could be.'

'That's exactly why someone would choose here to get rid of him,' Laing countered.

'Look,' Knox said. 'It's your job to plan for the worst-case scenario, and you're doing a very good job of that. But you need to draw the line at paranoia. I'm not prepared to tell the Russians we can't protect one of their heads of state for an evening.'

Knox ushered Laing out into the corridor, expecting a slightly awkward ride together in the lift. But, their meeting over, the younger officer strode away from Knox while he was still shutting his office door, and opted to take the stairs down to the School Hall.

Knox wondered if Laing was going to seethe over their encounter until it completely slipped from his mind as he walked the short distance through Shepherd Market to Green Park tube station.

The morning clouds had evaporated, and a tentative spring heat was starting to creep into the day.

Knox took the tube to Piccadilly Circus, then changed onto the Bakerloo line, switching from one aluminium carriage to another, and rode two more stops to Regent's Park. He should have been more discreet, cleaned himself of any potential tail by chopping and changing direction, but he didn't have the time, and he was too excited to find out who was waiting for him. By the time he reached Ulster Terrace, which ran along the outer rim of the park, adrenaline was pumping through him again.

As he crossed over the road in front of the entrance to the Broad Walk he saw two people he recognised sitting on a bench looking back at him. A woman and a man from two different times in his life, who shouldn't be there and who shouldn't know each other.

The woman was Abey Bennett and the man, impossibly, was Jack Williams.

CHAPTER 19

Knox had been shot before, but this felt like he'd just been hit square in the chest by a cannonball. The wind was knocked out of him and every bone in his body seemed to shatter and fuse simultaneously. Time and the world stopped as confusion overwhelmed him.

What he was seeing couldn't be real, yet it was there in front of him. Jack Williams couldn't be alive, but he was, sitting next to Abey Bennett and looking at Knox as if it had been days instead of years since they'd last seen each other – and as if he hadn't somehow come back from the dead.

Knox was stuck with shock until a high-pitched blast jolted him out of his paralysis.

He realised he was standing in the middle of the road, blocking the path of an angry-looking woman in a bright yellow Austin Mini. He stepped slowly up onto the pavement as the Mini screeched behind him.

Bennett got up, leaving Williams on the bench.

'Long time, no see,' she said to Knox as they both reached the wrought-iron gate at the entrance to the Broad Walk.

It was five years since the two of them had met, when Bennett was desperately trying to prove she could be more than just a file clerk in the US embassy on Grosvenor Square and Knox had been suspended from MI5 while hunting a Soviet mole who had buried their way deep into the Service. They'd made a formidable team, pushing each other when they both felt on the verge of giving up, finding the traitor Knox had started to fear might only have existed in his head, and proving that Bennett was a better spy than any CIA field agent in London.

They'd kept in touch from time to time via the odd letter and inter-agency gossip. Knox missed Bennett and her unrelenting determination, and always hoped their professional lives would cross paths again. But this wasn't the reunion he'd expected.

Five years, and she still had the exact same jet-black, close-cropped hair, and the bright blue of her eyes hadn't dimmed at all.

'How?' he stammered. 'How is this possible?'

'He turned up in Santo Domingo,' Bennett said. 'Somehow he knew who I was. When we worked out who he was I asked if I could bring him home.'

Knox looked past Bennett to Williams. He still seemed uncannily serene, like what was happening didn't defy all rational or fantastical reason.

'Is it really him?' he asked.

'As far as we can work out,' Bennett replied. 'But he's not in good shape.'

Knox's head snapped back to her, his face instantly switching from astonishment to concern.

'He hasn't made a lot of sense,' Bennett continued. 'He doesn't know where he's been or how he ended up in the Dominican Republic.'

'The Russians?'

'Maybe. Probably.'

'I need to get him to White.'

'That's not possible.'

'What? Why?'

Bennett inched closer to Knox.

'He told us he was the Wolf,' she said, her voice low even though there was no one near them to hear.

Knox's eyebrows rose. He knew the myth of the Wolf, and he mostly thought the idea of a Soviet master assassin running riot across the globe was precisely that – a myth.

'That's ridiculous,' he said.

'Sure,' Bennett agreed. 'But it's not something you can take back once you've said it. Hoffman wants a real hoopla. Make handing him over very official and very political.'

Hugh Hoffman was the new CIA chief of station in London. Michael Finney, who had been COS for decades, had finally stepped down three months ago. It was widely known that Hoffman wanted to 'shake up the place', and apparently thought that producing a missing British agent who had claimed to be a Soviet operative would do exactly that.

'And then,' Bennett continued, 'all hell will break loose.'

Knox knew she was right. If Hoffman got his way, Williams would have to be carted off to prison, or somewhere worse, and a blindsided Holland would be hauled in front of the cabinet to explain the inexplicable.

'Why are you here, then?' he asked.

'He's still in my custody,' Bennett replied, 'until Hoffman makes his scene. I didn't want you to find out what had happened after it was too late.'

'How long do we have?'

'Long enough to talk.'

Bennett's hand reached out, but she stopped herself before she squeezed Knox's arm in a gesture of un-spy-like empathy. Instead she just nodded at him and crossed over Ulster Terrace to where she could still see the bench but also give the two men a little privacy.

Knox watched her go, took a breath, and walked over to the bench and the best friend he never thought he'd see again. Up close, Williams looked older than the seven years that had passed. He was thinner, his hair longer and more lank than Knox had ever seen it. But it was definitely him.

Questions tumbled over each other in Knox's head. There was so much he wanted to ask, so much he wanted to say. In the end, he sat down next to Williams and simply said, 'It's good to see you, Jack.'

'It's good to see you too, Richard,' Williams replied.

The voice was unmistakable. That trademark tone of charismatic flippancy that ran through his well-educated Hertfordshire drawl. But Knox could detect a shadow of something else in it too now.

'How are you?' he asked.

'I've been better,' Williams replied. He smiled, but it looked more like a grimace.

'Did the Americans treat you well?'

Williams looked down at the gravel path in front of the bench, and gripped both his arms, like he was trying to hold on to himself. 'No.'

Knox looked at his fingers. They were bony and stained yellow. Williams had never smoked.

When he tilted his head back up, his eyes had completely changed. They weren't calm any more. They were focused so fiercely on Knox it felt like they were boring straight through him, which they were, towards Bennett.

'I asked her for help and they tortured me. You can't trust her.'

'You told Bennett you were the Wolf,' Knox said, instantly regretting the insinuation he hadn't intended.

'I had to,' Williams replied. 'I had to make them think that so they'd want to know who I really was, then bring me back to you. So you could help me.'

'Help you with what?' Knox asked.

Williams leaned forward again, gripping his arms even tighter, as if the words he was about to say were physically trying to stop him from uttering them.

'There's going to be an attack. Here in London.' His words were rushed, urgent. 'Soon. But I don't know when. The Americans scrambled my head. Everything's upside down and turned around, and I need you to straighten it out again.'

'An attack on who?' Knox asked.

'I-I'm not sure,' Williams said, the urgency in his voice turning into anger. 'But you have to believe me.'

Every fibre of Knox's being wanted to. Even with no evidence, even with the state of him, Knox wanted to believe Williams.

'Alright,' he said, making his voice as soft as possible. 'What can I do?'

Williams sighed and turned away, his fingers finally slackening their grip as he looked along the Broad Walk towards Parliament Hill in the distance.

'I need to rest. I don't know how long it's been since I slept. I can feel myself breaking apart.'

Knox glanced at Bennett across the road. He could tell she'd noticed Williams's outburst, and guessed they only had a few more moments together before she'd come back and say their time was up.

Then Knox saw the red roof of a double-decker turning into the far end of Ulster Terrace and realised he actually had mere seconds to decide what was going to happen next.

Should he leave Williams to the fate the CIA wanted, paraded through Whitehall and then disappeared off to be put through more hell? Or should he betray Bennett and help the friend to whom he owed a debt he never thought he'd be able to repay?

There was no choice. He was going to save Williams.

'Do you remember Geoffrey Pyke?' he asked.

Williams's face went blank for a moment, but then he nodded.

'Good,' Knox said. 'Follow me.'

He got up and started to walk towards the gate. As he heard Williams's feet start to crunch on the gravel behind him he signalled to Bennett to stay where she was and that they'd come over to her.

Knox and Williams reached the edge of the pavement at the same time as the double-decker momentarily blocked Bennett's view of them. Then, when it had passed, Williams had vanished and Knox was lying in the gutter.

'What the hell happened?' Bennett shouted as she ran over the road and the bus turned round a corner and disappeared into Marylebone. 'Where's Williams?'

Knox pulled himself up, massaging the shoulder he'd landed on.

'He's gone,' he said.

CHAPTER 20

'You're sure it was him?' Holland asked Knox.

After ten minutes of questioning the director general's voice was still an even balance of amazement and suspicion.

'Yes,' Knox replied. 'Completely.'

He was sitting again in the single chair that faced Holland across his desk. There was no way he could've gone straight after Williams with Bennett on his tail, so he'd returned to Leconfield House.

Knox reasoned that Holland had been as much of a patron to Williams as he'd been to himself, so he deserved to know that he was still alive as quickly as possible. He also wanted to warn Holland about what Hoffman was planning, and make sure that it would be him who was put in charge of bringing Williams back into the fold.

Knox hadn't expected Holland to rave and cry at the news that one of his missing agents had finally been found, or announce that he was going straight to Grosvenor Square to lodge a formal complaint with the CIA about their treatment of an MI5 officer. But he was surprised by just how cool the director general was being.

'And you have no idea where he'd go?' Holland asked.

'Under normal circumstances I'd expect him to go to Rabley Heath, but these aren't normal. He could have gone to ground anywhere.'

Holland's reply to that was a sceptical, 'Hmm.'

He was right to not be entirely convinced by what Knox was telling him, because Knox actually knew exactly where Williams had gone. At least, he hoped he did.

And that wasn't the only thing he was keeping from Holland. He'd neglected to repeat Williams's warning that some horrible event was about to befall the city. Williams had said himself that he couldn't trust his memory, and Knox needed to have a longer conversation with him in less dramatic circumstances to establish if the threat was real before he gave Holland something else to worry about.

'Well,' Holland continued, 'I don't have any issue with Hoffman's little spectacle being snuffed out. But we need to bring Williams in. He's not safe alone and neither might be anyone who he comes into contact with.'

'He's confused, but I don't think he's a threat to the public,' Knox said.

'I'm sure you don't. But that doesn't mean he isn't one.'

Knox was about to protest again, but a look that Holland very rarely gave him stopped him before he could speak.

'You know I've never given the theory of the Wolf much credence – it's too convenient, too easy – and I'm not about to start,' Holland said. 'But Williams is still a highly trained and, by your own admission, unstable agent who needs to be contained.'

Knox winced internally at Holland's choice of words. Williams wasn't an animal to be caged, he was a colleague and a friend who needed protecting.

'This isn't the time to let anyone make a fool out of us, or for us to make a scene of our own,' Holland continued. 'I'll celebrate Williams's return once he's in our care. Now find him. Before the Americans do.'

***

Less than half a mile away Bennett was enduring a similar conversation with Hugh Hoffman in his office on the fourth floor of the US embassy. Similar in subject but not in tone.

'You're a damn embarrassment,' Hoffman shouted, loud enough for most of the rest of the building to hear.

Bennett had never been in Michael Finney's office when he'd been the London COS and she'd worked down in the embassy's subterranean archives, but she knew it had been relatively modest, at the back of the fourth floor that the CIA occupied entirely, and just large enough for his desk and a small meeting table. Hoffman, however, had taken over one of the large, glass-walled conference rooms that looked out over Grosvenor Square as his personal dominion. No one could cross the fourth floor without passing his expansive office and seeing what was going on inside, and being seen themselves – a tactic by Hoffman to remind everyone who worked for him that he was the boss, and that he was always watching them.

'I couldn't know that was going to happen,' Bennett said.

For twenty minutes she'd been trying to defend herself whenever Hoffman stopped his tirade to catch his breath. Hoffman was a large man with a thick Tennessee accent. He had the kind of voice that sounded like it was permanently angry, and he usually was. If it wasn't for the change of scenery, Bennett could have been back in Santo Domingo, arguing with Gibson.

'He's an enemy asset. You didn't think he was going to make a run for it as soon as he could?' Hoffman replied.

Hoffman was also, uncommonly for a high-ranking CIA officer, extremely open about his politics. He was a red-blooded Republican who thought Kennedy had been too timid with Castro and Khrushchev, and that President Johnson should be spending even more of his time and the federal budget fighting communism abroad instead of being distracted by his so-called 'war on poverty' at home.

'The British aren't our enemy,' Bennett said, more than a little astounded that she was having to defend America's relationship with one of its most important and closest allies to a CIA chief of station.

'Everyone is our enemy,' Hoffman said. 'The only difference is how much. This might be their backyard, but I'm not about to let them forget who's really in charge around here. The Brits have been dragging their heels for years, letting their country get infested with Reds. It's like they forgot what we fought the war for, or that they still owe us for bailing them out.'

Bennett forced herself not to correct Hoffman about the geopolitics of World War Two, or get sucked into more debate about Cold War allegiances.

'And now they've invited the damned chairman of the Council of Ministers to swan about London while Wilson fawns over him.'

The CIA had found out about Kosygin's secret summit with Wilson weeks ago thanks to one of their sources in the civil service. Hoffman was, unsurprisingly, as furious about it as he was about the UK being on the verge of re-electing a left-wing government.

He paused to take a breath, and Bennett took the opportunity to steer the conversation back towards something close to a purpose.

'Let me help find Williams,' she said. 'I have a connection with him, and his friends.'

Hoffman smiled. 'Oh you're not going to help find him. You're going to do it. By yourself.'

'I'll need support,' Bennett said. 'I can't do this without a ground team.'

Hoffman shook his head. 'No way.'

'He could be anywhere in the city, or the country, by now.'

'That's your problem. You got yourself into this mess so you can get yourself out of it, without dragging anyone here down with you. Get him back in twenty-four hours, or you're out. And I'll send people after him who won't be as friendly as you're so keen to be.'

CHAPTER 21

One and a half thousand miles away, Major Natalya Yegerova was also being kept up to date about the day's events in London.

In the run-up to Kosygin's trip to the British capital, all *residentura* spies in the Soviet embassy and Directorate S's illegal operatives spread throughout the city were on high alert and feeding constant reports to Moscow. Yegerova read everything that was sent to Directorate S, and anything else that arrived at the Lubyanka she could get her hands on. She was particularly interested in the sudden appearance of a low-level CIA agent who should have been on the other side of the Atlantic, sweating in the Caribbean sun, and her eventful meeting with the director general of MI5's right-hand man in Regent's Park.

'Tell me again what the message said about the third person,' she said to the junior Directorate S officer standing on the other side of her narrow desk. 'Precisely.'

'Our agent described him as white, in his late thirties or early forties,' the young man repeated. 'They said he looked thin and confused.'

It wasn't standard protocol to include so much description in coded message bursts. But on this occasion Yegerova wasn't going to issue a reprimand.

'And they were certain he arrived with the American?' she asked.

The officer nodded. Just as Knox had been followed from Leconfield House, Bennett and the man with her had also been shadowed to Regent's Park from the American embassy.

'Good,' Yegerova said. 'You may go.'

The officer nodded, turned on his heel and waited until he was out of Yegerova's office before rolling his eyes.

Yegerova had found her first traitor when she was ten, the summer after the end of the Great Patriotic War. She'd seen a worker stealing potatoes from the collectivised farm in central Georgia her mother had been left to run after her father had been marched to his death at Stalingrad, along with half a million other Soviet souls. The thief had been severely punished, and Yegerova had been heavily rewarded, and singled out for her burgeoning zealotry.

She'd been a Little Octobrist, and had already traded her red five-pointed-star pin badge with its portrait of a young Lenin for the red neckerchief of the Young Pioneers. When she turned fourteen she graduated to the Komsomol, the All-Union Leninist Young Communist League. By then, the local Party had serious ambitions for her to continue the legacy of Georgia's greatest Soviet child, Joseph Stalin. However, Yegerova's own ambitions stretched further than attending youth rallies in Tbilisi and giving rousing speeches about the humble value of endless work at farms and factories. She wanted to follow Stalin's footsteps all the way to Moscow, and she wanted to join the KGB.

She'd never forgotten the feeling of glorious justice that had filled her after she'd informed on the potato thief. She knew the Soviet Union was under constant threat from enemies within its own ranks as well as from the West, and she wanted to root out as many of them as she could.

'Do not go beyond yourself,' she'd been told when she'd announced her desire to attend School 101, more formally known as the Higher Intelligence School, the advanced KGB training centre on the fringes of the Soviet capital, when she was twenty-one. 'They will just look down on you.'

'Then I must go,' she'd replied, full of her ever-present righteousness. 'We are all comrades and if they disagree then I will expose them. And if they disregard me then they won't suspect me, and that will be their mistake.'

Her application had been accepted, and she'd left Georgia for good the following spring. As her old mentors had predicted, she'd been alternatingly taunted and ignored by the other students. They thought she was a backward farm girl, and she thought they were all apostate metropolitan elites. She was surrounded by people who had been sent to the KGB by their families to be handed jobs that would keep them clean and dry and, if they played the game they'd been born into right, give them unquestioned power.

Her fellow initiates had started to change their minds about her when she'd reported enough of them for smoking, excessive drinking, and other unacceptable and un-Soviet activities. They ostracised her, played tricks on her, even threatened her. But she remained resolute, and her would-be tormentors eventually ended up bending first, finally seeing her as the immutable moral force of nature that she was. By the end of their time at School 101 her classmates found it easier to either act properly and piously whenever she was around or come up with excuses to never go anywhere near her.

She hadn't expected to be assigned to Directorate S when she'd graduated, or to stay there for the last six years, overseeing operations and managing illegal operatives without ever leaving the Lubyanka. But she was happy she had been. KGB headquarters was her monastery, and she was its most faithful abbess.

She didn't even mind that her office was so small that she could reach out and touch both sides of it with her arms if she stood up at her desk, or that it had clearly been carved out of some dead space between two other rooms, because it had been created just for her.

Working in the Lubyanka also gave her ample opportunity to uncover more potential traitors. And now her attention was firmly on Rykov, a man whose rapid rise and disregard for the solemn responsibilities given to him were both going unchecked.

Yegerova didn't share the view that his assumption of General Medev's responsibilities at the scientific directorate after his death demonstrated loyalty and dedication to duty. She thought it was insubordinate. She also didn't believe that Line Z was working for the greater glory of the Soviet cause. She thought Rykov had a different agenda for his department, one that would only benefit him and his rampant ambition. And she'd decided that what was happening in London might be the perfect way to expose it.

CHAPTER 22

Knox was more careful when he left Leconfield House again. This time he retrieved his Jaguar from the car park and drove the short distance north up Park Lane, past the Dorchester Hotel, and into a side street behind Marble Arch tube station. Then he left his car behind, dropped into the network of underpasses that ran beneath the triumphal arch that had ended up incongruously perched on top of a roundabout, and completed a convoluted figure of eight through the dark, permanently damp passages before descending further underground and taking the Central line east to Tottenham Court Road, the Northern line south to Leicester Square, and then the Piccadilly line back west to Knightsbridge.

The tube was one of the easiest places to get lost in London. The combination of tunnels, lifts, escalators, and seven lines built independent of any order made it a nightmare to navigate for the uninitiated. However, Knox knew that spies of every nationality spent long hours learning the tricks and shortcuts of the subterranean maze, and he wanted to take extra precautions before he reunited with Williams just in case someone was tailing him.

Harrods was its own kind of riddle. The vast emporium was a knot of departments that wanted to sell the fabulously wealthy anything their hearts desired as soon as they stepped through its doors. And its meandering pathways were designed to make it as hard as possible for them to leave again. Knox knew it almost as well as he knew the tube.

MI5 had quietly used Harrods as a training ground for decades, and both Knox and Williams had spent their fair share of time trying to slip through the book department or across the antiques gallery without being spotted before retiring to the food hall for a slice of meat pie or a sandwich.

Knox tested his muscle memory now, weaving between perfume counters, behind pillars and up and down gaudy escalators and staircases for almost half an hour. He even stopped briefly in the food hall to buy a large Melton Mowbray pork pie. Unfortunately for him, the three Soviet illegals who had tracked him to Knightsbridge were wise to his game and simply waited outside, watching from the far side of the Brompton Road until he emerged again and headed down into the tube once more.

The Russian agents shadowed Knox in rotation, each one only riding for a few stops in the same carriage as him before swapping places with each other. When Knox went above ground at King's Cross two of them followed him up into the railway station, taking off their jackets and folding them over their arms for a quick and simple change of appearance, then followed him back down into the tube ticket hall, where their comrade was waiting for them, and onto the Piccadilly line to Holborn and the Central line back to Marble Arch.

They followed him, keeping their distance, to his Jaguar. Two of them got into the black Ford Cortina that they'd also driven from Mayfair an hour and a half ago, while the third peeled off and disappeared towards Hyde Park.

Knox now headed east across the city, weaving another elaborate path that took him over the river twice before ending up in another quiet side street just off Finsbury Circus in the heart of the City. From there, he walked along the edge of the bomb-site-turned-building-site that the new Barbican housing estate was slowly rising from. Then, at the edge of Smithfield Market on the corner of Charterhouse Street and Poultry Avenue, he prised open a door that had been designed to look both permanently shut up and derelict, and walked down five flights of stairs.

Smithfield was one of London's oldest markets, and had been supplying meat and livestock to the city for centuries. In the 1940s the War Office's Combined Operations Headquarters had requisitioned a large cold-meat store deep beneath it and used the frigid space to test Pykrete, an experimental super-hard but lightweight compound of ice and sawdust dreamed up by Geoffrey Pyke. Senior members of the army and navy had hoped to use it to create huge floating refuelling stations for Allied aircraft and convoys in the Atlantic. But the war ended before Pyke had been able to prove the viability of his wonder material, and then the Combined Operations Headquarters had been promptly disbanded. No one had thought to officially return ownership of the deep store to Smithfield, and there was no one for the market to ask for it back from, so it was left empty and forgotten, by everyone except MI5.

Every morning the market's Victorian halls were a chaotic stampede of delivery vans and crates piled high with fresh, bloody carcasses, but by the afternoon they were all scrubbed clean and quiet.

The sound of Knox's footsteps echoed down the stairwell to the cold store. The only other noise was the occasional low rumble of a Metropolitan or Circle line train in the tube tunnel that ran along the northern side of the market.

Enough electricity had been kept flowing for lights to stay on in the store and the lower half of the staircase. But even with power to the cooling systems shut off years ago, Knox still felt a chill run through him as he got closer to his second incredible reunion with Williams.

Their meeting in Regent's Park had been brief, a cry for help Knox had instinctively reacted to, but he didn't know what he was now walking into. Williams might be about to tell him about a terrifying threat to national security he had managed to pull from the tangle of his mind, or Knox might be about to face his long-overdue reckoning for sending his best friend to his death.

The last thing he'd anticipated was to be grabbed as soon as he walked into the cold store and pulled into a hug so hard he couldn't believe he was being held by the same gaunt man he'd sat next to a few hours before.

'Thank God it's you, old man,' Williams said when he finally released Knox from his embrace but kept a tight grip on his shoulders.

Old man was a private joke between Knox and Williams, an ironic reference to the world of club room conversations and gentleman's agreements they'd found themselves part of as young, fast-rising members of MI5. Hearing it again after so many years warmed Knox's heart, and sliced straight through it.

'Expecting someone else?' Knox asked.

'Honestly,' Williams replied, 'I had no idea.'

He seemed completely transformed from the fragile figure in Regent's Park. His voice was now full of humour and energy. He let go of Knox and walked over to a low line of dusty crates.

'I woke up about ten minutes ago. No idea how I got here. But that seems pretty par for the course at the moment.'

'Well, I'm glad you stuck around,' Knox said, relieved but also concerned that Williams didn't seem to know how he'd made his way to Smithfield after jumping on the backboard of the bus on Ulster Terrace and crouching between its rear seats out of Bennett's view.

'I decided someone would arrive sooner or later and tell me what was going on.' He paused for a moment, then added, 'I'm glad it was you.'

'Do you remember Regent's Park?' Knox asked.

'Of course,' Williams replied, an edge suddenly creeping into his voice. 'Most of it, anyway.'

'Who was there with us?'

'Abey Bennett. My mind's not a complete wreck.'

'Sorry,' Knox said. 'I know this must be frustrating, but I need to ask you a few more questions.'

He joined Williams on the row of crates as the rumbling echo of a tube train hummed through the store.

'What about before the park?' he asked.

'There are shards, fragments of places and people, but I don't know when or where it all belongs.'

'That doesn't sound like much fun,' Knox said.

'It's bloody terrifying,' Williams replied, his voice softening again. 'But what can I do?'

It was a sad statement, but in a strange way it reassured Knox because it was exactly what he'd expect Williams to say.

He remembered the waxed paper parcel he was holding and handed it over, watching Williams's face twist into a grin as he unwrapped the pie and devoured one of the thick wedges it had been cut into.

Knox knew he should give Williams a chance to eat, rest, build up some strength, and hope more of his memories fell into place. However, he was too impatient to ease off for long. He wanted to know more about the attack Williams was so scared of, and where his best friend had been for the last seven years. But not in that order.

'What's the last thing you remember from before...' he started, but was suddenly unable to complete the question.

Williams took another bite of pie, then his body abruptly stilled. He didn't look like he was searching his memories, he looked like he wasn't thinking at all.

'The *Surcouf*,' he said, flatly. 'Diving under and approaching the hull. That's it.'

'I'm sorry,' Knox said. His voice was a whisper as he finally said to Williams what he'd repeated to his ghost every day for seven years.

Williams's jaw moved. But he wasn't clenching it to hold back his anger. He was chewing. After a long, silent moment he swallowed.

'One of those things,' he replied, his voice still strangely even.

Knox had never dared to imagine forgiveness for what had happened to Williams – what Knox had let happen to him – but he couldn't believe Williams was dismissing it so easily and casually.

Whenever Knox had had this conversation in his head he'd fantasised every response Williams might give: sobbing into his arms, or screaming at him, or attacking him, and Knox taking punch after punch because he deserved them all. But he hadn't prepared for this reaction.

Williams had another bite of pie, then offered a wedge to Knox. He took it. The pastry was tough, but it crumbled and melted as it started to mix with the fat and meat in his mouth. It was delicious and he hated it.

'What happened to everyone else?' Williams asked when he'd swallowed his pie.

Knox stared at the crumbs on his fingertips as he said, 'They were fine.'

'Well, then,' Williams replied, wiping his hands. 'Just one of those things.'

The two men fell back into silence. There was no way Knox could ask Williams any more about the *Surcouf*, or the supposed attack on London, now. He couldn't even look him in the eye.

Knox felt like they could stay seated next to each other under Smithfield forever, stuck in their own personal limbos. But after a few more moments of unbearable quiet their solitude was interrupted.

Two men appeared in the doorway of the cold store. Knox had no idea who they were, or how they'd managed to get down five flights of half-lit stairs without making a single noise, but their sudden materialisation jolted him out of his despair. He felt Williams tense next to him too.

'It's polite to knock,' Knox said, standing up as the two strangers stepped into the store.

One of the men was in an open-collared shirt and blazer, the other was wearing a leather bomber jacket.

'Is there something we can do for you?' Knox asked.

'Not you, him,' the man in the blazer said in accentless English, pointing at Williams.

'He's busy,' Knox said, moving between them.

'Not any more,' the man replied, squaring up to Knox as his partner kept guard on the door.

It was months since Knox's last fitness test, and longer since he'd had any close combat training. He prepared himself for a messy fight. But before he could land a first hit or take a blow, Williams launched himself past him.

He was incredibly fast, and precise. He slammed his left elbow into the nose of the man in front of Knox, breaking it with a single, wet crunch that sprayed the old meat store with fresh blood. Then he stamped his foot down on the toes of the second man, distracting him with pain so he could inflict more by driving his opposite knee into his crotch.

Knox could only watch, stunned, as Williams spun back, grabbed the man with the broken nose, who was now stumbling round in a daze, and slammed his head against the bare brick wall. Then he did it again, and again, until the would-be attacker's body crumpled onto the floor.

Knox couldn't tell if the man was unconscious or dead, and neither could his accomplice in the leather jacket, who had bolted for the staircase. He made it to the second turn in the stairs before Williams caught his trailing ankle, pulled his leg out from under him, and sent him crashing onto the concrete. Then Williams leaned over him and somehow used his own slight weight to pivot and twist the man over the old rusty handrail and down into the void. The sound of his neck cracking as he landed in front of Knox echoed up and down the stairwell.

Knox looked up at Williams just as his face turned from cold, hard determination to a cool curiosity about what had just happened.

'Time to go, I suppose,' Williams said.

CHAPTER 23

Knox caught up with Williams at the dark halfway point of the stairs, where the glow of the electric bulbs faded but the weak light from the jimmied-open door to the street couldn't quite reach. Williams was slowing down. Whatever energy he'd managed to summon in the cold store was already draining away. That was good, but also bad – Knox needed him calmer but not worn out, because they still needed to put some distance between themselves and the bodies at the bottom of the stairwell.

Knox had had a few seconds to check if the man in the cold store was dead. He was. Knox had also gone through his clothes to see if they gave any clues about where he was from or who had sent him, but there were no telltale foreign labels or scraps of paper in his pockets. Knox didn't know if the men had been KGB, or CIA, or someone else. Or if there were more of them waiting outside.

They reached the top of the staircase and Williams doubled over, against the wall and away from the handrail and five-floor drop, trying to catch his breath.

'It's about a mile to my car. Can you make it?' Knox asked him, knowing already that the answer would be no.

Knox peered through the gap in the door. Rush hour was just beginning and he could see a few people heading to the nearest tube station or bus stop. But no one looked like they were loitering, or paying well-disguised attention to the half-open door as they passed it.

'Wait here,' he said. 'And don't talk to any strangers.'

Knox stepped casually out into the street, as if he was simply leaving his office for the pub or to take the train home to the suburbs, then, when he was twenty yards from the doorway, he burst into a sprint.

He calculated he could get to his car and back in fifteen minutes. He'd have to be pretty direct, but that didn't matter so much – if someone was waiting for them then they already knew where they were, and Knox could worry about losing them later when he and Williams were properly mobile. He also hoped that if someone was watching the doorway and saw him racing away from it they'd be more likely to follow him than go and see what had happened all the way down in the store.

In the end it took almost twenty minutes for Knox to run down Little Britain, through Postman's Park and its memorial to people who died saving the lives of others, and along London Wall to where he'd left his Jaguar, then drive back to Smithfield.

By the time he pulled up in front of the doorway and Williams slipped into the passenger seat, and almost immediately fell asleep, Knox had decided where he was going to take him – the only place he could take him.

As they drove through the early-evening traffic, and started to wend their way up to the old, rich hill that stood over the north of the city, Knox tried to process what had just happened and found that he couldn't. Williams had brushed off his apology, then apparently forgotten their conversation had even taken place as he quickly and coldly killed two men. And now he was sleeping peacefully next to him, seemingly without a care in the world.

***

Williams was unconscious, but he wasn't asleep. Sleep would have meant rest, recovery, rejuvenation. Williams was denied all of that. The exhaustion that had pulled him out of the chaos and confusion of the waking world had only dragged him down into something much worse.

Just like he'd told Knox, his mind was a maze of fragments. Each shard was a slice of the terror that he'd experienced over the last seven years. One instant he was trapped underwater, blinded by filthy darkness and gasping at mouthfuls of acrid, cold liquid. Then he would be caught up in a surge of people, screaming as booming explosions rained debris on them. Then he would be suspended, weightless and deprived of all sense and feeling apart from unspeakable dread and anxiety that echoed around him.

One moment Williams was being smothered by great, choking forces. The next he was pinned upright, trapped between walls so hot they seared the naked flesh of his arms. Then he was falling to his knees, naked in a blizzard, hard rock cutting at his feet and knees as a gale of ice sliced every inch of the rest of his body.

He fought against invisible hands that held him down, then flung him through a black void, smashing him through his memories. He felt dizzy from vertigo, disoriented as his mind and body were spun, pushed, and pulled in every direction, and crushed and stretched beyond breaking point.

He shouted and railed, his voice piercing and booming, then silent and strangled. He reached out, straining to hold on to something, no matter how nebulous or jagged. But his mind refused him an anchor, and he kept tumbling through hell.

***

Knox only heard the quiet groans and saw the slight muscle twitches of someone dreaming. He had no idea how much his best friend had endured, the horror he was still being subjected to by his own mind, and how close he was to being completely torn apart. He just saw the man who had been miraculously returned to him, and who he was now being given a second chance to save.

Half an hour after they left Smithfield, they arrived at their destination in Highgate.

Knox nudged Williams awake and watched a look of timid recognition slowly spread across his face. He knew the large, old house that Knox had parked in front of. It was a place referred to ironically in the Service as 'the cottage', because it was anything but one. And it was a place Williams had been to countless times in his previous life.

It was Wytchen House, the home of James and Sarah Holland.

CHAPTER 24

Bennett avoided indulging in self-pity too often, because when she did it was intense. Her return to London hadn't been the glorious one she'd spent quite a lot of the last five years hoping for.

She knew she'd screwed up – she'd been cocky, miscalculated how both Williams and Knox would act, and let her asset slip out of her grip. But she didn't have the luxury of getting to wallow in her failure. She had to fix it. She also had to eat.

After she left Hoffman's office she went down to the canteen that took up most of the embassy's first subterranean level. She ignored the stacks of white bread and jars of peanut butter and jelly that were left out at all hours to help embassy staff whenever they suffered pangs of hunger and homesickness, and instead chose a large corned beef sandwich.

Her pride, her desire to prove Hoffman wrong, and her fear of who he might send after Williams if she failed meant she needed to get to him first. But, as she found herself a seat far away from the secretaries and low-level diplomatic assistants on their breaks, she struggled to come up with another, bigger reason.

Williams was still a mystery, but no one else in the CIA seemed to care about that. MKULTRA had chewed him up and spat him out, and now he was just a pawn Hoffman wanted to use to score some cheap points over an ally. Bennett had no idea where he could have fled to. He might have rushed straight to Leconfield House, or into the arms of an MI5 team waiting somewhere out of sight while Knox caused a distraction. But she doubted it. She also doubted he was just wandering alleys or curled up in an old, dirty yard somewhere. He was alone and confused in a city that had changed a lot in the time since he'd gone missing, but even if he couldn't fully trust the memories that were guiding him, there were still some skills and instincts no spy ever forgot.

Knox had told Bennett a little about the mythical figure of Jack Williams. She knew they'd met in France at the end of the war, that Williams had taken Knox under his wing, and that Knox had repaid him by introducing him to Holland and MI5.

'He was one of us,' Knox had said.

And what had that got him? He'd sacrificed his life for what he believed in, for the West, only to now come back from the dead all these years later to find his own side trying to finish him off.

She hadn't told Knox the whole story of his resurrection. She hadn't admitted anything about what Williams had endured at Haina. Or the journey to get him to London, which included a flight to New York where he'd been questioned one last time to see if there was any last scrap the CIA could squeeze out of him, then tidied up, given a hastily made passport that would get him through London Airport, and bundled onto the back of an overnight Pan American flight, where for eight hours one of his wrists was handcuffed to his seat and the other was attached to Bennett's.

Williams didn't deserve what he'd been put through. But as she ate the last of her sandwich, she reminded herself that he'd still been a spy and, as Bennett kept discovering herself over and over, no spy could ever be entirely blameless. As Gibson had so ineloquently put it, nobility wasn't part of the job description. Intelligence officers lived and worked in uncertainty and opportunity, in the moral in-between. On top of that, he'd still appeared out of thin air on the other side of the planet, known private information about her, and claimed to be a Soviet super-agent. He couldn't be an angel, and Bennett doubted he was a devil, but she still wanted to know exactly where in between the two of those he fell.

She decided she needed to learn more about her prey if she was going to hunt him down, so she went to the one place in London where she might find something to help – the floor directly beneath her.

The archives had been Bennett's domain when she'd been stationed in London. After being forced to accept her posting, her superiors had dumped her in the embassy's basement and tried to forget she existed.

She didn't enjoy the sensation that washed over her as she pushed open the swing doors and stepped inside. It felt like after so much hard work for so long the universe had brought her back where she belonged.

She wasn't sure if she should be surprised or not that in five years the place hadn't changed. The lights were still kept low, the clerks' desks were still piled high with the unending supply of requests or filing generated by the people who got to work above ground, and it was still very, very quiet.

Bennett knew there would be at least a couple of clerks somewhere out in the stacks but they didn't seem to be anywhere close to her. She figured that was probably for the best – she didn't want anyone asking her any questions about why she was there or what she was looking for.

Her anonymity lasted five minutes, until a clerk carrying a large pile of folders crashed into her back as she leaned over an open file drawer.

'Can I help you?' the clerk, a young black woman wearing thick glasses, asked as she balanced the pile of folders she'd managed to stop spilling out of her arms onto the edge of the file drawer.

Then a mix of recognition and excitement flashed across her face as she looked at Bennett properly and realised who she'd just bumped into.

'Oh my God,' she said, 'you're Abey Bennett.'

It was the second time in a week a complete stranger had known who Bennett was, and she didn't like it.

'I didn't realise I was famous,' she said.

'Round here you are,' the other woman said, thrusting out her hand for Bennett to shake. 'I'm Eloise, ma'am, Eloise Harpel, and I think you're amazing.'

'Sorry?' Bennett replied, cautiously reaching her hand out.

'Abey Bennett, the clerk who became a field agent.' Eloise adjusted her glasses as she enthusiastically shook Bennett's hand. 'You're an inspiration to just about all of us down here. I have to go get the other girls so they can meet you.'

'No,' Bennett said, a little more urgently than she'd intended.

As much as her ego might enjoy the boost of meeting the other clerks, she needed to be discreet, which meant as few people as possible knowing she'd been anywhere near the archives.

'Sorry, I'm in a rush right now,' she said. 'But I'd sure appreciate a little help if you've got a few minutes.'

'For you,' Eloise replied, 'anything.'

'Great,' Bennett said. 'I need to see any files we have on Jack Williams, an MI5 agent listed as MIA in 1959.'

'They'll be down the back,' Eloise said. 'The back' was slang for dead local records that were kept in the deepest depths of the archives.

'And any mission reports from the last seven years that included an unidentified enemy agent or external actor.'

This was a double gamble by Bennett – that she could trust Eloise, and that she was the type of clerk who spent her downtime poring over old files looking for things other people missed, just like Bennett used to when she first started believing in the Wolf.

'I think I can find a few,' Eloise replied, her smile turning conspiratorial. 'Give me twenty minutes.'

Bennett watched Eloise set off into the stacks, smiling herself as the other woman paused at the end of a row and cautiously peered round the corner before disappearing down it. Then she set to her own work, finding the set of file drawers that covered current serving members of MI5 so she could refamiliarise herself with her old friend Richard Knox.

She wasn't entirely comfortable with what was effectively prying into Knox's recent past. She told herself she was only doing it to help him, and Williams, but she knew that was only partly true. She was also doing it to help herself. Knox was the closest person to Williams, and Bennett couldn't shake the feeling that Williams's escape from Regent's Park wasn't as much of a surprise to Knox as it had looked.

She read through the CIA's version of Knox's service record. It turned out the agency had noted the closeness between him and his fellow agent and friend, even speculating after Williams's presumed death that Knox might not recover from the loss. Then she read about the agency's assessment of the time he'd spent as MI5's grand inquisitor at the start of the decade, endlessly hunting moles and undermining Service morale until he'd finally been proved right.

She lingered over the official write-up of the mission that had brought the two of them together, relishing the grudging praise that had been handed to her as the CIA 'member of staff' who had helped secure the defection of a key Soviet scientist, and blown the cover of a KGB asset working inside MI5.

The last five years of information was more patchy. With most of Knox's time spent travelling the Commonwealth dealing with old colonial problems, he'd fallen a little off London station's radar. What scraps of information there were about him seemed to describe a different person to the man Bennett knew – a man who did what he was told, avoided rocking boats, and was apparently no longer terrified of flying.

Bennett slipped Knox's files back into their drawer as she heard Eloise's footsteps returning. She didn't want to give away more clues about the less than heroic mission that had brought her down into the archive. But Eloise didn't ask her what she'd been doing while she was gone, or why she wanted the files she'd fetched. She just quietly handed them over and waited for Bennett to read them.

It took Bennett ten minutes to scour the reports Eloise had collected. They covered agent extractions gone wrong, the deaths and disappearances of politicians and businessmen all over Europe, and a lot of questions that had been left unanswered. Some of these questions seemed conspicuously large to Bennett, others almost too small to notice. There was the Italian tycoon's yacht that had inexplicably sunk in the middle of the Mediterranean, the CIA informant gunned down on the wrong side of the Berlin Wall, the three Turkish nationalist generals who died mere weeks apart, one of a heart attack, one of an aggressive cancer, and one during a live fire exercise.

Like so much to do with the Wolf, there was no discernible pattern that connected them. But if they weren't random, the only thing that could explain them was a highly trained operative working to some secret agenda who was extremely good at covering their tracks.

Bennett was impressed by Eloise. Sometimes accidents did happen, and coincidences were often exactly that, but the file clerk had a gift for spotting the not quite right. Bennett almost took another gamble and asked her if she was a fellow believer, but stopped herself.

Instead, once she was done reading she just said thank you, and promised to stop by for a longer chat next time she was passing through Grosvenor Square. From the smile that instantly returned to Eloise's face as she took the records off Bennett, ready to return them to their dusty, neglected homes, it looked like she believed her.

CHAPTER 25

Knox felt a little like a poor, distant relative whenever he visited Wytchen House, no matter how many times he'd been there to see Holland or his wife, Sarah. Williams had always been more comfortable in the rarefied surroundings of the home that had been in Sarah's family of high-ranking politicians and business leaders for generations. But, as they both got out of the Jaguar and approached the front door, Knox could tell that his friend's timid recognition was rapidly turning into terror.

Knox suddenly wondered if bringing Williams here was the right decision after all. He was still astounded by how fast and fatally Williams had acted in Smithfield. He looked scared now, and he'd looked scared before he'd killed the men too. What if something happened here to provoke him? What if some impulse drove him to assault Holland or Sarah? Would Knox be able to stop him? Knox told himself Williams had acted in self-defence in Smithfield, and that they were very unlikely to face another attack in the refined environs of Highgate.

'Don't worry,' he said, glancing up and down the street, double-checking they hadn't been followed. 'They'll be happy to see you.'

It also occurred to Knox that the Hollands might not be at home. There was plenty to keep the head of MI5 at his desk late into the evening at the moment, and Sarah kept her own busy schedule of functions and meetings across the city that blended the social, political, and charitable. But a few moments after he knocked on the front door it was opened by Sarah, whose hands flew to her mouth in surprise as Knox stepped aside to reveal Williams standing nervously behind him.

'Oh lord,' she said to Williams, as she ushered them both into the grand, wood-panelled hallway. 'I didn't believe James when he told me you were alive, but here you are.'

Then she hugged him.

Sarah was the consummate spy's wife. She was as smart and shrewd as her husband, and as discreet – they kept very few secrets from each other, personal or professional.

'James,' she called out, 'we have guests.'

The three of them marched in a line into the drawing room, where Holland was waiting, standing in the middle of a large, intricately patterned rug like a headmaster about to tell children on their first day at school what he expected of them.

Holland looked at Knox, then Williams, then his wife. After what felt to Knox like a long and damning silence, he strode over to Williams, shook his hand and said, 'Welcome home.' Then he turned to Knox and added, 'we need to talk.'

Sarah took her cue and tempted Williams out of the room with the offer of a cup of tea. Williams, visibly relieved by Holland's reaction, followed her.

'It's really him, then,' Holland said once he and Knox were alone.

'It is,' Knox replied.

They moved to the twin high-backed chairs next to the fireplace. Low, flickering flames produced the odd quiet pop and crack.

'It didn't take you long to catch up with him,' Holland said. It was clear from his tone he knew Knox had lied to him in Leconfield House, but also that he understood why.

'Me and a couple of other people,' Knox said.

'How was that?'

'It turned out worse for them.'

Knox told Holland about the unexpected appearance of the two men he hadn't been able to identify, and their equally surprising deaths. He also finally told Holland about the attack Williams had mentioned in Regent's Park.

'I haven't got any concrete details out of him so I don't know how legitimate the threat is.'

'Or if it's a memory of an old operation,' Holland said. 'Or simply a figment of a fevered imagination.'

Holland's conclusions were among the possible ones Knox had also reached – he knew there'd been plenty of times in the war, and after, when Williams had been involved in life-or-death missions that could have become jumbled in his head – yet hearing someone else dismiss Williams's warning instinctively compelled him to defend it.

'I think we should take what he's telling us seriously,' he said.

'We will,' Holland replied. 'When he's fit to be debriefed.'

'What if we don't have time for that?'

'No verified intelligence has indicated any imminent threat to London, or anywhere else in the country for that matter. I can't make decisions based on one sentence from someone who isn't in their right mind.'

'He's still an MI5 officer,' Knox said. 'He's earned our faith, and he's our responsibility.'

'I'm fully aware of all my responsibilities, Richard. But he's now proven he's dangerous, and as soon as he steps inside Leconfield House the Americans will get wind, register a formal protest and create exactly the kind of incident I've been told by the PM to avoid at all costs. He doesn't want another Vassall or Profumo before the election. And he doesn't want anything to derail the summit.'

'This is different,' Knox said. 'This isn't a double agent, or a minister who can't control his libido.'

'No, it's one man's confused words.'

'It's Jack Williams.'

'Who the prime minister doesn't know. If we do anything to draw attention to the Service then he'll view it as a political move against him.'

'I don't much care what Wilson thinks right now,' Knox said.

'Well you should,' Holland replied, a hardness in his voice that Knox rarely heard. 'It's your job.'

Before Knox could apologise the door opened and Sarah walked back into the room.

'The tea lasted all of a minute,' she said as she sat down on the chaise longue opposite the two high-backed chairs. 'I'm afraid I had to sacrifice your soup, darling.'

Holland huffed.

'How is he?' Knox asked.

'Like he's fit to burst or fall apart at any moment.'

She adjusted a pleat in her skirt, an unusual sign of nerves, and smiled at Knox. It was the kind of smile that told him he wasn't going to like what she was about to say.

'He's still Jack, at least most of him,' she said. 'He knows who I am, and where he is. But part of him doesn't. He seems to slip from moment to moment, almost like there's someone else in there with him.'

'Someone we don't know and can't necessarily trust,' Holland said, adding a twist to the knife his wife had just politely driven into Knox's chest.

Knox had to stop himself from jumping to Williams's defence again.

'So what can we do?' he asked.

'We keep him out of the way,' Holland replied.

'He needs our help. We need to know what the Americans did to him, and why someone else is after him.'

'And we're going to help him,' Holland said. 'Quietly.'

'Where?' Knox asked. 'Whoever came after him today will be watching Kemp House, and Rabley Heath, and he can't stay here—'

'Actually,' Sarah interrupted, 'maybe he can. He could use the spare room.'

The spare room was Sarah's name for the heavily fortified fallout shelter that MI5 had clandestinely excavated under Wytchen

House in case the Hollands found themselves at home in the event that a nuclear-tipped ICBM crashed into London.

'Then what?' This time it was Holland asking the question.

'Then Richard can take him to the house in Deal for a few days. Take in the sea air, start to recover, spend some time with a familiar face.'

'I'm not needed for a few days,' Knox said, jumping on Sarah's suggestion before Holland could dismiss it.

If the director general wanted to sweep Williams under the carpet, Knox should at least be the one holding the broom. He didn't want anyone else looking after him or trying to prise what he may or may not know from his addled brain.

'Laing has everything well in hand for Kosygin's visit,' Knox continued. 'He doesn't need me, but Jack does. If he's going to let anyone help put the pieces of his mind back together, it'll be me.'

Knox had no idea if that last sentence was true, but he hoped it was.

Holland mulled over the idea for what seemed like an eternity. Knox glanced at Sarah more than once, and each time she gave him a reassuring nod.

'Fine,' Holland said finally. 'He can spend the night in the bunker, which will be locked for everyone's safety, then Richard will take him to Kent in the morning. And none of us will talk to anyone else about this.'

CHAPTER 26

The Pushkin Museum of Fine Arts wasn't used to hosting formal dinners, and Rykov didn't usually spend his evenings in his dress uniform, but he made exceptions for special occasions.

Justas Paleckis, the ex-president of the Lithuanian Soviet Socialist Republic, was in Moscow. Rumours were abounding that he was being lined up to become the new chairman of the Soviet of Nationalities – the head of the upper chamber of the Supreme Soviet, a position of extreme political power. So, several high-ranking members of the Council of Ministers, the KGB, and its military counterpart the GRU, were spending the night flattering him and currying favour with him over food, alcohol, and speeches.

The dinner was a good place for Rykov to be seen.

A long table had been laid down the central void of the one of the museum's larger, columned galleries, with the space's usual statuary occupants shoved back against the walls and surrounded by serving trolleys.

It had been a fairly dreary and drawn-out event, and Rykov, seated two thirds of the way down the table between a tedious member of the Second Chief Directorate and a drunken representative from the Byelorussian SSR, had resorted to sneaking water instead of vodka for every other toast to try to keep himself somewhere near sober.

Eventually, when the oldest of the politicians, soldiers, and spies started to fall asleep in their chairs, the people who would still be expected at their desks the next morning started to make their excuses and leave.

Polished Volgas were lined up like a rank of taxis on the sweeping approach that led up to the museum. Their drivers sat behind their steering wheels, quietly stamping their boots in their footwells to stop their feet getting too cold and swearing at the heavy rain that was throwing up fresh dirt and mud they would need to clean off their cars before they could finally go home to a warm bed.

As soon as people started appearing at the top of the museum's entrance stairs, the row of engines turned over and cars began jockeying to be the one who could get to the bottom of the steps first. Rykov followed the other dinner guests, who were hastily pulling coats over their suits and uniforms. But when he spotted his driver he signalled for him to pass him an umbrella through his window then follow him as Rykov crossed the path to where another figure, sheltering under a tree and their own umbrella, was watching the departing quests.

'I'm sure I could have arranged an invitation for you,' he said to Yegerova.

Her jacket and skirt were dry, but Rykov could see her shoes were soaked through from standing in the rain.

'I'm not here for this,' she said. 'I'm here for you.'

Rykov smirked, thinking she probably wouldn't have enjoyed spending the night in the museum anyway – she would have found it far too extravagant, the seven-course meal that had been laid out for them over the course of three hours positively debauched.

'Then let's take a walk,' Rykov said, moving away from the museum entrance and out onto the pavement of Ulitsa Volkhonka. 'We don't want people to gossip.'

'Perhaps they should,' Yegerova said, watching Rykov's car creep past her.

'What can I do for you on such a lovely evening?' Rykov asked as he stepped round a puddle.

'Two of my agents were killed in London today,' Yegerova replied.

'That's terrible, but it's got nothing to do with me.'

'They were trailing an asset the Americans were handing over to the British. A missing MI5 officer.'

'How did they die?' Rykov's voice was still flippant, but the question was direct.

Yegerova stumbled over her reply. 'We don't know. They were watching MI5 headquarters, they followed their target, then they vanished.'

Rykov smiled again. 'So they may have just disappeared off into the sunset. I'm surprised you noticed. You have so many operatives swarming over London you're bound to lose a couple from time to time.'

'Your senses may be dull from too much vodka, but the Soviet Union is surrounded by enemies on every side, and they are all working against us. The only way to guarantee our safety is to be constantly on guard.'

Rykov sidestepped another pool of water. 'I'm fully aware of our need for eternal vigilance. But I'm not the one who's been misplacing agents.'

Yegerova stopped, forcing Rykov and his car to pause as well.

'The missing MI5 officer is called Jack Williams,' she said.

Rykov looked confused, but not surprised. He'd spent a long time training himself to never look surprised. 'Should that name mean something to me?'

'Yes, because he's your asset. The one you lost in Santo Domingo.'

Rykov stepped closer to Yegerova. Their umbrellas bumped into each other, dislodging a small flood of droplets around them.

'I didn't have an asset in Santo Domingo. And I don't have one in London,' he said.

'And I believe you are responsible for the death of two loyal KGB operatives,' Yegerova replied.

Rykov stepped back again. 'You can believe whatever you want,' he said. 'But we aren't living in the purges any more; if you're going to throw around accusations, you'd better be able to back them up.'

It was another implicit threat for Yegerova not to overstep her position. But it didn't seem to cow her. In fact, now she smiled at Rykov.

'We have his confession,' she said. 'Smuggled out of the CIA base at Haina. He told the Americans he was the Wolf.'

The myth of the Wolf also lived in the Soviet Union. No one in the KGB or the GRU admitted to being behind it, which only increased the belief among some that one of them must be. There had been considerable speculation that it was the work of Line Z.

'The Wolf is a fable,' Rykov said.

'Perhaps,' she replied. 'But I won't let your fantasies run loose and risk all our safety. Contain them, or I will.'

Rykov sighed and signalled for his driver to pull over. A moment later the car drew up next to him and the rear passenger door opened into his hands.

'You can threaten me all you want about something that doesn't exist,' he said as he got in the car. 'But it might not get you as far as you hope.'

Then he shut the door and the car pulled away, leaving Yegerova standing alone in the rain.

As the Volga passed Vodovzodnaya Tower and turned onto Kremlevskaya Naberezhnaya along the north bank of the Moskva, Rykov started to think that he might have underestimated Yegerova.

The Wolf was indeed a creation of Line Z, but it wasn't what believers on both sides of the Iron Curtain thought.

They assumed the Wolf was one person, their codename a translation of the Russian word *Volk*. It wasn't. Its name came from the German word for folk – a reference to its true scope and to where one of the most important projects for the survival and security of the Soviet Union had been born at the end of World War Two. One of the projects Rykov had been personally responsible for since he'd joined Line Z.

CHAPTER 27

The slanting sunlight dazzled the surface of Lake Annecy. The water moved like liquid glass, not frozen but almost. In the far distance the jagged teeth of the Dents de Lanfon mountains were blunted by snow and, closer, so were the tiled roofs of the medieval town that gave the lake its name.

In summer, Annecy would be teeming with tourists enjoying the crystal-clear waters that fed the lake from mountain streams and snowmelt, and snaked through the old canals that cut between the town's narrow stone arches and passageways lined with cafes and market stalls. But now it was too cold for anyone but locals and a few travellers passing by on their way to the last of the season's skiing higher up in the Alps.

Just the locals, the skiers, and a woman called Anna, who was standing on the high diving platform at the Plage de l'Impérial on the edge of the lake.

She looked like she belonged up above the water, wearing a maroon one-piece swimsuit with her long hair tucked under a black cap. The fine features of her face were calm, composed, seemingly unaware of the icy wind that was picking up and sending ripples across the surface of the lake ten metres beneath her.

The Plage was closed. It was a victim of the dwindling fortunes of the hotel next to it, which had tried and failed to bring the glamour of Monaco to the mountains and had shut down permanently after the last summer season. However, it had taken Anna a considerable amount of effort to negotiate her few days of rest and recuperation with her employers, and she was going to spend them doing exactly what she wanted. So, for the last two evenings, just before sunset, she had picked the simple lock that had been chained across the gates of the Plage, changed into her swimsuit, and practised her diving.

She craved the cold, the feeling of it wrapping round her and numbing every inch of her skin. She stood perfectly still on the diving board, breathing slowly through her nostrils to suck the chill deep down into her. Then she raised her arms, sprang off her feet and jumped into a graceful arc that took her into the brutal, brief oblivion of the freezing lake.

When she broke the surface again and gasped air back into her lungs, she floated in the water for a moment and looked across the empty pontoons that lined the lake and would fill with rowing boats and pedalos once spring finally arrived, towards the Jardins de l'Europe with its lawns and flowerbeds that were kept pristinely manicured all year round.

She saw a man in a heavy coat leaning against the wrought-iron railings of the Pont des Amours on the edge of the park staring at her. She held up both her arms, flailing as if she was drowning. Then, when she saw the man tense upright, she threw her head back, let out a loud laugh, and started swimming with deep, even strokes back to the diving board.

Five minutes later, Anna had dried herself off and changed into a thick jumper, trousers, and her own winter coat.

She re-locked the entrance to the Plage and walked towards the town. The man was gone by the time she reached the Pont des Amours, either off raising the alarm or feeling like a fool for the trick she'd played on him. So was the sun, which was now too low in the sky to reach over the mountains.

She passed the Hôtel de Ville and the Église Saint Maurice and turned onto the Place Saint-François de Sales. Then, where the square opened up next to the Quai de l'Île, she stopped in front of the Auberge de Savoie to consider the simple menu that had been pinned up outside the restaurant and was fluttering in the breeze creeping into the town.

In a few months the Auberge would swell to twice its size, with tables and chairs set out under the trees in front of its varnished wood doors. But tonight the trees were bare and the restaurant was manned by a small staff serving a severely reduced clientele.

To anyone watching, Anna's decision to go into the Auberge might have seemed spontaneous, but she'd eaten there the last two nights and she'd only paused outside to check that the menu hadn't changed from the hearty Alpine fare she had enjoyed so far.

Anna's job regularly took her to some of the world's finest restaurants, where she was wined and dined by wealthy, powerful people on immaculate morsels of extravagant cuisine that inevitably left her hungry. Anna was an animal; it took a lot of energy to keep her in the athletic shape she needed for her work, and she relished the chance to fuel herself with plates full of meat, cheese, and potatoes for an hour in a quiet restaurant.

After her meal, she descended into the warren of dark, cobbled streets that led to her hotel on the Rue Sainte-Claire.

Les Deux Salons, at first glance, lived up to its name. Beyond its old oak doors were two modest rooms – the first acted as a foyer and was given over entirely to a reception desk, and the second was scattered with chairs for the hotel's guests to rest over coffee or cognac. But beyond them, corridors and staircases stretched out into the buildings on either side, which Les Deux Salons had spent almost a hundred years cannibalising, room by room.

The hotel was quiet when Anna opened the front door and stepped inside. She hadn't encountered any other guests in her few days in Annecy, but her surreptitious glances at the board of room keys whenever she came and went had told her that at least three other rooms were currently occupied. They were spread out, far apart from each other – a tactic employed either by the hotel management or her employers to ensure maximum solitude and anonymity.

Anna hoped to pass through the foyer in silence, retrieving her key from the old man in the faded black double-breasted jacket who permanently sat behind the reception desk without having to talk to him, but he produced an envelope from under the desk as he slid her key over to her.

'A telegram for Madame Maier,' he said in heavily accented English.

Anna had checked into Les Deux Salons under the name Maier. It was the surname in the passport she'd shown when she'd checked in, but it wasn't hers.

She'd sized up the man as soon she'd arrived at the hotel. He was in his sixties but looked seventy, aged not through exertion but by inactivity. She could tell he was the type of man who twenty years ago would have come up with some excuse to accompany her to her room or drop by and knock on her door at the end of his shift. But, luckily for the both of them, he no longer had the energy or inclination to leave his desk or harass solo female travellers.

Anna made a show of opening the envelope so that he couldn't see what the note said, and he made a show of looking away, even though they both knew he would have read the telegram when it arrived.

It was an address for another hotel: the Hôtel des Bergues in Geneva.

Anna folded the telegram, slid it back into the envelope.

'I'll be checking out this evening, and I'll need a car,' she said.

Her soft, rich voice had been cultivated over years of training to make whoever she used it on do whatever she wanted without question. And it worked.

'Yes, madame,' the man replied. 'When will you be leaving for Geneva?'

Anna noted his slip, but didn't acknowledge it. 'In an hour.'

'Very good. Your bill has, of course, already been settled.'

'Of course,' she said, then took her key and left him to arrange the taxi that would take her over the border into Switzerland.

Anna's room was on the elegant side of bare – just a bed, a small table and chair with a mirror, a window that looked out onto a small square, and an equally simple bathroom.

It took her half an hour to shower and change into a fresh set of clothes, and pack everything else including her still-wet swimsuit and cap into a case that she would not be taking to Geneva with her.

She spent her remaining time wiping down every surface in the room to make sure she hadn't left any fingerprints behind her. She didn't need to do either of these things herself – by morning her luggage would have been removed, her room meticulously cleaned before the chambermaid arrived, and her name in the hotel register smudged beyond recognition. But it was a ritual that she enjoyed, and it helped her mind prepare for returning to work.

As her taxi drove her out of the town and up into the mountains, Anna saw that at last the sun had completely set. The white roofs now glowed in moonlight, and the lake looked ominous, dark, and inky.

She also briefly wondered what would happen to the old man.

Her employers didn't like loose ends, and he not only knew her assumed name and what she looked like but also, thanks to the telegram, where she was going. Perhaps they'd be lenient and let him forget that she'd ever visited Les Deux Salons, or perhaps he'd shortly find himself knocked unconscious, dragged through the old streets of his town, and dropped overboard in the middle of the lake with several cobblestones attached to his ankles.

As usual when it came to anyone's life other than her own, she found that she didn't really care either way.

CHAPTER 28

Williams woke up three times in the night.

The first time he knew who he was, and where he was. He remembered talking with Knox in the Hollands' kitchen and being told that everything was going to be alright but that they needed to leave the city for a few days. He also remembered agreeing to spend the night in the fallout shelter under Wytchen House, and hearing the heavy metallic clunk of the lock as he settled down on the large, old sofa Sarah had had moved into the narrow space in place of the military-issue camp bed that MI5 had installed.

He spent twenty minutes staring at the domed ceiling, repeating over and over what he could still recall – the three conversations with Knox in Regent's Park, the cold store under Smithfield, and in the house above him – trying to cement them in his shifting mind before he slipped back into unconsciousness.

The second time, he was plunged into a waking nightmare. His body pulled him up to stand to attention in front of the sofa. He could see the walls of the bunker dissolve, and an endless line of people stretch out on either side of him. They all wore the same dark grey smocks and trousers – a uniform Williams saw on himself when he looked down at his body – and all stared, dead-eyed, straight ahead.

Voices shouted orders out of the dark. English turned into French, then German, then Russian, then Chinese. Williams realised he could understand all of it, and somehow knew what he was supposed to say to each command, barking his responses in time with everyone else in the infinite line.

At some invisible signal, the two men on either side of Williams stepped out of the line, faced each other, and started yelling. They got louder and louder, their shouts echoing deafeningly in the void that had replaced the bunker, until one of them lunged at the other, grabbed him in a chokehold, and pulled his arm tighter and tighter across his windpipe until he crushed it and the man collapsed dead on the floor. Then, as the attacker silently returned to his place next to Williams, the walls started to rematerialise, cutting off the line of phantom people and leaving Williams falling slowly backwards onto the sofa.

The third time was a completely different kind of horror. This time, the man who woke up wasn't really Williams. He wasn't really a person at all. He was a beast, driven by a single, bloody desire: to kill.

He wanted to break out of his bricked-up cage. He wanted to prowl the rooms above it and hunt the people who had trapped him. But most of all, he wanted to kill. To snap bones, break skulls, slit throats, and slice arteries.

He tore at the sofa, ripped its cushions, and stamped on the frame until it cracked. He clawed deep scratches into the concrete lining of the walls. He hit the locked door over and over, ramming it with his shoulders, kicking it with his feet, and punching it with all his strength until his knuckles were bruised and bloody.

And through all this, a face hovered above him. A twisted visage of a man with ashen, bruise-marked skin stretched across his skull, screaming silently from a mouth full of blood and cracked teeth.

It was only when Williams's energy was completely drained, when he had no more feeling in his fists or air in his lungs, that his desperate mind forced his body to stop and compelled him to pile some of the sofa cushions next to the door, curl up on them, and fall back into an exhausted sleep.

CHAPTER 29

Knox lay in his bed in Kemp House the next morning thinking about being careful what he wished for. He'd wanted change, and now he had it. He'd also wanted his best friend back, and now he was. But neither of these things had happened the way he'd hoped they would.

Instead of pressing Holland to cancel Wilson and Kosygin's summit and use the full might of the Service to work out who was responsible for what Williams had gone through, he'd volunteered to be figuratively and literally sidelined. And Williams might have risen from the dead, but had all of him returned?

The Hollands had agreed that Knox should be the one to tell Williams about their plan to shut him in a dungeon overnight and then drive him out to the coast for a few days of rest and, hopefully, no excitement.

He'd taken it well, to Knox's relief. As he finished his second bowl of soup, he'd agreed to do whatever they thought was best. He'd seemed fine in the Hollands' kitchen, some of his old irreverent charm poking through, and the closest he'd been to the old Williams yet. But Knox was still worried about him. Especially because when he'd asked him how he'd managed to kill the two men in Smithfield and the attack he'd mentioned in Regent's Park, he seemed to have no idea what Knox was talking about.

As soon as Knox had left Highgate he'd regretted leaving Williams locked up and alone. And by the time he'd got back to Soho he'd worked himself up again and had wanted to call

Wytchen House to persuade Holland to order in every MI5 officer still in the country to find proof of the attack on London he hadn't even been sure was real. But he knew he'd just be overruled and Holland would tell him again that, at least for the moment, Williams needed to be handled with kid gloves, and everything he said taken with a very large pinch of salt.

Knox was trying to think like that, but doing so just revealed a bigger, more serious problem that was lurking beneath everything else.

He didn't feel forgiven.

Williams's fast, almost casual pardon had sat on him all night, and he'd come to the unpleasant conclusion that it was too good to be true. It had been given too easily, too freely, by someone with a muddled, unstable mind. Knox didn't know if Williams even remembered their conversation about the *Surcouf*. And if he did, had he been so quick to dismiss it because it was a wound that had long healed over? Or had he been trying to spare himself the pain of something that had terrorised him as much as Knox for seven years?

The smell of coffee drifted into his bedroom as Knox mentally prepared for the day ahead. By now Leconfield House would have been told that he wouldn't be coming in, and the bodies of the two men Williams had killed would have been removed from Smithfield, along with any signs that anyone had been anywhere near the cold store. In an hour Knox would collect Williams from Wytchen House, take him on the long drive to the Kent coast, and hopefully start to help his friend put himself back together, and work out what he needed to do to earn true absolution.

Knox finally let the enticing aroma pull him out of his bed. Then he remembered that he didn't have any coffee in the flat.

He slid out from under his white cotton covers, slipped on a dark grey robe, and stepped out into the open-plan living area, where he found exactly who he was expecting waiting for him, leaning against the kitchen counter next to two porcelain cups Knox didn't own full of fresh coffee.

'Good morning,' he said to Bennett. 'I thought I was out of beans.'

'You are,' Bennett replied, handing Knox one of the cups. 'The guys at Bar Italia kindly obliged.'

Bar Italia was the twenty-four-hour cafe on Frith Street that Knox had spent incalculable hours in over the years, first with Williams and then by himself. It was also where he'd first encountered Bennett – though he hadn't known it at the time.

'I didn't know they did takeaway,' Knox said as he sat down at the dining table. 'Last time I saw someone ask they were laughed out of the place.'

'I was real nice about it,' Bennett said, joining him at the table.

'I suppose everything changes eventually.'

'Most things.' Bennett looked around at the room that had been an empty white box the first time she'd quietly let herself into Knox's flat. 'Usually for the better.'

'Usually.'

Knox took a long sip. He tried to recall the last time he'd shared a drink with someone in his flat, as part of either an interrogation or a seduction, and drew a blank.

'I've missed this,' Bennett said, taking her own sip.

'Breaking into people's homes?'

Bennett smirked. 'Decent coffee. I've been stuck on American instant for too long.'

'Sounds rather joyless.'

'It is, but it gets the job done.' Bennett savoured another mouthful of the rich, dark liquid, then added, 'Are we going to talk about Regent's Park?'

'We probably should,' Knox replied.

'Where is he?'

'Who?' Knox asked.

'You know who. Jack Williams.'

Knox took another sip of his coffee. 'I have no idea.'

'That's bull, Richard,' Bennett said, her tone not quite as light as it had been a few moments before. 'I just want to know he's okay.'

'I'm surprised you're so concerned for his welfare.'

'Technically he's still in my custody,' she said.

Knox put his coffee down.

'He's been through enough with you looking after him, don't you think?'

'What did he tell you?'

'That he came to you for help, and you used him.'

The words were heavy with betrayal. It was a cruel, abrupt precis of what had happened, but Bennett couldn't argue with it. So she said nothing.

Knox knew they both lived in the murky world between right and wrong. For him, that meant he always had to be sure his moral compass was at least pointing in the right direction. It was a quality they'd once shared, but it seemed like in the last five years other forces had taken control of Bennett's needle.

'If you were going to deny it, that was your chance,' he said.

After a long pause Bennett finally spoke. 'He doesn't know what he's saying.'

'And you've turned into an agency stooge, incapable of taking responsibility for your own actions.'

'That's not fair.'

'Please, show me some evidence to the contrary,' Knox shot back. 'We're supposed to be fighting torturers, not handing people over to them.'

'You have no idea what I'm fighting,' Bennett almost shouted, before she got up from the table and paced a loop of the open-plan. 'I'm trying to do the right thing, but if I don't bring him in I'll be fired, and I won't be able to do much good then.'

Her sentiment might have been genuine, but to Knox it was still an evasion.

'Are you doing much good now?' Knox asked.

The question was deeper, more philosophical than he'd meant, and more cutting.

'Look,' she said, 'I don't like what Hoffman's planning, but now you know about it you can cut him off, when I have Williams back. I know how much he means to you.'

'You do,' Knox replied. 'And you still let this happen to him.'

Bennett took a breath, leaning against the kitchen counter.

'I want to help him,' she said. 'And I want to work together so we can both win.'

'There are no winners in this scenario.' Knox's voice was hard. 'A British citizen and MI5 officer has been physically and mentally abused by the CIA, because of you, and now you want to hunt him down so he can be paraded down the Mall like some trophy. So, thank you for your kind offer of assistance, but you can consider yourself absolved of your responsibility. We'll take care of him now.'

'Really?' Bennett said. 'Because you already lost him once.'

It was a knee-jerk reaction to Knox's personal attack, and probably the worst thing Bennett could have said.

'Get out,' Knox said through clenched teeth.

'I'm sorry, Richard,' Bennett replied. 'I didn't mean that. This isn't how I wanted this conversation to go.'

'I'm not interested in what you want,' Knox said.

Bennett stood frozen in place for a few moments, seemingly trying to decide what she should do next. Then she put her half-full cup of coffee on the table next to Knox's and left the flat without another word.

CHAPTER 30

Bennett's attempt to reconcile with Knox hadn't gone to plan.

After reading up on Williams in the CIA archive and the hole he'd left in Knox's personal and professional life, she was convinced there was no way Knox would have just let him disappear after Regent's Park. And she'd hoped that even though they hadn't seen each other in years he'd still think that they, no matter what the agendas of the powers they worked for might be, were still allies. But she'd underestimated just how deep the wound in the centre of Knox was, and how long it would take to heal over after she'd reopened it.

She stormed straight past the lift door across from Knox's flat and into the staircase that spiralled around its shaft to the bottom of Kemp House. Halfway down, she paused on a landing to catch her breath and stop her body and brain from spinning in circles.

Bennett had wanted to know what plot Williams and Knox had concocted in the few minutes they'd had together, but there was no way Knox was going to tell her now. She'd also wanted to tell Knox exactly what had happened in Santo Domingo, explain that she'd thought she was helping Williams and that she felt ashamed for what he'd been through.

She'd arrived at Kemp House prepared to accept the blame she deserved, fully. But she'd fudged it. She'd got defensive, and let Knox's anger get to her. Now, she couldn't see a way back from what she'd done to Williams or what she'd said to Knox.

Bennett started down the stairs again, but after three more floors she came to an abrupt halt and a smile cracked the scowl her face had hardened into.

'Nice try,' she said.

She'd had an agenda in Knox's flat and, of course, so had he. Their conversation was never going to be easy, but he hadn't even given her a chance to lay the situation out calmly before they'd both let things escalate. Bennett had hoped to leave with information that would save her skin, and maybe lead her to Williams. Instead, she'd left wanting to crawl into a hole, kicking herself as she did. Which, it now occurred to her, was exactly what Knox had intended. He hadn't just wanted her gone, he'd wanted her angry, distracted, and doubting herself.

In another life his ploy would have worked. Five years, or even five days, ago she would have let the argument sit on her, weighing her down. However, after all her run-ins with Gibson, she was quicker to realise when people were trying to deflect her away from seeing what they were really up to. And to work out how she could use that to her advantage.

So, as she walked over to the blue and cream MG 1100 she'd borrowed from the embassy, she didn't plan on driving back there, or to the dishevelled hotel in South Kensington that had been grudgingly booked for her by one of the diplomatic secretaries. But she was happy to let Knox sit in his flat, thinking he'd pushed her across a burning bridge.

CHAPTER 31

Knox wondered if Bennett would try to follow him to Highgate, or if she'd retreat straight to Grosvenor Square to lick her wounds. He'd wanted to push her, and was stunned at where they'd ended up. Half a decade apart was bound to change both of them, but Knox could barely recognise the person Bennett had turned into. She'd once been driven by her hatred of people who had completely sacrificed their morals for power. Now she was an apologist for them. Worse, she was becoming one of them.

His mix of anger and disappointment was still simmering as he parked in front of Wytchen House, walked up the short path to its porch, and was greeted by an old Irish setter as the front door opened.

'Hello, Stella,' he said, reaching down to scratch behind the dog's ears as she circled his legs. 'Is your father here?'

'He's with James and Jack,' Sarah answered from the doorway, beckoning them both inside.

'How was the night?' Knox asked when they were all in the hallway.

'Eventful,' Sarah replied. 'We're in the kitchen.'

Knox followed Sarah and Stella into the large Shaker-style kitchen at the back of the house. It was a well-used and much-loved room. Knox had eaten plenty of meals at the large oak table that took up most of the space.

Beyond the kitchen's French doors an immaculately maintained lawn was surrounded by borders of late-blooming cyclamen, budding hydrangeas and high stone walls crawling with vines. And inside them, Holland sat at the head of the table, watching MI5's head of research and development bandage Williams's knuckles.

'What are you doing here?' Knox asked White.

'Playing doctor,' he replied.

'Are you okay?' Knox said, this time to Williams.

'I am,' Williams replied, sheepishly. 'But I really do feel terrible.'

He sounded like the same almost-Williams-of-old Knox had left in the bunker last night.

'We don't know what happened,' Holland said. 'But at some point in the night Williams took against the bunker door, and the sofa.'

'For which he has already apologised profusely,' Sarah said as she let Stella out into the back garden.

'Can you remember anything?' Knox asked.

'Shreds again,' Williams replied, flexing his hands in their bandages.

Knox could see the mix of pain and frustration on Williams's face as he half-clenched his fists. He didn't want to be the cause of more, but he also needed to keep probing.

'Of what?'

'Voices. Shouting, twisted faces. Fear, anger.'

'Like you told me yesterday in Smithfield?'

Williams nodded.

'Could it be something to do with the attack you were trying to warn me about in Regent's Park?'

Holland and Williams both frowned at Knox's last question. Holland because he'd made it clear before Knox left last night that he didn't want Williams pressed too hard on the attack in case his confused mind felt forced to invent an answer to it. And Williams because it looked like he was trying to do just that.

Knox wanted to give his friend one more chance to show that he should be taken seriously. Unfortunately, Williams couldn't come up with the proof.

'I can remember the park,' he said. He smiled briefly, then sighed. 'But it's hazy. And the harder I try to focus on it, the blurrier it gets. I'm sorry, old man.'

Now Knox frowned as well.

'I don't like this,' Holland said. 'I think it would be better and safer for all concerned if Williams was put under secure observation.'

'We can't,' Knox said, almost before Holland had finished.

The director general's eyebrow lifted a fraction, a sign of surprise and a request for his deputy to explain why he was suddenly arguing against exactly what he'd demanded twelve hours ago.

'Abey Bennett paid me a visit at home this morning,' Knox said. 'The Americans aren't going to let this drop. We have to get Jack away from the city and out of harm's way.'

Knox was happy for Holland to think his change of heart was out of a newfound desire to avoid a blow-up with Grosvenor Square that might affect the Kosygin summit or leak to the press before Wilson's precious election. But it wasn't. His motivation was the same as it had been since he'd seen Williams sitting on the bench on the Broad Walk, staring glassy-eyed back at him: he had to keep his best friend safe.

'Should we still consider Miss Bennett a friend of the Service?' Holland asked.

Knox shook his head. 'Not at the moment.'

'And if she or someone else from the CIA follows you?'

'Then they'll be out of your hair, and we can lead them on a merry chase.'

'There are other interested parties.' Holland was referring to the two dead bodies from Smithfield, which had resisted all attempts at identification overnight.

'Hopefully they've been warned off. But if not, it'd still be better if they were hunting us while you're busy with Kosygin.'

Knox, Williams, White, and Sarah all waited for Holland to decide what was going to happen next.

He looked down at the oak tabletop, his eyes following the grains in the wood as if they were different paths laid out before him. Then he looked up at Knox and said, 'Deal.'

Ten minutes later, White left Wytchen House, with Stella in tow.

After Holland had given his blessing once more for Knox to go to Kent, Sarah had taken Williams to find another change of clothes, and White had given Holland and Knox his assessment of Williams's mental condition, which was why he'd really been summoned across the heath from his home in Hampstead.

'I'm as much of a psychologist as a doctor, but from what I've read, the things I've heard about the interrogation techniques the CIA and KGB are experimenting with, and what I've just observed, I'd say he's been subjected to intense, prolonged trauma. Possibly for as long as he's been missing.'

'Is that why he's suppressing his memories?' Knox asked.

'Probably,' White replied. 'It's a natural defence mechanism. Like flinching away from fire after you've been burned. The brain doesn't want to go near anything that could hurt it.'

'Even if that thing's in your head.'

'Especially then.'

'Do you think MKULTRA has been at him?' Knox asked.

'I wouldn't be surprised,' White replied.

'Could they have brainwashed him, or erased his memory somehow?'

White and Holland both snorted at Knox's question. Both men knew about MKULTRA and some of the things it had achieved through distinctly questionable means. But they disliked the rumours that swirled around it and seemed to credit it with almost magical abilities to play with people's heads.

'I think what happened to Williams is most likely just plain old human cruelty,' White said.

'So, what does he need?' Holland asked.

'Therapy, drugs, probably both,' White said. 'But mostly time. A lot of the mind is still uncharted territory. It can't be rushed.'

Once White had gone but before Sarah finished helping Williams get ready for his journey to the coast, Holland took Knox into the living room. Knox expected the director general to tell him again not to do anything that might rock political boats, or be too willing to believe whatever sliver of memory or dream worked its way out of Williams's broken mind, but he didn't.

'Are you sure you can take care of him?' Holland asked quietly once he'd closed the living-room door behind them.

'I'm not going to let him go again,' Knox replied.

'Good,' Holland said. 'Drive carefully, and if his memories suddenly return and there's something we do need to act on, get back here as fast as possible.'

***

Five minutes after White left, Knox and Williams stepped out of Wytchen House, got into Knox's Jaguar, and drove away. A few moments later, the black Ford Consul that Laing had signed out of Leconfield House an hour before pulled away from the kerb fifty feet down the road and followed them.

Laing's dislike of Knox had turned to distrust when he'd taken his concerns about Kosygin wanting to go to the ballet to him and he'd dismissed them.

At the very least, he'd thought Knox would order him to reassign enough Watchers to make sure the Royal Opera House was covered for the whole of the next forty-eight hours. And when he hadn't, Laing had done it anyway.

He'd expected word to reach Knox overnight, and that he'd be dragged over the coals for his prudence this morning. But when he'd arrived at Leconfield House he'd been told by one of the secretaries from the fifth floor that Knox had been called away and wouldn't be contactable for a few days. And then, on his way back down to the School Hall, he'd heard one of the engineers from the R&D department complaining about a project review delayed because White had been summoned to the cottage.

Laing couldn't resist putting two and two together and deciding that MI5's most senior officers were meeting secretly. He was extremely curious as to why. So, he'd quickly checked that everything for the summit was still well in hand, then gone down to the garage and signed out a car.

He'd driven straight to Soho and had reached Berwick Street just in time to see Knox leaving Kemp House. Now, he'd just watched him drive away from the director general's home with a man he didn't recognise.

Laing wanted to know who Knox's mysterious passenger was, and where he was taking him.

CHAPTER 32

Laing didn't know it, but he wasn't the only person watching Wytchen House. Angus Gaulke, whose real name was Pavel Utkin, had also been staking it out all night.

Gaulke was a Directorate S illegal who had been in London for almost three years and who, by fluke of regularly being in the wrong place at the wrong time, had done very little. Normally, his surveillance shifts involved following members of MI5 around the capital and then driving out of the city in his midnight blue Morris Oxford Farina, which had an R-354 Morse code radio set hidden in its boot, to send an encrypted message burst to Moscow detailing whatever had or, more likely, hadn't happened that day.

Last night he'd been slowly making his way north to send a short and mostly pointless report when, by sheer chance, he spotted a grey Jaguar he recognised in the traffic ahead of him. He'd decided to take the initiative for once and followed it up to Highgate, where he'd watched Richard Knox and another man go into Wytchen House, the home of the director general of MI5.

Half an hour later Knox had left alone and Gaulke had continued on to a motorway lay-by twenty miles outside the city, where he added a short note about what he'd just seen to his report. He stayed at the side of the road with his engine and lights switched off, leaning into the boot, waiting for the standard acknowledgement message that usually only took a few minutes to reach him all the way from the Lubyanka. When he hadn't received it after ten minutes he started to worry slightly. But after another ten it arrived – except that it wasn't a simple confirmation of receipt, it was instructions to return to Highgate and wait for support.

His backup arrived at four in the morning. Gaulke had been at least half asleep in his tilted-back seat, parked sixty yards up the street from the cottage, so hadn't noticed the woman suddenly appear next to his window, tapping on it and gesturing at him to unlock the passenger-side door. The woman had two rucksacks with her, which she slung into the back of the car. And she was silent. They watched the house together, mutely, for hours until the sun rose.

Gaulke didn't mind that his career as an illegal agent had been rather pedestrian. He hadn't been driven to join the KGB by fervent devotion, he'd just wanted to get as far away from Tukchar, his home village on the edge of the Caspian Sea, as possible, and had happened to have a knack for English. He liked life in the West. He preferred the freedoms he'd gained here to the ones he'd lost by leaving the Soviet Union. And he enjoyed his quiet cover life, which consisted of an administrative job at a distiller's company, a small flat in West Kensington, and an on-off relationship with a Scottish schoolteacher who lived three streets away from him.

But, as he watched another man he didn't know with a dog leave Wytchen House, followed by Richard Knox and the man he'd left there the night before, and then another car that had pulled up down the street moments after Knox's Jaguar had arrived half an hour ago, Gaulke wondered what he'd got himself into.

CHAPTER 33

Patrice Labarre couldn't believe his luck. Normally, the French financier's trips to Geneva consisted of endless meetings with people begging him to invest in some hare-brained scheme, and barely any time to devote to the city's more enjoyable pursuits.

So far this visit had followed the usual pattern. He'd spent his whole morning listening to two very well-bred but also very dim Englishmen trying to convince him that all they needed were a few tens of thousands of francs to fund an expedition in the Arabian Gulf that was guaranteed to reveal a hitherto undiscovered oilfield that would make them all millionaires. Labarre was already a millionaire, but from the slapdash presentation the two men had made to him he doubted they'd be joining him any time soon. They hadn't even suggested taking Labarre to lunch at one of the restaurants along the Quai de Mont-Blanc to wine and dine him – probably, Labarre guessed, because they couldn't afford to – so, after wishing the Brits goodbye and good luck, he'd had to make do with returning to the Hôtel des Bergues and eating alone.

He was now free for the afternoon, and was content to spend it indulging in working his way through the hotel restaurant's selection of miniature, Michelin-starred desserts, until he noticed a woman sitting at the bar that ran the entire length of the long room watching him. She was the kind of woman who demanded attention. She was perched on a high stool and her whole body was visible over the shoulders of the few other diners who were still lingering at their tables. Her hands and forearms were covered by long, black silk gloves. She wore no necklace or earrings.

They stared at each other, neither breaking eye contact for a full minute as a smile started to curl the edges of the woman's lips.

Labarre took one last bite of his air-light profiteroles and made his way over to the bar.

'Bonjour, mademoiselle,' he said.

'Bonjour, monsieur,' Anna replied in her deep, trans-European accent.

'What is your name?' Labarre asked.

'Cosette,' Anna replied.

'I don't think so,' Labarre said, looking her up and down. 'I think you're more of a Fantine.'

'Then that's who I shall be.'

'And what brings you to the Hôtel des Bergues?'

Anna took a sip of her Martini, still keeping her eyes fixed on Labarre's as her hand reached out for her narrow-stemmed, wide-brimmed glass, brought it to her lips, and returned it to the bar.

'Boredom.'

Five minutes later they were in Labarre's suite.

Labarre was a good fifteen years older than the woman he'd christened Fantine. He knew he wasn't particularly attractive. His thin hair and sallow face had never naturally drawn gazes from the opposite sex. But he also knew that money was just as alluring as looks, and he'd always made it clear to anyone who might be interested that he had plenty of that.

He removed his jacket, tie, and shoes as Anna slipped into the bathroom to freshen up, and lay back on his large bed, propped up on the thick goose-feather pillows. When Anna emerged a few minutes later, Labarre was faintly disappointed that she was still wearing her dress. But that feeling quickly evaporated as she climbed onto the bed, straddled him, pulled off one of her gloves and tied it over his eyes.

Labarre's excitement grew visibly as Anna slowly dragged her fingers down his chest and along his legs before she gently climbed back off the bed, reached her gloved hand under the end of it, pulled out the silencer-tipped pistol that she'd hidden there an hour earlier, and put a bullet in his crotch and another in his neck.

Pain and shock ripped through Labarre. His mind couldn't process what had just happened to him. His arms flailed wildly at his throat and face as blood spurted out of his neck, staining the white pillows red, and into his lungs, slowly drowning him.

As the last embers of life drained out of Labarre, and two blooms of dark red spread across the bed, Anna quickly opened the wardrobe, retrieved the large leather holdall she'd planted there along with the pistol, and changed into the beige cashmere jumper and dark trousers that were folded inside. She also removed the small black patent-leather and gold-chain Chanel handbag that had been hidden under her new outfit before repacking the holdall with her dress, the glove that she'd kept on, and the gun. She untied the other glove, which had slipped down round Labarre's neck and was now soaked. She looked at his dead, blank eyes for a moment before she pushed his head to the side with the tip of her finger, prompting another weak gurgle of blood to seep out of his neck. Then she dropped the wet glove into the holdall, put it back in the wardrobe, and left the suite.

Anna didn't know who Patrice Labarre was, or why he had to die, only that he must, because her superiors at Line Z had decreed it.

She had no idea that Line Z knew Labarre spent his professional life investing in whatever could make him richer, and his personal life funding the political causes he believed in. He was a fervent nationalist, and an ardent, right-wing capitalist. He was also France's single biggest secret donor to the Quebec sovereignty movement, and funnelled vast sums of francs to the Ralliement National. This was a problem for the KGB, because they were also supporting Quebecois freedom via quietly backing the Marxist-Leninist Front de Libération du Québec.

The prospect of a sympathetic breakaway state in North America that might even one day become a Soviet satellite was too tempting for the KGB to ignore. So, while rubles flowed into an untraceable bank account in Zurich destined for the Front de Libération, in Ottawa the KGB *residentura* and a team of Directorate S operatives were constantly working to destabilise the Ralliement National – including operations like tricking the local MI5 SLO into believing that it was actually being funded by Russia.

Unknown to them, Line Z was also working to bring down the right-wing party.

Anna's orders had been brief, just a coded note in the holdall that she'd collected when she'd checked into the Hôtel des Bergues late last night. She wasn't given any instructions about how Labarre was to be killed, only that his death needed to look bloody and painful.

She'd slipped into his room in the morning to prepare her trap, then walked over the Pont du Mont-Blanc to Rue du Rhône, where she'd bought the silk gloves – a personal flourish that would help her create the character of the high-class prostitute she would use to ensnare Labarre, as well as ensure she didn't leave any fingerprints in his suite that would need removing along with the holdall after she'd left.

It had been a calculated risk to shoot Labarre twice. One pop of a silencer could be misheard or ignored by someone in the corridor outside the suite, but not two in quick succession. However, Anna had decided the likelihood of someone passing Labarre's room in the middle of the afternoon at the very moment he was being killed was low enough to take the chance. Plus, the obliteration of his manhood would provide the impact that Line Z wanted when news of his death reached whoever it needed to.

She walked through the quiet hotel foyer, transformed by her new outfit into a rich businessman's wife, congratulating herself on another successful job. She didn't give any thought to the poor chambermaid who would discover Labarre's body in a few hours when she came to turn down his bed for the night, or the hotel manager who would have to spend the rest of his week dealing with enquiries from the police and Labarre's office in Paris.

As she settled in the back seat of another taxi and told the driver where she wanted him to take her, she opened the Chanel handbag and memorised the name that was printed next to her photo in the passport that had been left in it for her. Then she double-checked the time on the BEA ticket tucked inside it and decided she had time to have something to eat at the airport before her flight to London.

CHAPTER 34

Knox drove south into the centre of London and then over Waterloo Bridge. He had hoped taking Williams on a little sightseeing tour might help reconstruct some memories, but the man in the passenger seat next to him didn't seem to register anything as he stared out of the window at the city passing him by.

When they were somewhere near Blackheath, Williams finally spoke.

'He doesn't believe me, does he?' he said.

Knox could hear the quiet hurt in his friend's voice, and knew he was referring to Holland.

'He has faith in you,' Knox replied. 'But he also needs proof.'

'And I can't give him any.'

Williams shifted in his seat to look almost sideways out of his window, as if he was turning his back on Knox and the conversation. Knox switched on the radio. For once, the presenter wasn't talking about the election – they were interviewing some American who was trying to convince Londoners to join an international day of protest at the end of the month against the Vietnam War.

'It's been a year since the American people started to realise the truth about our illegal occupation of Vietnam,' the interviewee said.

'But what impact do you think non-Americans could have on your military policy?' the presenter asked.

'It's the duty of everyone in the free world to stand up and speak out against President Johnson's violent imperialism,' the American replied.

Knox dialled through static before he picked up another station. This one was playing a loop of 'Day Tripper' by the Beatles, 'These Boots Are Made for Walkin'' by Nancy Sinatra, and 'The Sun Ain't Gonna Shine (Anymore)' by the Walker Brothers. Knox lasted three cycles before he turned the radio off. By then they were on the A20, which would lead them all the way to Kent and most of the way to Deal. Williams had remained silent as they'd travelled out of London, but the sudden quiet brought his attention into the car.

'I'm guessing you've listened to those a few more times than I have,' he said.

Knox smiled. 'How are you feeling?'

'Fine,' Williams replied.

Knox knew it was a lie.

'Try having a nap,' he said. 'We've still got a good hour and a half to go. Maybe if you rest some things will come back to you.' He wanted to add, 'like if you remember forgiving me, or killing two men in front of me, or where you've been for seven years without me,' but didn't – Knox knew he needed to take things slow if Williams was going to be able to answer everything he was desperate to ask him.

'No,' Williams said, his voice suddenly firm. 'I need to stay awake. When I sleep I lose whatever grip I have on things and it all falls out of place.'

Knox glanced down at Williams's lap and his two bandaged hands.

'What can I do?' he asked.

'Tell me about what I've missed,' Williams replied.

'Well, Vietnam is still rumbling on. The Russians have built a wall through the middle of Berlin. And Castro's still running Cuba.'

'I didn't mean what's been going on in the world,' Williams said. 'I meant with you. Tell me about all your adventures.'

Knox suddenly struggled to think of how to describe what he'd been doing lately that didn't sound disappointingly prosaic.

'I've mainly been spending my time cleaning up other people's messes,' he said.

'Wasn't it ever thus?' Williams replied. It sounded like it should have been a joke, but his tone was flat.

Knox wanted to start at the beginning, tell Williams how much things had changed after he'd lost him, about the leave of absence Holland had given him and then how the director general had had to drag him back into Leconfield House and convince him to get on with his life and job. But he also wanted to give him the time and space Sarah and White were convinced he needed, and which he was now tacitly asking for himself. So, he jumped ahead a few years.

He told Williams about the mole hunt he'd gone on with Bennett five years ago, and how that had changed the trajectory of his career and led eventually to his recent trips to Australia and Canada.

'Richard Knox jetting off around the globe,' Williams said. 'You used to lecture me every time I went up in a plane.'

Knox and Williams had used to joke that together they made the perfect agent. Knox was the brains – cautious, methodical, always questioning every angle of attack – and Williams was the brawn. He'd had an unquenchable thirst for adventure. He'd been the one who had jumped at the chance to train with the navy divers, and who had learned to fly at Shoreham Airport, a small airfield outside Brighton. He'd spent long summer evenings spiralling and diving over the town and sea while Knox watched anxiously from the ground, waiting for him to make it safely back down to the flat stretch of grass the airport called a runway.

'Airliners are a bit different to those balsa-wood boxes you used to love so much.'

'I don't know,' Williams said. 'It sounds like the thing that's really different these days is you.'

'Oh, I'm the same old me,' Knox replied.

Silence fell between them again as the A road got quieter and the countryside they passed through greener. They were getting closer to the Kent Downs, and the rolling hills that stretched out ahead of them were starting to colour with early spring flowers.

'I just realised I have no idea where you live,' Williams said after ten minutes.

'I've got a flat in Soho,' Knox said. 'I told you, same old me. But I'm hardly there these days.'

'Spending all your time above the clouds?'

'And at Rabley Heath.'

Williams's eyes widened at the mention of his ancestral home.

'Someone needed to take care of the place,' Knox said. 'So I've been squatting in the gatehouse. I hope you don't mind.'

'No, no, of course not,' Williams stuttered. 'I'd completely forgotten about the old manor. At least I think I had. It's good that you're looking after it. Someone ought to.' He looked away for a moment before turning back to Knox. 'I'd like to see it again, sometime.'

'We can,' Knox said. 'As soon as this is all over.'

He watched Williams's brow furrow and gaze fall to his lap. He realised he'd let their reminisces stretch too far into the past. He needed to change the subject to something that might help jog Williams's memories without depressing him.

'Do you remember Belfast?' he asked.

Williams's head snapped back up, his mouth in a wide grin. 'Remember it? I think I still have the hangover.'

Belfast had been a rite of passage for junior MI5 agents for decades, and Knox and Williams had served there for a few months in the late forties, shortly after their recruitment into the Service. Still reeling from the war, the government hadn't wanted to fight any more battles the country couldn't afford, and had grown increasingly terrified of the prospect of someone using violence to finally solve the Northern Ireland question one way or the other.

The two young officers had been briefed on all the talk rattling around Whitehall about angry Catholic nationalists and fervent Protestant unionists. But after several weeks of backstreet meetings and shadowing operations, Knox and Williams had concluded that for the moment talk was all it was. The Irish and the Northern Irish, like the rest of Europe, weren't ready to take up arms again just yet. So for the rest of their deployment, Knox and Williams had spent their mornings dutifully filing their observation reports and their afternoons and evenings in the pub.

'We had some fun,' Williams said.

'Yes, we did,' Knox agreed.

He was buoyed by Williams's positive reaction to one of their most formative experiences in MI5, and wondered what else he could help him remember from their early days in the Service.

'What about St John Clare?' he asked.

Williams's face went blank for a moment while he tried to place the name, then his smile came back, even broader than before.

'The Red Tory,' he said, his smile growing wider. 'The barnstormer in the top hat and tails who was secretly working for the Hungarians.'

St John Clare was a young right-wing firebrand who had seemingly come out of nowhere to be elected as MP for North Devon in 1951 when Churchill was voted back into 10 Downing Street. He was as close as Britain came to having its own Joseph McCarthy, campaigning loudly for witch hunts against suspected communists, until he suddenly and quietly stepped down and triggered a by-election in 1953.

'Hated everyone except dyed-in-the-wool Conservatives, but was more than happy to take Budapest's money,' Knox said.

It was MI6 that had first uncovered the signs of Clare's hypocrisy and potential betrayal of his nation, and it had done it entirely by accident.

Hungary had been occupied by Soviet forces since the end of the war, so most Western intelligence about the country had to be gathered clandestinely. An MI6 analyst had been comparing a new set of undercover photographs taken in the Hungarian capital with some old file images when they realised that one of the people in the background of a photo taken in 1947 of Liberty Bridge, the first of the city's crossings over the Danube to be rebuilt after the Nazi retreat, looked remarkably like Clare. MI6 had passed their discovery on to MI5, and Knox and Williams had been sent down to Dorset during the 1952 parliamentary winter recess to ask Clare to explain himself.

'I've never seen anyone crack so quickly during questioning,' Knox said.

'What questioning?' Williams said. 'We were barely through his front door before he broke down and confessed everything.'

It had taken roughly ten minutes for Clare to tell them that he'd spent the last five years taking money from a 'representative of the Hungarian government' he'd happened to meet during his holiday in Budapest for information he passed on about the British upper class.

Clare's family was landed gentry, which made him a perfect source, and he was already rich, but he wanted more money. He also wanted power, which had drawn him into politics. When he'd become an MP he'd discovered that notoriety came with its own kind of influence. The more famous he became for stoking anti-socialist fires the more people wanted to know him, and the more he could demand from Budapest for the gossip he heard from his new friends.

'He was so scared of going to jail I thought he would have done anything we asked him to,' Williams said.

'And I thought he was going to kiss us when we told him what was going to happen,' Knox replied. 'No more pieces in the press, no more grand speeches in parliament, just a few months of actually doing his job and dealing with his constituents' petty concerns about potholes and missing cows before fading away into obscurity.'

Knox waited for Williams to make another quip, but instead he saw his face cloud again.

'Another charlatan,' Williams said quietly.

They drove on. Ten miles outside of Folkestone Knox slowed at a junction, checked his rear-view mirror, turned right, and headed south.

'This isn't the way to Deal,' Williams said.

'You've been before?' Knox asked.

'No, but I can read road signs. What's happening?'

'We're being followed,' Knox said, as casually as possible. 'Have been since London. They're quite good, but not good enough.'

Williams slouched in his seat and fought the urge to turn and look behind them.

'What type of car?' he asked.

'A Ford Consul. Which means it's one of ours, or someone who wants to look like one of ours.'

'So what's the plan?'

'We're going to find out what they want.'

CHAPTER 35

Stubbornness had driven Laing to follow Knox all the way to Kent. He should have turned round as soon as he'd realised Knox was heading out of London, and gone straight back to Leconfield House. But, instead of relishing the fact that Knox wouldn't be spending the next twenty-four hours stepping on his toes, he'd trailed his superior for almost two hours into the English countryside, keeping his distance but never letting the Jaguar out of his sight, even as the roads got quieter and quieter.

Laing watched Knox turn south just outside Ashford, and a few moments later he did the same. He'd been lucky that Knox had kept a fairly leisurely pace all the way from London – there was no way his pool Consul would have kept up with the Jaguar if Knox had really opened up his engine.

As the hills of the Downs faded into the distance and the two cars started to pass through ever-shrinking villages and hamlets, Laing let his mind range across all the possible excuses it had come up with for what was happening since he'd left Highgate. Was there a simple, innocent explanation for why Knox had driven a stranger from the director general of MI5's home to the Garden of England? Or were the Service's most senior officers up to something they didn't want anyone to know about, and using the summit as a distraction? Laing didn't like that possibility, mainly because it would mean they were using him to help create their cover while also keeping him in the dark about their plans.

He was momentarily distracted from his spiral of thoughts by a flock of birds bursting from the hedge that ran along the side of the road, flapping up into the wide blue sky in every direction.

A second later, the source of their sudden take-off appeared: a plane flying so low it looked like it was going to crash into the row of bushes.

The aircraft crossed the road just fifty feet off the ground and only a hundred in front of Laing's car, yet even that close it looked tiny to him, like someone had strapped a couple of wings across the top of a Mini. It was a Piper PA-18 Super Cub, with a cabin barely large enough to fit its pilot, and a wingspan of only thirty-five feet.

Laing watched it get lower and lower beyond the hedge, and guessed there must be an airstrip on the other side.

He looked back at the road just in time to see Knox's Jaguar make another turn outside a town of small pastel buildings with brown pitched roofs and a single tall, square church tower. And then he was distracted again, by the Doppler roar of a motorbike overtaking him. It was travelling too fast for him to make out any details, and it was only when it slowed momentarily to take the same turn Knox had that Laing saw there were two people on it. If they were a couple out for a countryside ride they seemed to be in a hell of a rush to get it over with.

Laing dropped down through his gears as he approached the junction so Knox wouldn't spot the Consul if the motorbike made him glance in his rear-view mirror. Then he turned into the next stretch of country road.

The hedge that had blocked his view of the little plane's final descent continued along one side of his path, but on the other the flat fields that had replaced the Downs now gave way in quick succession to a series of wide marshes and then a vast shingle beach.

Laing had arrived at Dungeness.

He continued on, unconsciously slowing down as he processed the abrupt and dramatic change to the landscape around him. He passed a small, quiet car park, where he saw a couple of wet dogs being coaxed into car boots and the two helmeted riders from the motorbike dismounting their metal steed. For a moment, he thought Knox had somehow vanished, sucked down into quicksand or swallowed up by one of the marshes, but then he saw the Jaguar over to his right, still heading away from him down a barely visible path.

Laing's wheels crunched as they drove over chunks of rock that had been smoothed by tides for centuries then blown onto the narrow strip of tarmac that ran across what was technically Britain's only desert. There was no wind now, not that there were any trees with leaves and branches to sway in the breeze – the expanse of shingle was only broken by the occasional stunted bush or brave flower, fisherman's huts that looked abandoned and stood far away from the sea and, in the distance, the squat, hulking profile of a nuclear power station.

Dungeness was an eerie, remote place. It was that remoteness that had led to this stretch of the Kent coastline being chosen for the power station. Strangely, the addition of its series of grey, featureless boxes had made the place seem even more desolate. The power station looked completely alien, and it was impossible to believe that anyone at all worked there, let alone hundreds of scientists and engineers, or that the track Laing was driving down and the narrow-gauge single train line that ran alongside it didn't just continue beyond the odd aberration and on into oblivion.

As Laing passed yet another wind-beaten hut with window shutters closed up and old strips and blocks of metal strewn across the shingle in front of it, he noticed that Knox's Jaguar wasn't as far away as it should be. In fact, it was stopped in the middle of the track ahead of him. Laing swore at himself. He'd been so focused on imagining the schemes that might be afoot and then mesmerised by the strangeness of Dungeness that he hadn't realised that he hadn't just been following Knox, but that Knox had also been leading him to exactly where he wanted him – possibly even all the way from London.

He slowed to a halt twenty feet behind the Jaguar, turned off his engine, and waited for Knox to make his next move.

***

'What do we do now?' Williams asked as Knox watched the Consul come to a stop in the Jaguar's rear-view mirror.

The glint of the sun on the second car's windscreen meant that Knox and Williams still didn't know who had followed them all the way out to Dungeness.

'You stay put,' Knox said. 'And I'll see what this is all about.'

Knox opened his door and got out of the car. He didn't hold up his hands, but he moved slowly enough to tell whoever was behind him that he wasn't a threat. However, he also left his door open so he could dive back into the car if he needed to.

He filled his lungs with a couple of deep breaths of briny air, then stifled his surprise when he saw Laing get out of the Consul.

'It's good to see you, Simon,' Knox said. 'But you've come a long way just to give me the morning status report.'

'Everything's ready for tomorrow,' Laing said, matching Knox's relaxed tone. 'But I wanted to talk to you about something out of the ordinary that I've noticed.'

'What's that?'

'Members of MI5 harbouring and transporting unknown individuals.'

'Nothing for you to worry about,' Knox replied, leaning against the side of the Jaguar.

Laing stepped forward into the gap between the two cars. 'If there's a secret operation running over Kosygin's visit I should know about it.'

Knox wondered if the young agent was aware just how insubordinate he was being.

'Everything we do is secret,' he said. 'But this doesn't concern Kosygin, or you. I'm just out for a drive.'

'Who with?'

'That's none of your business.'

Laing looked like he wanted more of an answer than that, but before he could ask another question Knox looked past him and tensed, pulling himself back up off the Jaguar. Laing twisted his head and saw what had drawn Knox's attention.

Another car was driving down the track towards them.

It was an MG 1100, painted blue and cream, and the closer it got the louder its engines, and the wheels on stray bits of shingle, sounded. Beyond the new car, Knox could also see two people walking in their direction, along the edge of the narrow train line. They were still a fair distance away, but he could tell they were a man and a woman, both wearing anoraks and waxed trousers, with rucksacks strapped over their shoulders and binoculars slung round their necks – a pair of optimistic birdwatchers who were probably very confused at stumbling across this unexpected scene in the middle of their coastal ramble.

Knox and Laing both watched the MG stop ten feet behind Laing's Consul, adding to the curious, stationary convoy. Laing didn't know who the short, dark-haired woman who got out of the car was, but Knox did, and he was both surprised and not to see Bennett.

***

Williams recognised the new arrival too. The sight of Bennett took him back to meeting her on the street in Santo Domingo, then to his cell in Haina, and finally to his reunion with Knox in Regent's Park. For the first time in a long time it felt like he was observing his memories with some kind of objectivity instead of being caught up or lost in them. And, oddly, instead of adding to the dread that he'd felt building inside him all day, Bennett's appearance seemed to calm him.

He looked down again at his bandaged hands still resting in his lap, then he opened his door, got out of the car, and moved round the front of the Jaguar to stand next to Knox.

***

A breeze was starting to pick up, carrying the sounds of the distant sea inland. But everyone on the track could still hear the two birdwatchers getting closer to them over the white noise of crashing waves.

It wasn't until the couple crossed over the tarmac behind the MG that they appeared to decide to veer sharply off towards one of the dilapidated huts between the road and the marshes.

When they were far enough to be out of earshot, Bennett was the first to speak.

'Nice day for a drive,' she said to Knox.

He didn't react.

'Who are you?' Laing asked her.

She ignored him.

'I had a feeling you'd find each other eventually,' she said to Knox and Williams.

'Have you been following me, Abey?' Knox asked, trying again to keep his tone light, and wondering if someone had managed to secrete a tracker somewhere on his Jaguar after all.

'Actually, I followed him,' Bennett replied, finally acknowledging Laing's existence.

He didn't look happy about it, and neither did Knox.

'I'm here for Williams,' she said.

'Is this a handover?' Laing asked.

'No,' Knox answered.

'Yes,' Bennett countered. 'I need him back.'

'Then you've come a long way for nothing,' Knox said.

Bennett took a step forward, and Knox moved in front of Williams. The wind was building, getting louder as it moved the sea and shook the shingle.

'I gave you time together as a friend,' Bennett said, almost shouting. 'That time's up. This has to happen.'

'I don't think I have to do anything,' Knox replied.

'Don't you?' Bennett said. 'I thought you were all about duty. And loyalty.'

'I am loyal,' Knox shot back. 'To people who deserve it.'

'And I'm not on that list any more?'

Before Knox could spell out again the reasons why she wasn't, he felt Williams's hand on his arm.

'She's right, old man,' he said, in what sounded like a whisper against the wind. 'This has gone on long enough.'

Knox opened his mouth, but nothing came out.

'Whatever battle I have to face I can't ask you to fight it for me,' Williams said.

'You're not asking,' Knox managed to say.

'I know,' Williams replied.

Neither Bennett nor Laing had heard Knox and Williams's exchange, and both looked confused as Williams started to walk past Laing towards Bennett.

He was a foot beyond Laing when they all heard the gun go off.

CHAPTER 36

Laing's body spun as he fell to the ground. The bullet had ripped through his left thigh, the force of it kicking his leg out from under him. He landed hard on the tarmac, and the sound of his head smacking against it before his neck had a chance to tense and protect it was almost as loud as the gunshot.

Knox and Bennett instinctively ducked behind their cars. Then after a split second spent checking they hadn't been hit, they both looked at Laing, dazed and lying exposed in the gap between the Consul and the Jaguar, and Williams, who was bizarrely still walking towards Bennett. He'd slowed down, but he looked completely unaware of what had just happened, or the danger he was in.

'Jack,' Knox shouted. 'Get down!'

But Williams ignored his instructions, and just kept slowly walking further away from him.

Knox had to stop himself from launching out from behind the Jaguar. Instead he raised his head to peer through its side windows at who was attacking them.

He could see the two birdwatchers standing behind a low rusted metal locker next to one of the huts. The man had his binoculars held up to his eyes, and the woman was kneeling against the locker, her rucksack resting on the top of it, fluttering in the growing wind, and a folding sniper's rifle in her hands.

If this had been a movie, Knox would have shuffled back to the open driver's door, reached into the car, pulled out a hidden revolver, and come up firing, But this wasn't a movie, and Knox had no gun.

He heard Laing groan and looked over at Bennett, who had also shifted along the MG and was crouching behind its back wheel, tentatively looking through the car's rear windows at their attackers.

'Get behind the car, Simon,' Knox said, hoping the still-high wind would stop his words travelling to the birdwatchers' ears.

Laing moaned in response and reached out his arm to drag himself behind cover. The response from the birdwatchers was immediate – one bullet into the Consul's headlight that showered Laing in glass, and another into its bonnet that started petrol dripping onto the road a foot from him.

Williams was now between the Consul and the MG, completely exposed again. Knox needed to get him to safety, but he needed to help Laing too. He edged forward, daring to lean his head out past the Jaguar's rear bumper.

The reaction was swift again as an inch of tarmac exploded next to Laing's prone body. It was a clear warning shot to Knox to stay exactly where he was.

'Help Jack,' he called out to Bennett as he ducked back behind the car.

By now, Williams had almost reached the MG and Bennett, taking advantage of the birdwatchers' focus on Knox and Laing, had already moved forward to the front tyre. As soon as Williams reached the square nose of Bennett's car, she reached up and pulled him down, rolling him over her to land behind the rear wheel.

They were all pinned, and Laing was still stuck in the open, grimacing as he held his leg that was seeping blood, and staring at the trickle of petrol that was inching closer and closer to him.

Knox looked past Laing to Bennett and Williams. She signalled that they were fine, then gestured towards their attackers, silently asking what they should do next. Knox could only answer by shrugging his shoulders. He raised his head to take another look at the birdwatchers, but before his eyes were level with the glass of the window another bullet had slammed into the Consul's engine, eliciting a shriek from Laing and turning the trickle of petrol moving towards him into a stream.

The wind shifted and suddenly the row of cars became engulfed in a bubble of silence. Knox and Bennett could still see shrubs that had managed to grow taller than a few inches being battered by gusts of air, but all they could hear were Laing's groans and the constant drip of engine fluid.

'Are you okay?' Bennett whispered to Williams.

He didn't reply. She shoved his shoulder, trying to provoke some kind of response, but he just stared dead ahead, as if he was spellbound. She hit him again, but he didn't seem to feel it.

Knox was watching, and he was as scared by Williams's lack of reaction as he was at not knowing what the birdwatchers were doing. For all he knew, they were creeping across the shingle, their footsteps muffled by the wall of wind Knox and the others were trapped behind, ready to flank the row of cars and pick them off one by one.

He slid down onto the ground to look under the Jaguar's chassis but couldn't see anything other than car tyres, tarmac, and shingle. The temptation to stand up was overwhelming, but he knew that would probably result in a bullet in himself or Laing. His only option was to wait.

Wait until the man with the binoculars suddenly appeared at the rear of Bennett's car and the woman stepped between the MG and the Consul, with her rifle trained on Knox.

Bennett tried to scramble to her feet to protect her and Williams, but before she could get far the man slammed her head against the metal trim between the two driver's side doors, and bundled her unconscious body into the back of her car.

The woman then started to walk backwards, keeping her rifle pointed at Knox, who could only stay where he was, impotent with anger as he realised the two of them weren't wearing waxed trousers after all – they were wearing biker leathers.

The man paused as he stood over Williams, who was still staring blankly into space, apparently unsure of what might happen if he touched him. The woman glanced down at him, shifted the rifle in her hands, and jabbed the butt of its grip against his temple, knocking him unconscious as well, before turning her aim back on Knox.

The man then hefted Williams's body next to Bennett's, climbed into the driver's seat, started the MG's engine, and moved over to the passenger side. It took the woman two seconds to get in the car, hand the rifle to the man, put the car into reverse, and accelerate away down the track.

CHAPTER 37

Lieutenant Maksim Starikov had come to a very unpleasant realisation. He was going to die, trapped in a metal tube hundreds of metres under water. This terrifying and absolute certainty had arrived abruptly twenty minutes ago as he'd lain in his bunk deep in the gut of the *Yorsh* and started to notice the bulkheads close in around him.

He was suffering from acute and intense claustrophobia.

At first, he'd told himself he was just feeling sick, having a bad reaction to the meal he'd eaten alone in the submarine's small mess at the end of his last shift – probably to something the cook or another member of the crew who didn't appreciate the presence of the KGB had slipped into his food. But the queasiness that had woken him up had quickly faded, replaced by a deep, churning fear in the pit of his stomach, and an unstoppable, creeping belief that the submarine was shrinking.

He reached out and touched the bulkhead at the end of his bunk with the boot he'd been too tired to take off after spending eight hours relentlessly walking and watching every inch of the *Yorsh*. He was sure the thick metal plate was closer than it had been when he'd first boarded the submarine in Murmansk, and when he'd last stretched out his foot a minute ago.

Starikov's breathing, which was already shallow, started to quicken as he fought to convince himself this was all just in his head. He couldn't understand why he suddenly felt like this seven days into the voyage. All he could think was that for the first four days of cruising around the North Sea and English Channel he'd been too overwhelmed by the strangeness of life underwater. And, of course, he'd actually had a job to do then, ensuring that no one in the *Yorsh*'s skeleton crew was doing anything that could jeopardise their mission. But for the past three days, since he'd last breathed fresh air and looked at something that wasn't a metal plate, dial, or disdainful crew member, he'd had nothing to do. And neither had anyone else.

He should have got up as soon as he'd started to feel trapped, and walked the submarine again to prove to himself that it wasn't really getting smaller, but he couldn't face the prospect of his rational mind being wrong and ending up stuck in a tangle of pipes or pinned between a control panel and a bulkhead as the pressure of the ocean and his psyche squeezed around him.

Now, however, the shift change was starting and he didn't have a choice. Luckily, the few other members of the crew who had been off shift with Starikov and were still in their bunks didn't look his way as he tentatively swung his legs out of his, pulled on his uniform jacket, and slowly stood up, his eyes on the deck plate above him to check it was still where it was supposed to be. Then he made his way through the cramped mayhem that briefly consumed the submarine as half of its crew perched narrow braided caps on their heads and the other half removed theirs, to see Captain Tokorev.

***

Tokorev was supposed to obey the same shift pattern as the rest of the *Yorsh*'s crew, but with no second in command and being very curious about the odd shape this shakedown cruise had taken, he'd decided to spend as much time as possible in the submarine's control room, only retiring to his quarters for brief naps when he felt tiredness start to take over his muscles.

He was on his way to his own narrow bunk for a few minutes of rest when he saw Starikov approaching. Tokorev still hadn't warmed to the KGB officer, who had spent the last three days stalking his crew and getting in the way of even the most basic and mundane procedures. But he could tell just from looking at the younger man's face that he wasn't in a good way, and ushered him into his quarters without a word.

Tokorev had seen enough junior submariners succumb to claustrophobia to know the warning signs. Usually recruits who couldn't handle the lack of personal space, sunlight or fresh air that came with life on a submarine were weeded out early on in the selection process, and the ones who fixated on the constant possibility of the tube they were stuffed inside crumpling under the weight of the ocean depths only lasted a few short trips away from their base. The KGB, Tokorev guessed, gave their officers no such training, or any reprieve if they weren't cut out for serving beneath the waves. And this was a serious issue, because if someone didn't calm Starikov down then he could very easily become a risk to the rest of the crew and a threat to the success of their mission, however peculiar that mission currently was.

'Have we received fresh orders?' Starikov asked as Tokorev closed the door to his quarters behind them, unbuttoned his uniform jacket and sat down at the small desk next to his single bed.

'You would know if we had, Lieutenant,' Tokorev replied.

Tokorev's quarters weren't much bigger than Starikov's own bunk, but the KGB officer still managed to find enough space to pace up and down.

'Perhaps we should surface ahead of schedule,' Starikov said.

'Why would I disobey direct instructions?' Tokorev asked.

Tokorev knew he needed to divert Starikov away from the precipice he was rushing towards, but he couldn't resist needling the young man a little while he did it.

'The ZEVS system might be malfunctioning,' Starikov offered.

'Disobeying orders and questioning the Soviet Union's mastery of technology. I don't think I'd advise it.'

Starikov stopped in his tracks, apparently realising the implications of what he'd just said. Tokorev laughed, relieved he'd so quickly and easily managed to insert an even greater fear than death into the KGB officer's head.

'Don't worry,' he said. 'I won't tell anyone what you just said. And between the two of us, I have my own reservations about what we're doing sitting out here in the middle of the ocean.'

The last orders the *Yorsh* had received had been simple and confusing – to head slowly out of the Channel at near-surface depth, and then dive, hold position in the open Atlantic, and await further instructions. The submarine had now floated steady, minus a few metres or so of drift, in the same spot for almost seventy hours.

'What are we waiting for?' Starikov asked.

The question had none of the distrustful tone that usually accompanied enquiries from the KGB. Tokorev wondered if he wasn't just managing to calm Starikov down, but also perhaps starting to get through to him about the realities of their lives and duties.

'I don't know,' Tokorev replied. 'But I find it better to think about it not so much as waiting but more as lying in wait.'

He watched as Starikov's addled mind slowly began to entertain this new possibility – that they hadn't just been left or forgotten out in the ocean, but that they were there for a reason, however invisible or incomprehensible to them.

The lieutenant's body finally relaxed, and Tokorev gestured for him to take a seat on his bunk. He might be a grizzled old cynic, but Tokorev was also a patriot, and he wanted to remind Starikov that he was one too – not to the KGB, or even the Soviet Union, but to Mother Russia.

The captain was old enough to remember the long revolution of 1917 and the civil war that had followed. As a scared child he'd watched a decaying Russian empire collapse around him and witnessed the rise of the Soviet Union from its wreckage. And he'd pledged to protect this brave new version of his homeland with the same fervour with which he'd mourned the death of the old one.

'Do you know what the true definition of capitalism is?' he said. 'There isn't one. It has no ambition other than to spread around the world, consuming every last corner of it like a cancer. It doesn't want peace, it only wants victory. A whole planet of workers toiling at their own cost for someone else's benefit. At least with communism we all have the chance to reap the rewards of what we sow.'

He slipped his jacket off, tossed it onto the bunk next to Starikov, and undid the top buttons of his shirt.

'We helped the capitalists save the world, twice,' he continued. 'And what did it get us? Millions dead, and betrayal. They are, at their most basic level, simply what we are not. And so, we must be forever locked in conflict with them. We may never win the battle, but we will never stop fighting. We can do nothing else. It is our nature. And Russians are very patient people. So we must be content to bide our time.'

Starikov's body stiffened again and sat him upright on the bed, but this time not out of fear. The rhetoric was working.

'And while we lie in wait,' Tokorev said, as he leaned behind himself and opened the drawer of his desk, prompting the bottle of vodka inside to roll and bounce off its sides, 'we drink'.

CHAPTER 38

The nurses at the quiet country hospital were more than a little surprised when a grey Jaguar screeched to a halt on their short drive and a man with a blood-stained scarf wrapped round his thigh was rushed through their front door.

Knox had dragged Laing away from the pool of petrol that had started to soak his jacket, checked his thigh, and seen that the bullet from the sniper's rifle had passed straight through it. Then he'd pulled an old chequered wool scarf out of the boot of the Jaguar and fastened it tightly above the two holes in Laing's leg.

By then the two attackers, and Bennett and Williams, had disappeared beyond the marshes. Even if Knox had left Laing where he was, jumped in his car and chased off after the MG, the chances of finding and catching it in the network of lanes and roads that led inland were maddeningly small. So, swallowing his shock and anger, he helped Laing up onto his good foot, then supported him as he hobbled to the Jaguar's passenger seat. Knox then completed a delicate three-point turn so they didn't end up with their wheels trapped in the shingle, and set off to find Laing some medical attention.

Knox wanted to get back to London as fast as he could, but he knew if he drove straight there he might arrive with a dead colleague in the seat next to him. However, he still didn't want to lose too much time, so instead of driving further east to Folkestone or Dover he headed west, down through Jurys Gap, back to the coast, and through Camber to Rye, where he saw signs for the small hospital on its outskirts.

Neither of them said anything for the duration of the journey, Laing concentrating on the pain in his leg and Knox doing his best to maintain a decent speed while avoiding any bumps or potholes in the country roads. But, the closer they'd got to Rye, the heavier he'd become on the accelerator, because with each glance he stole at Laing the younger man looked more pallid and anaemic.

'Not much we can do for him here,' the middle-aged matron said to Knox after he'd deposited Laing in a wheelchair and two nurses in starched white uniforms had whisked him away to a bed on the hospital's single, empty ward.

Knox could tell that she wasn't going to be fobbed off with some made-up excuse about Laing's injury – neither he nor Knox were dressed for game hunting or some other rural pursuit that might have explained the bullet holes and lost blood.

'I just need you to patch him up a little,' Knox said, after he'd described an edited version of what had happened. 'So I can get him back to London and a proper hospital.'

If the matron was offended by Knox's use of the word *proper*, she didn't show it. And, as her hospital's only doctor was out on house calls tending to a minor spring flu outbreak, there wasn't anything she or her nurses could do other than patch Williams up and send him on his way with cleaned and dressed wounds and some very strong painkillers.

'Don't dilly-dally,' the matron told Knox as he transferred Laing back into the passenger seat of the Jaguar, which was stained from his blood. 'He needs properly stitching up, and a transfusion.'

'I'll make sure he gets both,' Knox replied as he turned over the engine and pulled away from the hospital.

Knox drove them through the High Weald, along more narrow roads that wound through woods and fields and eventually connected to an A road that would take them back into London.

Aside from his occasional shrieks and groans, Laing had been silent since he'd been shot. Knox now decided this was the result of obstinacy rather than shock, and that it was time to shake him out of it.

'How old are you?' he asked.

Knox already knew the answer to his question, but he thought it might be a good way to break the ice that had formed between him and his second passenger of the day.

'Twenty-six,' Laing answered as he watched the blurred verges go by faster and faster as Knox sped them back to the city.

'Not many people around that age.'

'No.'

Knox hadn't expected him to suddenly open up and tell him his life story, or even thank him for taking him to the hospital and probably saving his life, but he wanted a bit more from Laing than monosyllabic answers.

'I would have made the same call,' Knox said. 'In Canada.'

'What?' Laing said, surprise replacing petulance.

'I'm serious. I read your report and my instincts told me to do exactly what you'd done as well.'

'But you didn't. I did, and I was wrong.'

'I've been wrong plenty of times myself. The only difference between the two of us is that I've made enough good bets to outweigh my bad ones.'

Laing moved his bandaged leg, shifting the weight that had crept onto it. 'Did any of them get you shot?'

'One did, actually,' Knox said, unable to stop a wry smile spreading across his face. 'As it happens, the last time I encountered Abey Bennett. Welcome to the club.'

Laing's surprise turned to shock. 'That was Abey Bennett?'

Knox realised Laing really had no idea what he'd driven all the way from London into the middle of, and decided that after what he'd got for his trouble he deserved to be properly brought in on what was going on. He added some colour and detail to how he'd come to meet Bennett on their joint mission that was still a fairly well known part of MI5's recent history, and told him about Jack

Williams, whose story was less well remembered. Laing knew Williams's name, but only from reading it on the memorial to lost Service officers in Leconfield House.

'I shouldn't have come after you,' Laing said after Knox had explained why he'd taken Williams out of London instead of coming into MI5 headquarters and spending the day twiddling his thumbs.

Before Dungeness, Knox would have agreed with Laing. But while he could blame Bennett's appearance there on him, it wouldn't be fair to heap the responsibility for the attack on his shoulders too. They'd all been blindsided, and were all now suffering for it. Laing had lost a lot of blood, Knox had lost Williams again, and he had no idea what his best friend and Bennett were currently being subjected to.

'I don't think any of us could have predicted how today was going to turn out,' he said. 'I'm sorry you got caught up in it.'

'Do you think they were KGB?' Laing asked.

'It's likely. We can send someone down to take a look at the motorbike, though I doubt they left their logbook for us to find.'

Laing exhaled, and Knox guessed it wasn't from pain but from making the connection that he had when he'd seen their attackers up close: they were the pair that had screeched past Laing's Consul and Knox's Jaguar just before they'd reached the beach, and had possibly followed them, and Bennett, all the way from London.

'Still,' Knox continued, 'process of elimination points that way. They certainly weren't MI5, and Bennett's been hung out to dry on this by the new London COS. But we don't know for definite who's been holding Williams all this time, or what they've done to him.'

Laing thought for a moment, then asked, 'What if he wasn't a prisoner? What if he was an asset gone rogue, and the Russians want him back?'

Knox had to stop himself from slamming on the brakes. Laing had leaped straight to the one possibility that Knox absolutely refused to consider.

'There's no evidence to suggest Williams is anything other than a victim in all this,' he said, firmly. 'Any speculation has to start from that point.'

'Either way, the DG will have to insist that Wilson can't meet Kosygin while a KGB hit squad has kidnapped an MI5 officer and CIA agent.'

Knox wasn't so sure. He'd wondered about that exact point while Laing was being treated, but it now felt like there were too many unknowns and variables in play to make a solid bet on anything, including how Holland would react when he found out what had happened at Dungeness.

'We'll see,' he replied.

CHAPTER 39

If Anna ever forgot where in the world one of her jobs had taken her, she'd be able to work it out just from where she was staying the night. No matter how high- or low-end, every hotel had certain subtle qualities that betrayed their nationality. And Durrants on George Street in Marylebone was quintessentially British.

The hotel's ground floor was all wood-panelled walls and over-waxed chesterfields. But it was also pleasingly quiet, and the staff were discreet and fastidious. The surname on the passport Anna had used to travel from Geneva was Lopez, and if the hotel manager, a short man in a three-piece suit who Anna guessed was in his mid-fifties, had any suspicions about her not sounding entirely Spanish he hid them well. Durrants was a long-standing favourite of the continent's globe-trotting elite, who often travelled with names that didn't match their accents and who preferred to retain their privacy and avoid London's larger, flashier hotels like the Dorchester or Claridge's.

The manager, keen to make a good impression, also showed Anna up the split imperial staircase to her suite, which was considerably brighter than the foyer. The walls were papered in a light, floral pattern, and Liberty print fabrics covered the bed and framed the two tall windows that looked across George Street towards the back of Hertford House, the imposing mansion on Manchester Square that had once been both the Spanish and French embassies.

'Your luggage arrived this afternoon,' the manager said, pointing at the suitcase on the mahogany stand next to the suite's large wardrobe. 'With instructions not to unpack it,' he added, anticipating any criticism his new guest might have had at the level of service she was receiving.

'It's perfect,' Anna replied, reassuring him that he'd done the right thing. 'Thank you.'

Once he was gone, Anna stretched out the slight stiffness she felt after the flight from Geneva and the long rush-hour taxi journey from London Airport to Marylebone. Then she picked up her new luggage – a brown leather monogrammed Louis Vuitton suitcase – carried it over to the bed, and opened it. Inside was a small toiletry bag and a change of clothes, along with an exceptionally ugly gown, a large envelope filled with sterling notes, and a card with an address near Shepherd's Bush in west London on it.

There was a knock at the door as she was laying out the unstructured, billowing georgette evening dress and wondering just how inappropriate it was for the task at hand. Instinctively, she calmed her breathing to near nothing, rose up onto the balls of her feet, and silently skipped across the room to the door.

She wasn't expecting any visitors, so she readied to either defend herself or attack whoever was waiting in the corridor. However, as she flung the door open all she saw was a porter, holding a large, flat parcel.

Her face transformed into a wide smile, instantly disarming the shocked young man.

'The manager sends his apologies,' he said, holding out the paper-wrapped package, 'that this didn't arrive before you did.'

Anna took the parcel.

'Did he arrange the delivery?' she asked, adding a stern edge to her voice.

'Erm, no,' the porter stuttered, suddenly nervous.

'Then there's really nothing to apologise for,' Anna replied, smiling broadly again and slamming the door in the porter's face.

Anna felt the parcel as she carried it back into the suite. It was heavy and hard-edged. Solid enough, she decided, to have crushed the porter's windpipe with one sharp thrust, if she'd wanted to.

It would have been crude, and inaccurate, to describe Anna as a psychopath. Anna was more than that. She delighted in the pain she caused, relished her craft, and always understood exactly what she was inflicting on people. The only thing she didn't know was why she did it, but that wasn't her job.

Anna had been found by the Soviets in the bombed-out husk of Dresden in 1945.

Allied air raids had destroyed more than half of the city in the cold early months of the year, and by the time the Red Army marched into its rubble-strewn streets the rule of law, along with most other signs of civilisation, had collapsed.

Tales had spread, among the people who had managed to survive the bombings and a harsh winter with barely any protection from the elements and even less food, of a ghostly killer haunting the city's ruined buildings, murdering the weak and the sick. Some called this spectre the angel of death, others the angel of mercy.

After several months spent ignoring the rumours, and a few more impatiently waiting for them to fade, KGB investigators were sent to end them once and for all. The agents were astonished when they discovered that the real, flesh-and-blood human who had been steadily adding to the city's mass of corpses was a beautiful twenty-one-year-old woman. They were even more stunned when she openly confessed to all the murders and recounted the gruesome details of each one, starting with her first two victims: her parents.

Anna's mother and father had been scared of their daughter for most of her childhood. She was a pretty child, and her beauty had only grown as she got older. But so had the darkness that seemed to sit deep within her. She was quick to anger, and sought revenge for even the smallest slight. By the time she was ten, they suspected she was responsible for at least three broken bones among the local children. They tried their best to shelter her from the world – and the world from her.

When the war started, she was kept in the family home in the south of Dresden almost all day with her mother while her father worked long hours in a munitions factory in the west.

The whole family was at home the night the RAF dropped the first wave of bombs on the city. They rushed to their cellar as they heard the explosions getting louder and close enough to shake the walls of their house and smash her mother's prized collection of Dresden's famed porcelain. Then a direct hit brought their home down on top of them.

When the dust from the blast began to settle, the ringing in Anna's ears was replaced by the screams of her mother as she tried to dig her husband out from under the rubble that had crushed his body and was forcing blood out of his mouth with every shallow breath. Anna, who was serenely calm in the chaos, understood that nothing could be done to save her father. So she picked up a large chunk of brick and used it to cave in his head. Then, when her mother's screams got even louder, delirious and desperate, and Anna realised there was no way she could survive without the man who had been by her side for forty years, she strangled her.

The KGB agents didn't know whether to lock Anna up or execute her, put a bullet in her head and bury her somewhere in the city to be forgotten. But Ivan Egorov, the head of the newly established Line Z, had another idea. He wanted to recruit her.

Line Z was only a few months old, one of the many experiments the KGB had dreamed up to work out how to take advantage of the new territorial and collateral resources the Soviet Union had acquired after defeating Nazi Germany, and to prepare for the predicted cooling of relations with its wartime allies.

Anna was sent to a military base near Bernau bei Berlin, a small town north of the German capital that had also been bombed by the Allies and left to rot by the Soviets.

Bernau itself might have been festering, but the now-Soviet military base in the woods outside it was full of life and activity. Red Army soldiers had been moved into its barracks; stylised murals of their comrades standing proudly under hammers, sickles, and stars had been painted over the outstretched wings of the Reichsadler eagle and wreathed swastika; and Line Z had requisitioned one of the compound's large halls as its own private training ground.

Anna slept, ate, and honed her killing skills in the cavernous building along with the rest of Line Z's early initiates. Conditions were tough, lessons hard, and punishments for disobedience severe. The trainees shivered in winter, sweated in summer, and any of them who baulked at the orders they were given or started to question the morality of their instructions would quietly vanish from the hall overnight.

Anna thrived under Egorov's strict rules, much to the surprise of the KGB psychologists, who had believed she would never succumb to any kind of authority. What the people who tried to analyse her had failed to appreciate was that Anna was more than happy to relinquish responsibility for such trivial matters as who she must kill and why they must die, and focus simply on how she was going to execute them. She didn't care if her victim was a homeless German accused of stealing food for his family, or a Red Army soldier who had been caught acting unpatriotically, she obeyed her commands without question.

She became the first graduate of Line Z's Bernau academy, and then a founding agent of the Volk programme. Twenty years later, she was still its most effective assassin. She had finally lost count of how many lives she'd brought to abrupt ends. But the KGB hadn't. In two decades she'd murdered nearly three hundred people under orders from Line Z – orders that had almost entirely been followed to the letter.

On rare occasions, Anna hadn't restricted her creativity solely to killing and had taken it upon herself to change certain minor parameters of a mission. For any other agent such behaviour would have brought about their own execution, but Anna had earned a little length on her leash.

And, as she unwrapped the large square book the porter had delivered, which had a set of architectural blueprints and a gilt-edged invitation card tucked inside its cover, and looked again at the gauzy dress and thick envelope of money, she decided that this mission would be one of those times.

CHAPTER 40

Rykov stood in the small triangle of weak sunlight that was still managing to penetrate the courtyard in front of the columned dome of the Kremlin senate building. He didn't like waiting for anyone, but he had a standing appointment at this time every week that he made an exception for.

The Kremlin senate had been a seat of political power in Russia ever since Catherine the Great had ordered its construction. Lenin and Stalin had both had studies and apartments in the building, and Lenin was now interred in his mausoleum a hundred metres away on the edge of Red Square. Rykov had always thought the high wall that cut between the senate and the mausoleum was a rather neat symbol of the transition the old grandfather of the Soviet Union had made from power to spectacle – and the removal of Stalin's body from the tomb the two men had briefly shared a sign of the fleeting nature of fame.

Colonel General Aventin Churkin was the kind of anonymous, suit-wearing middle-aged man who would be dismissed as an accountant or lawyer in the West. He was, however, the deputy head of the first chief directorate of the KGB. Like every other line or department head in the first chief directorate, Rykov reported to Churkin. But his relationship with the colonel general was closer than merely being his direct subordinate. Churkin was also favoured by Brezhnev, and in the last couple of years had become something close to a patron to Rykov. However, both were careful to keep their alliance discreet and not bask too much in the glow of

Brezhnev's attention. They both knew how capricious the moods of politicians could be, and how frosty the general secretary had recently become towards Vladimir Semichastny, the chairman of the KGB, who had helped depose Khrushchev eighteen months ago.

Rykov watched Churkin step through the left-most of the three narrow doors at the base of the senate and button up his coat. Churkin's seniority meant he had to come into regular contact with the Council of Ministers and their individual offices. His weekly visits to the senate mainly involved listening to grievances and placating politicians over their latest, childish issues. But they also made him privy to their quiet gossip, fears, and ambitions.

With a split second of reluctance, Rykov left his little slice of sunlight and walked over to Churkin, falling into step beside him and matching his slow pace. Churkin never rushed anywhere, even in the depths of winter. Rykov knew he considered it a sign of confidence, a manifestation of the image of certainty the KGB must project at all times. And that he enjoyed how awkward some people felt when they saw a spy walking slowly towards them.

'Have you heard the terrible news from Cape Kennedy?' Rykov asked, his voice dripping with sarcasm.

The previous afternoon, America had launched the Gemini 8 capsule on top of a Titan II GLV rocket, carrying two astronauts, Neil Armstrong and David Scott, into orbit to attempt NASA's first extraterrestrial docking test. Ten hours after launch the mission had been aborted due to a critical systems failure and the Gemini capsule had splashed down 430 nautical miles off the coast of Okinawa, Japan.

Churkin didn't return Rykov's grin. 'A setback. And a minor one at that.'

Rykov dropped the small talk.

'How are the wheels?' he asked, his voice suddenly considerably lower.

'Greased,' Churkin replied.

'And the minds?'

'Changing.'

'Should we be concerned?' Rykov asked.

'I don't think so,' Churkin said. 'But it wouldn't hurt to send some flattery in Yuri Andropov's direction.'

'The head of the department for liaison?'

'He's in the ascendent. Brezhnev hasn't forgotten how he handled the Hungarian Uprising. I wouldn't be surprised if he replaces Semichastny soon.'

'What do Kosygin and Podgorny think?'

'Kosygin needs to be here to have an opinion, and no one cares what Podgorny thinks.'

It was a sign of the confidence between the two men that Rykov could ask such questions and Churkin could answer them so directly.

'The short leg of the stool,' Rykov said, recycling one of the better lines he'd heard the basement poet use a few weeks ago to describe the troika that currently led the Soviet Union.

'Someone always has to be the junior partner,' Churkin mused.

By now they were passing along the top of Ivanovskaya Square. To their right was the huge concrete and glass slab of the Palace of Congresses, Khrushchev's grand arena for mass events, and to their left was the cluster of cathedrals that reminded people of the higher power that had once held sway inside the Kremlin's red walls.

'The Party, the people, the Church,' Churkin said. 'One is always weakest, and only one is ever really in charge.'

'And we faithfully serve whoever that might be,' Rykov replied, finally drawing a smile from the older man.

'Politics is a tedious business. Stay in the shadows as long as you can. Speaking of which, what do you have to report?'

'All's well with the Volk,' Rykov replied.

'And Project Mykl?'

'Mykl continues as planned,' Rykov said.

Intelligence agencies all over the world enjoyed giving their operations oblique codenames, and the KGB was no exception. Volk had been chosen for its double meaning, and Mykl had been selected for its biblical connotations which, should the Americans, British, or anyone else ever happen upon it, would tantalise and confuse them in equal measure. The project was named after the archangel Michael, the warrior angel who was an eternal force of vengeance and retribution. It was also, Rykov hoped, about to become the Soviet Union's newest and possibly greatest weapon against the West.

'Good,' Churkin said, his voice suddenly gruff. 'We have let the Americans get too far ahead of us with their weapons and rockets. And there are rumours coming out of Beijing that Mao has finally finished licking his wounds and wants to try another great leap forward. We may soon find ourselves surrounded. Project Mykl needs to work. If it doesn't I will be the one seen to have failed.'

Rykov was offended. He'd been nothing but diligent and meticulous in his management of Volk and Mykl. Churkin had no reason to doubt him now.

'If anything goes wrong I will personally take responsibility,' Rykov replied.

'Rest assured, that would also happen,' Churkin said.

***

Yegerova had chosen the time and place of her ambush carefully. Her previous two encounters with Rykov had been mere scuffles. This was to be the real battle. So it was only right that it should happen in the very heart of the Kremlin, and fitting that she should be waiting to strike inside the Palace of Congresses, the palace of the people.

Yegerova was the only person in the whole building. The thin columns of concrete and glass created deep stripes of light and dark that stretched deep across the cavernous entrance hall. She stood in one of the lines of shadow, where she could watch Rykov and the colonel general without them seeing her.

She knew the two men met at the same time every week, and she couldn't think of a better witness to Rykov's fall from grace – or a better way to guarantee that it was lasting – than Churkin. She was sure that as soon as the deputy head of the first chief directorate heard what she was about to tell him he would instantly and permanently remove the quiet backing he'd given the head of Line Z. Rykov's disgrace would reflect badly on anyone associated with him, and in the KGB self-preservation always won out.

***

As Rykov and Churkin passed the entrance to the palace, Yegerova made her move, striding out into the cold.

'Comrade Colonel General,' she said, as she walked towards them.

The two men both groaned under their breath at the sound of her voice.

'Comrade Colonel General,' she said again as Rykov and Churkin stopped and turned to face her. 'I'm afraid I must report a grave and repeated breach of security by the head of Line Z.'

Rykov was torn between telling Yegerova to stop before she said something truly embarrassing and seeing just how big a fool of herself she was prepared to make. But Churkin made his decision for him.

'That is a serious accusation, Major,' he said, his tone as stern as it had been with Rykov a moment ago. 'I hope you're prepared to elaborate on it.'

'An asset of Line Z has been allowed to fall into enemy hands, twice, despite warnings from Directorate S.'

Rykov smiled. He'd warned her not to try to invoke a higher power over what he'd told her was pure fantasy. Now that she had, he'd happily watch her pay the price for it.

'I assume by Directorate S you mean you?' Churkin asked.

'I was the representative who shared our concern,' Yegerova replied.

'And how did you establish that this captured asset belonged to Line Z? Did Major Rykov tell you?'

'He didn't deny it.'

'That's not the same thing.'

'I believe this asset is also responsible for the disappearance of two Directorate S operatives, for which Major Rykov must be held responsible.'

'Do you have any confirmation of this?' Churkin asked. 'What if they just defected?'

'All of Directorate S is loyal,' Yegerova protested. 'Our agents would never betray the Soviet cause.' Then she turned so she was looking at Rykov. 'But we will know exactly what happened to them soon. We have captured the asset.'

Rykov's grin evaporated, and he had to clench his jaw to stop it from falling open.

'He was apprehended along with a CIA field agent on the southern coast of England a few hours ago,' Yegerova continued. 'They will be interrogated shortly.'

'What have you done?' Rykov hissed through gritted teeth.

'I have taken care of your mistakes,' she said.

The two majors stared at each other in icy silence, until Churkin spoke again.

'Major Yegerova,' Churkin said, 'you have overreached yourself.'

'Comrade,' Yegerova stuttered. 'You must—'

'I must nothing,' Churkin said, cutting her off. His voice was as hard and sharp as the blades of concrete that ran up the side of the Palace of Congresses. 'You presume to think you deserve to know about operations that are none of your concern. You would do well to remember that you're a very small cog in a very large machine, whose direction was set long before you learned the Young Pioneer promise.'

'I am only acting to protect the Motherland,' Yegerova replied, paraphrasing the youth organisation's recitation she'd known by heart since she was five.

'And yet you dare to order the unsanctioned kidnapping of an American agent? Do you have any concept of the retribution the CIA will inflict on our operatives around the globe for this?'

It was a rhetorical question and Yegerova wisely didn't try to answer it.

'You will release your prisoners immediately. Both of them. And then you will await your punishment.'

Yegerova looked shell-shocked.

'Yes, Colonel General,' she whispered.

Then she nodded stiffly at Churkin, turned, and began a swift retreat back to the Lubyanka.

Churkin sighed as she left, letting the officiousness drain out of him.

'You need to watch her,' he said to Rykov.

'I thought I was,' Rykov replied, still astonished by what had just happened.

'Then do it more closely.'

Rykov stiffened at the admonishment he knew he fully deserved.

'I apologise. I will ensure that this does not affect Volk or Mykl.'

'Yes, you will,' Churkin said, as he started to slowly walk away from Rykov towards the Trinity Bridge that would take him over the western part of the old moat that had once surrounded the Kremlin.

CHAPTER 41

Rykov walked the opposite way to Churkin, through the gate beneath Spasskaya Tower that led to the southern end of Red Square and Saint Basil's Cathedral.

He replayed the last ten minutes in his head. He could barely believe what Yegerova had done in Britain, or what she'd just tried to do to him in the Kremlin. He was overcome with an urge to change direction, head north to the Lubyanka and inflict some form of vengeance on her immediately. But, as he got nearer to Saint Basil's swirling coloured domes, he told himself that would just play into her hands, and confirm what she still only suspected. And he wanted to keep her in the dark, grasping to know what he and Line Z were up to. So, he continued walking to Kitay-gorod metro station, and rode the M7 line one stop to Taganskaya.

People survived life in the Soviet system in different ways. Some accepted obedience and anonymity, while others pretended to, and vented their frustrations secretly and impotently in basements. Yegerova had picked fanaticism, and Rykov had chosen deception. It was the foundation of everything he did, and everything he was.

He knew Yegerova thought he was the child of some old Muscovite bourgeois family who somehow held enough sway to avoid having all their money and influence confiscated. In reality, his beginnings were far more humble. He'd been born in the Soviet capital, but not into some powerful dynasty, and he hadn't been handed the opportunities he'd taken on a gilt-edged plate. He was a mere son of the proletariat, who had ideas and ambitions above his station. But he found it useful for certain people to believe the myth rather than the truth about him, which he'd let get lost in the fog of the past. If people knew he'd come from nothing, they'd think they could send him back there.

He walked along Goncharnaya Ulitsa, then up the stairs of his apartment block to his front door. His home was large, one of the bigger properties the KGB had requisitioned for its officers, but it was also modest, and not that dissimilar to Yegerova's. He knew this because he'd visited hers a year ago while she was busy with one of her important little ideological quests at the Lubyanka. He'd gone looking for anything he might be able to use against her one day, but had found nothing. He kept his apartment fairly unremarkable and devoid of personal touches for exactly the same reason. In fact, the only signs anyone actually lived there beyond the clothes in the wardrobe and food in the kitchen were the scrupulous lack of dust on any surface, and the set of large constructivist posters of hardy workers and tumbling athletes Rykov had hung in his living room. No one knew he only enjoyed them ironically.

As soon as he closed his front door behind him he started to strip, like a snake shedding its skin or a chameleon adjusting to its new surroundings. He hung up his coat and suit jacket, folded his trousers and shirt over a chair, and stood in the middle of his living room in his underwear. Then he dropped to the floor and started doing press-ups. He did a hundred every morning and every evening.

His exercise was another form of falsehood. His body was firm and strong and he worked hard, in secret, to create the appearance of effortless fitness. The press-ups were followed by rounds of star jumps, squats, and stomach crunches.

Likewise, the reason all his clothes fitted him so well was because every single item he owned, bought from the GUM state department store, had been impeccably tailored by an old babushka who lived two floors above him.

Deception was also the bedrock of his professional life. After he'd been rewarded for stopping the scientific directorate from falling apart after Medev had been killed, he'd toiled tirelessly to make Line Z into what it was today. By the force of his will he'd turned the Volk programme into a global apparatus of deceit. And now he was on the verge of doing the same with Project Mykl.

Project Mykl was Rykov's greatest invention and achievement. It was an extension of the Volk programme. An evolution, really. It wouldn't rely on the loyalty, or psychotic desires, of its operatives, because they wouldn't even know they were working for Mykl – for Rykov – and, when they received their orders, they wouldn't be able to resist them.

More than a sky filled with surveillance satellites or missile silos bursting with ICBMs, Rykov believed Project Mykl was the key to delivering final victory for the Soviet Union in the Cold War.

He'd been working on it for years, recruiting scientists, testing subjects, and quietly building political support for his grand experiment. Now, he was about to prove to Churkin that the faith he'd put in him was justified. However, as he finished his workout and poured himself an ice-cold glass of water his mind suddenly fixed on the warning Churkin had given him moments before Yegerova had appeared.

He wondered if the colonel general had known what had been about to happen. Or if there was something else going on that might pose an even more serious threat to the future of Project Mykl, and him.

CHAPTER 42

Bennett wasn't sure what she could taste. It was metallic, but it wasn't blood. It felt older, grittier, like decay and dirt. She knew the only way to work out for certain what it was – and where she was – would be to open her eyes and sit up. But she also knew that would make the throbbing ache in the side of her head worse.

Eventually her curiosity won out and she dared to open an eyelid a sliver. She could see a corrugated roof and a row of thin windows running along the top of a bare brick wall. She couldn't hear anything but her own, slow, even breathing. She opened her other eye, revealing more of the zigzag roof, but not much else.

She tried to ignore the pounding that came with every pulse of blood into her brain and turned her head, slowly in case some silent person was waiting to smack it again. She was in an abandoned warehouse or stripped-out factory, and she was alone.

A rough concrete floor stretched away from her to another bare brick wall topped by narrow windows. The only thing in the large, empty space apart from her was a pile of old rags in the shadow of the opposite wall.

It was still light outside. Bennett guessed she hadn't been out very long, which was preferable to the possibility that she'd been unconscious overnight.

She eased herself up onto her elbows, then shuffled back towards the wall. Her clothes and hands were smudged by the same dust that had coated the inside of her mouth. She felt her arms, legs, and body, but couldn't find any more injuries than the swollen bump just above her temple.

After she had taken stock of her body, she tried to do the same for her situation.

She had, briefly, succeeded in her mission to get Williams back, though she bet she wouldn't get a slap on the back from Hoffman any time soon. In fact, she wasn't sure she'd ever see Hoffman, or Williams, again. She assumed a team of KGB illegals had been behind the ambush on the coastal track, because there was no way MI5 would attack their own – and neither, she hoped, would the CIA. But she knew that whoever had followed her or Knox to Kent could just as easily be working for a Soviet satellite state, or the Chinese, or even a Western ally who had some unknown reason for thinking Williams was a prize worth risking a couple of mercenaries for. Spying was a global business, and it had more than its fair share of expendable freelancers.

Bennett also assumed that Williams had been the primary target. This was mainly because, as she'd been told multiple times over the course of her career, she wasn't worth a lot in the international intelligence market.

She blamed herself for what had happened, but she also blamed Gibson, Hoffman, and the whole CIA. She'd tried to do the right thing from the moment Williams had appeared in Santo Domingo and all she'd got for her trouble was more problems. She'd butted up against two station chiefs, driven a wedge between her and Knox, been shot at, knocked out, and was now apparently dumped and forgotten. She didn't know what had happened in Dungeness after she'd lost consciousness, but she guessed things hadn't gone well for the others, and that Williams was probably now somewhere being tortured yet again.

Bennett wondered what her mother would think of where she now found herself. She'd been so proud of Bennett when she was alive, even to the point of hiding just how bad her emphysema had got when Bennett was at The Farm – the result of a life lived in the Kansas dust bowl – and how little the treatment Bennett had fought for her to receive from the white doctors in Lakin had helped towards the end.

After her death, Bennett had worked hard to turn that pride into a fire that propelled her. It was the engine that kept her going, kept her constantly pushing forward and smashing through all the barriers the world put in front of her. But, in her determination to honour her mother, had she let it take her a long way down a wrong path? Could she carry on serving masters who didn't stand for what she was trying to? Was it too late to change direction?

She felt that old niggle of doubt inside her. The one that told her she should be in Lakin, listening to her brothers' inane ramblings and childish private jokes, or working at Pinkerton, kidding herself that life would somehow be easier for a half Native American woman as a private detective rather than a government one. But she refused to let the feeling take root and grow. Instead, she stamped it down, pulled herself up onto her feet, and decided it was time to try to start fixing things.

She began by seeing if she was trapped as well as abandoned. She traced the walls with her hands, looking and feeling for any signs of weakness or surveillance. She found nothing, until she came to a slim rusted door embedded into the bricks at the far end of the building. She figured it had to open outwards because there was no handle on this side, or scuff marks where it would swing across the concrete floor. She pushed against the slab of metal with one hand, then two, then her shoulder. It didn't move.

Then she turned round and realised she wasn't alone after all.

The pile of rags she'd disregarded wasn't a jumble of oil-stained sheets or worn-out overalls. It was Williams. He was curled over on his side, his face a few inches from the wall and his legs tucked up under his arms and a filthy blanket.

Bennett walked over to him. His eyes were closed, and his breathing shallow. He was either unconscious or asleep. She was about to lean down and try to gently shake him awake when she saw his hand that was gripping his shin and the edge of the blanket. She'd noticed the bandages wrapped round his knuckles when she was trying to get through to him, crouched behind her MG in Dungeness. Now they'd been removed and she could see why they'd been there in the first place. The back of his hand was a patchwork of bruises and scabs.

She'd been more irritated than scared by her unexplained incarceration. But now, looking at Williams, fear started to creep through her.

Bennett could tell the marks on his hand were the kind of injuries that came from inflicting even worse ones on someone or something else. From the midnight street in Miramar to the bench in Regent's Park, Williams hadn't shown any signs of being strong enough to harm anything, so what had changed in the last twenty-four hours? Had his mind finally given in and he'd lost control and hurt himself for some mad reason? That would explain why he'd acted so strangely in Dungeness, seemingly oblivious to the sniper shooting at him. Or had he attacked someone and they'd come looking for him, dragging Bennett into their revenge? Whatever the answer, she decided to let this sleeping dog stay lying.

***

Williams was dreaming of Santo Domingo.

He was standing on the same street where he'd met Bennett. But she wasn't there, and he wasn't ragged and sallow, and the whole street was blanketed in snow.

He turned through 360 degrees, searching for something or someone that might explain what was going on. But there was nothing. There wasn't even a horizon. After a hundred yards in every direction everything faded to a white haze. It was like he was trapped inside a frosted snow globe.

Williams didn't feel the cold, or the occasional snowflake that fell on him. He was numb, physically and mentally. He wasn't scared, or happy, or confused. He was calm, objective, dispassionate – as if he'd stepped into someone else's dream and was only there to watch whatever was going to happen.

The only noise was the distant lapping of waves. He felt compelled to walk towards them, and as he did the snow started to melt, causing trickles and then torrents of water to race ahead of him towards the ocean.

Small black mounds began to emerge from the snow all around him. The closer he got to the edge of the island, and the less snow there was, the more the mounds became visible, and recognisable. They were shoes.

By the time Williams reached the beach the snow was gone, and he was surrounded by stiff, lifeless bodies that had been hidden under it. There were hundreds of them, thousands maybe, stretching out into the haze.

They all wore the same clothes, and they all had the same face, half grimacing up at him and half gone, obliterated by some violent force that had torn away flesh and shattered bone.

***

Bennett didn't take her eyes off Williams from the other side of the warehouse. He stayed curled up in unmoving silence for fifteen minutes before he started to shift and writhe, and his breathing got heavier and less even between low moans and mewls.

Then suddenly he was up on his feet, sprinting straight at Bennett and staring right through her until he collapsed on the concrete a foot in front of her and screamed, 'Jesus sodding Christ.'

Bennett was frozen in terror. But, as Williams cradled the side of his head in both hands and whispered, 'Who the hell hit me?' she couldn't stop herself answering.

'The Russians, I think,' she said.

'It's always the bloody Russians,' he replied.

'How would you know?' Bennett asked, with more sarcasm than she'd meant.

Williams dropped his hands from his head, looked up at Bennett through the strand of hair that had fallen across his face, and smiled.

'Touché, Miss Bennett.'

'So you know who I am?' she asked as Williams tipped back off his knees and casually crossed his legs beneath him.

'Of course I do,' he replied, still smiling.

'What else is in that head of yours?'

'Lots of things. It seems like I've finally had some sense knocked into me.'

Bennett wasn't expecting a joke. Williams still looked frail and a little wild, but his character appeared to have completely changed. She didn't know if this new – or old – version of him was a temporary reprieve from the rambling, unhinged one she'd first met, but if he was going to be staying around for any length of time, and if they were going to get out of the warehouse, then she needed him on side.

'I owe you an apology,' she said. 'For what happened in Haina.'

She saw a shadow of the cold look she'd seen in the MKULTRA interrogation cell flicker across his face, and wondered if she'd just said a very wrong thing.

'Did you know what was going to happen to me?' Williams asked.

'No,' Bennett replied, hoping he believed her.

'Then it wasn't your fault.'

Bennett didn't fully trust this sudden forgiveness. But she also didn't want to dwell on it.

'What else has come back?'

'After Haina is all less of a blur now.'

He recounted their trip to New York and then over the Atlantic, matching details with Bennett's own memories. Then he filled in some of the blanks of where he and Knox had got to after he'd disappeared in Regent's Park.

The more they talked, the more grounded and coherent he seemed to Bennett. But she was still most amazed that, despite everything, he still had a sense of humour.

'Do you remember what happened when you went missing?' Bennett asked.

'Not completely,' he said, his face turning more serious. 'But I think my brain is trying to tell me. I've been having nightmares, but they feel more real than that.'

'Memories?'

Williams nodded. 'Or information.'

'Information about what?'

He paused for a moment, then said, 'I think I finally know why I'm here. I think someone wants to assassinate Aleksei Kosygin.'

'Kosygin? How?'

'I don't know, but I'm sure it's going to happen. Soon.'

Bennett took a moment to process the idea and, bizarrely, found herself believing Williams. She could think of plenty of forces, including inside the Soviet Union, who might want Kosygin dead. And killing him on foreign, Western soil could completely shift the balance of global political power.

'In that case,' Bennett said, standing up, 'we need to get out of here right now.'

'Why?' Williams asked, getting up onto his feet.

'Because Kosygin's in London,' she replied.

'Ah.'

Williams followed Bennett over to the locked, handle-less door. He watched her take three steps, then run full-tilt at it, slamming her shoulder into it, flinging it open, and stumbling out into an alleyway.

'I swear that was locked before,' she said as she righted herself.

'I believe you,' Williams said, suppressing a grin.

They both looked up and down the alley. There were more warehouses on both sides, and Bennett's MG next to the door she'd just burst through. A few hundred yards away the alley opened up onto some sort of high street. They walked to the junction just as a red double-decker bus passed through it.

'Where are we?' Bennett asked.

Williams looked at a street sign bolted above the window of a corner shop opposite them. It said Green Lanes.

'We're in Haringey, north London,' he said.

'How do you know?'

'This isn't the first time I've woken up in this neck of the woods with a splitting headache,' he replied, smiling again.

CHAPTER 43

Knox left Laing with a doctor he knew at Guy's hospital who was used to doing favours for MI5 without asking questions. Laing had wanted to go straight to Leconfield House and either argue the case that Wilson and Kosygin's summit should be cancelled or start rounding up Watchers along with any men the Met could spare. But Knox had assured him that he could handle Holland, and there probably wasn't anything they could do to increase security that he hadn't already thought of, and if there was then Knox would take care of it while he was getting his leg stitched back together.

However, as he followed the traffic across the Thames, Knox struggled to work out how he was going to explain the events of the day to the director general. His job had been simple, but instead of keeping Williams out of harm's way, he'd let him be kidnapped, along with Bennett.

Knox was headed to Highgate, but he stopped in Soho first. He parked the Jaguar half on the pavement in the narrow street that ran along the back of Kemp House. He wasn't sure if he needed a gin or a coffee before he saw Holland and tried to persuade him to authorise a rescue mission for two people who had vanished without a trace, but he found his legs carrying him past Berwick Street and along Old Compton Street to Bar Italia.

The place was quiet, it was the early-evening rush hour again, and more people were walking past its large windows than going inside for a quick caffeine fix.

Knox ordered an espresso from one of the barmen in a perfectly pressed white shirt and maroon waistcoat, and took his coffee to one of the stools that faced out onto Frith Street.

As he settled into his seat he finally succumbed to his frustration. Frustration that he'd lost Williams before he'd been able to really get through to him. Frustration over the cruel things he and Bennett had said to each other. And frustration at his growing fear that when he did go to see Holland and tell him what had happened, the response would be a mix of disappointment and inaction.

He stared into the small cup in front of him, trying to decide his next move. He needed to get both Williams and Bennett back. But he also didn't. Because, as he took his first sip of his espresso and glanced out of the window he saw both of them looking at him from the other side of the street.

Five minutes later, the three of them were gathered round the island counter in Knox's kitchen.

Knox almost couldn't believe that Williams was actually in Kemp House. He'd had fantasies of them drinking late into the night in his flat, sprawled across his sofa and lounger reminiscing about older, even more drunken evenings spent stumbling from bar to bar in Soho, or scrapes they'd got into for the Service where they'd snatched triumph from the jaws of defeat. Instead, he was listening to Williams repeat what he'd told Bennett on their short drive from Haringey about the twisted face that had haunted his nightmares and was on every body in his dream of Santo Domingo. The face of Aleksei Kosygin.

'Who do you think wants Kosygin dead?' Knox asked.

'The KGB,' Williams replied, without any hesitation.

Knox frowned. He couldn't see how that made sense. And he said so.

'I think it does,' Bennett countered. 'We know how fragile Kosygin, Brezhnev, and Podgorny's troika is. Brezhnev's hungry for absolute power and he's been stacking the KGB with supporters. If

Kosygin's assassinated here, Brezhnev will get what he wants, and Britain will be thrown into political turmoil.'

'But Wilson is sympathetic to Russia,' Knox said. 'Surely the Soviets would rather keep a left-wing government in power here than let the Conservatives back in?'

'Russia wants the West running in circles,' Bennett said. 'If he's killed here the election won't matter. Whoever wins will get the cold shoulder from President Johnson, along with the rest of NATO. Simple divide and conquer.'

It was dark logic, but Knox could follow it.

'You're sure?' he asked Williams.

Williams nodded. 'I don't know why, but it feels like things are finally starting to fix in place in my head. I think the KGB were holding me, I somehow found out what they were planning and escaped, or was helped by someone who wanted to stop all this from happening.'

'In the Caribbean?'

'It's not impossible,' Bennett said. 'The KGB likes to move their most valuable prisoners around, and Cuba is only about sixty miles from the Haitian and Dominican coast.'

That sounded a bit far-fetched to Knox, but then so did everything else.

'And now?' he asked.

'The same thing. Someone wanted us locked up. Maybe someone else didn't. Someone who doesn't want Kosygin dead. It feels like a big game is being played here and we can only see a corner of the board.'

'What about you?' Knox asked.

'I'm here with arms open and olive branches in both hands,' Bennett said. 'Plus, I'm way past my window for redemption with Hoffman,' she added with a smirk.

'If it reopens?'

'I'm not interested. And after the last couple of hours I think Jack's right. This is bigger than all of us.'

'We need to go see Holland,' Williams said.

Knox thought for a moment, then said, 'No, not yet.'

Just after 7:30 p.m., Knox's Jaguar turned into the underground car park beneath Leconfield House, and Knox, Bennett, and Williams went up to his office, where Knox requested every single one of Laing's files on MI5's preparations for Kosygin's visit, and all Russia-related Pipistrelle chatter for the last three months, from the night clerk.

After two hours of combing through everything, Bennett unfolded herself from the armchair next to the teak cabinet that ran the length of one of the walls, announced that she needed to stretch her legs, promised that she wouldn't leave the fifth floor or pick any locked doors, and left the two men alone.

'You made it to the top,' Williams said after he and Knox had spent another five minutes pretending to read the papers they were holding.

Knox looked at Williams, and then his office. They were sitting in the two chairs in front of Knox's desk that stood between the long cabinet and wide window that looked out across Mayfair.

'I did,' he said.

'You were always going to,' Williams said. 'That flat, the fifth floor. I'm proud of you. And I owe you an apology.'

'You do?'

'For my temper in the car, and under Smithfield.'

'You remember them?'

'I do. I even remember doing this.' Williams dropped the folder he'd been holding onto Knox's desk and held up his bruised, scabbed hands.

'What's changed?'

Williams shrugged his shoulders. 'Something must have happened in the warehouse, or in Dungeness.'

'You were near catatonic on the beach after the sniper started firing at us. Maybe that was some kind of trigger.'

Williams shrugged again. 'Maybe.'

Knox put his own file down on his desk. 'And you really think the KGB is behind all of this?'

Williams nodded. 'I know I'm still not exactly a totally reliable witness, but it's the only way I can think to make sense of everything.'

Williams told Knox more about the remnants of memory that seemed to be growing and knitting themselves together in his mind. He could now clearly recall days spent in cold huts with views across Arctic tundra, then hours in hot, stuffy offices with no windows that felt deep underground, and being part of crowds walking through city streets past towering buildings and hard-edged statues. The details he could conjure up had convinced Bennett when he'd told her about them as he guided the MG from Haringey to Soho. And they convinced Knox as well. Knox had never been to Russia himself, but he was sure Williams was describing parts of the world on the other side of the Iron Curtain.

'And now,' Williams said, 'whenever I close my eyes I see Kosygin's face.'

It was all, Knox thought, enough to drive anyone mad. And yet Williams was now calm, rational even, despite the incredible strain his mind had been under for God knows how long. Knox knew that by all rights Williams should be recovering in some bucolic countryside facility, having his mental and physical wounds tended to by experts, not caught up in whatever may or may not be about to happen in London. But he also wanted Williams close to him. And needed to finally take the opportunity Bennett had subtly created for him.

'The *Surcouf*,' he said. It was a statement and a question.

He held his breath, waiting to see what impact the name would have on Williams. Would he suddenly lunge at Knox, crazy with rage, or break down and sob into his lap?

'That's still hazy,' Williams said, after a long, agonising moment. 'I can feel the edges of it. The water, the cold, the dark. But I can't hold on to it.'

'It was my fault,' Knox said. 'If I hadn't sent you on that mission, none of this would have happened."

It was a sentence Knox had carried with him for seven years, and it hung between the two men until Williams gently batted it away.

'You don't know that,' he said. 'And you didn't send me. I wouldn't have gone through with the dive if we hadn't taken every precaution. Precautions you insisted on.'

'I sent you to your death,' Knox replied. 'And you went through something worse.'

'But I'm not dead, am I, old man? You shouldn't blame yourself.'

'But I do,' Knox whispered.

'Then stop.'

'I'm going to find whoever did this to you and make them pay.'

'I know. You never give up or let go of anything. And I want to help stop this attack on Kosygin. But after that I just want to rest.'

'That's what was supposed to happen in Kent. It didn't exactly turn out as planned.'

Williams smiled. 'Ah well, gang aft agley.'

'What?'

'Robert Burns. Our best-laid schemes sometimes just don't go the way we want them to. I'll lend you my copy if it's still in the library at Rabley Heath.'

'I'd like that,' Knox said, finally managing a tentative smile himself.

Then, with timing so perfect it was as if she'd somehow been listening through the soundproofed walls, Bennett opened the door and stepped back into the office.

'It's getting late, boys,' she said. 'What's the plan?'

Knox looked at Williams, the piles of paper strewn around the room, and his watch. 'We get some rest and talk to Holland first thing in the morning.'

'Do you think he'll dare pull the plug on the summit last minute?' Bennett asked.

'No,' Knox said. 'And I don't want him to.'

CHAPTER 44

Anna was up and out of Durrants early, wearing the light jumper and tailored suit trousers that had been delivered to her the evening before, and carrying her jacket over her arm with the envelope of money tucked in the inside pocket.

She strolled the short distance across Manchester Square and picked up a black cab on Wigmore Street that took her along the north side of Hyde Park west towards Shepherd's Bush.

She told the driver to drop her outside the tube station, which was starting to fill with the first waves of morning commuters, waited for the cab to pull away, then continued her journey further west on foot.

Shepherd's Bush had originally been just that – an area of shrubby grazing pasture for shepherds taking their animals into the city. Now, a sparse triangular green that Anna walked along the side of was all that was left of its ancient history.

A thin, weak drizzle started. It was the kind of rain British skies managed to produce on cloudless days, that didn't so much fall as fill the air. Anna guessed it would only last a few minutes, but she still slipped her coat on as she crossed over a junction into Goldhawk Road. A couple of minutes later she turned into Shepherd's Bush Market, a narrow alleyway of stalls and shops that hugged an old elevated train line. She passed fruit stands and a couple of cafes that sold nothing but tea and buttered bread to the few people who could fit round their small Formica tables.

Halfway along the market the front of a clockmaker's shop jutted out from one of the railway arches. It looked like it had been there for a hundred years. The wood frames of its windows were worn and chipped. The square panes of glass sitting inside them were warped and sunken with age, and at least half of them were cracked. The shop was dark, and Anna could barely see past the first row of clock faces into the gloom, but the door opened when she tried it.

Her eyes quickly adjusted to the lack of light, and she realised why she hadn't been able to see further into the shop from outside. It was only six feet deep. The shop was literally just a front. A wall of wood panels had been built into the arch, with another small door tucked far up against the right-hand curve of bricks.

Anna could hear humming and the shuffling of feet over the ticking clocks that surrounded her, and she silently glided across to the second door to see who was responsible for them.

On the other side of the panels was another, much larger room. This one took up the rest of the railway arch, and ended in a wall made of bricks of different shapes, sizes, and colours held together by rough mortar. The space was filled with workbenches covered in strange machines and odd contraptions. And bent over one of them was a very old man. He was bald apart from a ring of short white hairs around the crown of his head. The dark, wrinkled skin of his face and hands was stained with grime, and the thick-lensed glasses he was wearing were smeared with grease. He looked like a geriatric animal in its cave, and Anna wondered when he'd last left his workshop.

'Good morning,' she said after watching him tinker away at the stack of pipes and gears in front of him for another full minute.

He didn't seem to register Anna until he finished attaching a bronze tooth-edged disk onto the end of a short black stick. Then he turned towards the doorway and finally looked at her.

'Hello, hello,' he said, in an accent Anna placed somewhere in southern India. 'How do you do?'

'Very well,' she said. 'I've come to collect a package.'

The old man paused for a moment, then looked at a row of clocks lined up on a bench that all showed the same time – 8:40.

'The package, the package. Yes.' He wiped his hands on an oily rag hanging from his belt. 'I wasn't expecting you so early.'

'My apologies,' Anna said, smiling. She hadn't been given a time for her pickup, but she'd wanted to get it out of the way, and when it came to dealing with unknown third parties she preferred some element of surprise.

'No matter, no matter,' the man said as he scuttled over to a shelf that had been drilled into the arch and was piled high with more weird creations.

He pushed several aside, then delicately picked one up and carried it over to Anna. He offered it to her in his palms.

It was an elegant weapon. Two short and thin metal pipes seamlessly welded together and highly polished. Anna was surprised by how light it was as she picked it up out of his hands and held it up to her eyes. One of the tubes was a miniature rifle scope, with clear glass at one end and cross hairs at the other, and the second had a trigger cut into it so finely that Anna could barely feel it as she ran her fingers over its edges.

'May I test it?' she asked.

'Of course, of course.'

The man gestured at the wall at the far end of the arch and Anna moved further into the room to where she'd have a clear line of sight. She held the weapon up to her eye, picked a spot on the wall through the scope, and gently squeezed the trigger. She hit her target perfectly and silently.

'This is wonderful,' she said as she slipped the double tube into her trouser pocket. 'Absolutely ideal.'

'Good, good,' the man said. 'It was a pleasure to create.'

'Now, your fee.'

'Oh, yes, yes.'

The money in Anna's coat was to pay the old man for his expertise. But he wasn't going to get it.

Anna smiled again as she picked up a heavy spanner that had been discarded on one of the workbenches, walked over to the old man, and drove it into his stomach. Then, as he doubled over in pain, she brought it down on the back of his neck, smashing it into his cervical vertebrae and crushing his spinal cord. His legs fell away beneath him and, as he hit the floor, Anna raised the thick length of metal over her head and swung it at the man's head with enough force to crack his skull.

She left the dead man in his workshop, closed the door to the shop behind her, and stepped back out into the market.

The rain had stopped, but she kept her coat on all the way to the tube station. Then she took the Central line four stops east to Lancaster Gate, where she hailed another taxi and told the driver to take her to Bond Street.

CHAPTER 45

Eight hours after Bennett had gone back to her hotel in South Kensington and Knox and Williams had briefly argued about who would take the bed and who would sleep on the sofa in Kemp House, the three of them were back together in Knox's office, steeling themselves to go next door to see Holland.

'Is he an early bird?' Bennett asked.

'Usually,' Knox replied.

He was sure of the plan he'd run over and over in his mind as he lay in the awkward crevice of his sofa, but for some reason he found himself suddenly worried about putting it into action. Seemingly intuiting his anxiety, Williams gave him an encouraging smile. Knox smiled back.

An hour ago, Knox had quietly sneaked into his bedroom, where Williams was soundly sleeping, to get to his bathroom and a cold shower. Williams was lying on his front, topless, and the duvet had worked its way down to his waist. Knox recognised the swirl of scar tissue that stretched up his friend's side – Williams's souvenir from his time in France during the war – but he was shocked by how pronounced the ridges of his spine were, and the gashes and gouges that criss-crossed either side of them. His whole back had been turned into a patchwork of violence.

The injuries looked old. Knox could tell some had been treated while others had been left to heal on their own. He could also see differences in how they'd been inflicted – when Williams had suffered with clinical precision and when with brute force.

Knox had almost reached out to touch his friend, first to check it really was Jack Williams lying in his bed, and then to gently shake him awake and ask him if he'd remembered any more about who had put him through so much. But he stopped himself. Instead he laid out a dark grey Hardy Amies jumper and some trousers next to him on the bed and continued into the en suite.

When he was done with his shower Knox had found Williams dressed and waiting for him in the kitchen and full of his own questions and reassurances about Knox's plan.

The office slipped into silence until the telephone on the desk erupted into loud life. Knox let it ring a couple of times before he reached over and picked up the black Bakelite receiver.

'The director general is waiting for you,' the cool voice of Miss Albury, Holland's secretary, said through the earpiece.

'We'll be straight in,' Knox replied.

Holland looked in no way surprised when Knox, Williams, and Bennett stepped into his office a moment later. He did, however, look very irritated.

'Miss Bennett, how good to see you again,' he said, transforming momentarily into a genial host. 'And how are you feeling, Williams?'

'Much better, sir,' Williams replied.

'I'm glad to hear it.' Holland turned to Knox, transforming back into an annoyed master spy. 'Now, perhaps you'd like to explain why you're not in Deal, and why Laing is in Guy's, recovering from two sets of stitches to his thigh and a rather large blood transfusion?'

Knox told Holland about the drive to the coast and the ambush in Dungeness. Then Bennett continued the story about her and Williams waking up in the abandoned warehouse in Haringey, and Williams explained his vision of Kosygin and his belief that the Soviet leader's life was in imminent danger.

The whole tale took twenty minutes, and by the time they'd finished, Knox was sitting in the single chair that faced Holland across his desk, Williams was perched on the thick arm of the sofa Miss Albury had had installed for the large meetings Holland refused to have in his office, and Bennett was standing next to the window that offered a view across Mayfair that was almost identical to the one from Knox's office.

Knox could tell from the questions Holland poked each of them with that his curiosity had been piqued. He also realised why he'd been so nervous about this conversation. He'd craved a real mission, and now he had one: vindicating Williams and giving some kind of meaning to the hell he'd been through. But it was still up to Holland whether he'd be allowed to pursue it, or if it would just be swept even further under the carpet.

'It's too late to cancel the summit,' Holland said finally. 'Kosygin's already in the city.'

'I don't want you to,' Knox replied. 'Dungeness proved there are some very dangerous people at large. If we did, or launched some nationwide manhunt, we'd just drive whoever it is to ground. But I'm willing to bet they're in London right now, so we should use the opportunity we've been given to flush them out. And if they are Soviet illegals working against Kosygin, we can make a show of expelling them after he's gone.'

Holland took his metal-rimmed glasses off and slowly polished the lenses as he considered what his deputy was proposing.

'I'm still not convinced about the threat to Kosygin,' he said. 'But I agree that something strange is going on, and that the KGB's illegals have been getting a little too confident recently. You won't be able to get near Kosygin while he's in the Russian embassy, though if something happens there it wouldn't be our problem anyway.'

He slipped his glasses back on and looked at the clock hung between his door and a large painting of a crumbling castle on a headland surrounded by churning waves.

'However, with Laing still recovering no one should be surprised if you stepped in to supervise our security arrangements,' Holland continued. 'Kosygin will arrive at the Trades Union Congress in an hour, then he'll be at the Foreign Office with the prime minister, foreign secretary and president of the Board of Trade in the afternoon. I want you to go to both and watch who else turns up.'

Knox nodded, suppressing both a smile and his relief.

'I'll come too,' Bennett said. 'If Richard does spook anyone it'd be good to have another pair of eyes watching.

'And vice versa,' Knox added.

'Agreed,' Holland said.

'What about me?' Williams asked. 'I might recognise someone.'

'No,' Holland replied. 'I want you here. It's clear you were the target in Dungeness, so I don't want to put you at risk. I also want you to spend the day with White. Who knows, he might be able to help you fill in the rest of the gaps in your memory.'

CHAPTER 46

Unusually for a politician, Kosygin was running early. He'd already arrived at the Trades Union Congress headquarters for his meeting with George Woodcock, its general secretary, by the time Knox and Bennett reached Great Russell Street.

The security Laing had arranged was subtle but formidable. As Knox and Bennett walked beneath *The Spirit of Brotherhood*, the weathered bronze statue that loomed over the entrance to Congress House, Knox recognised several MI5 and Met officers standing guard and walking circuits around the building, looking like they were staff. They all knew who he was too, and didn't react at all to his unexpected arrival.

'Everything in order?' Knox asked the plain-clothed constable sitting behind the reception desk.

'Yes, sir,' he replied.

'Good. I'm going to take a look around.'

'And the lady?'

'Is with me.'

'Very good, sir.'

The TUC's real staff had been told not to come into work this morning. Only a few members of Woodcock's inner circle knew why. Knox was sure the building had been checked for people who shouldn't be there. He was concerned about someone who was supposed to be there but who might have an ulterior motive – someone from the Soviet delegation, Woodcock's office, or, worst of all, MI5 or the police.

'Should we go floor by floor?' Bennett asked as they walked along a large window that looked out over the building's hexagon-tiled inner courtyard at another sculpture, this one of a skeletal woman cradling a dead child against a towering green marble backdrop.

Knox shook his head. 'We don't have time to search the whole building. They're meeting in the conference hall in the basement, so we should assume if someone's here they aren't messing about on the upper floors.'

'You sure about that?' Bennett said, pointing at the hexagons, which, Knox now realised, weren't just ornamental tiling but skylights that gave direct lines of sight into the conference hall from all round the building.

'Good point,' he said. 'We'll go up, then down.'

Bennett took the lift while Knox climbed the staircase. It took them ten minutes to check every office and potential hiding place on the top floor, then another ten on each of the next two floors down. The building was deserted, but that only added to Knox and Bennett's joint fear that that just meant they hadn't found whoever they were hunting yet.

After another set of empty offices and meeting rooms, they reached a level low enough that no sniper, no matter how skilled, would be able to angle a shot into the basement from it.

Knox checked his watch. 'Fifteen minutes before they're due to finish.'

'Better hope they're not early for that too,' Bennett replied. 'I'll go see if anyone's loitering outside or twitching blinds on the other side of the street.'

They split up in the foyer. Knox watched Bennett walk back out into Great Russell Street, hoping there wasn't a hidden sight trained on her, then went down the wide spiral staircase that led to the underground conference hall.

Two guards stood outside the large doors Kosygin and Woodcock were on the other side of, discussing the finer complexities of combining socialism and unionism. Knox stood in line with them, snatching glances at both while listening for any commotion in the room beyond.

After five minutes of quiet murmuring he heard the sound of scraping chairs and moving feet. Then the doors opened and Aleksei Kosygin and George Woodcock walked past Knox, each followed by a small coterie of advisers. It was the first time he'd seen either man in the flesh, and he was struck by how normal Kosygin seemed, and how farcical Woodcock's famously bushy, unkempt eyebrows made him look.

Knox fell into step with the two guards and followed the group up to the ground floor and out onto the street where three diplomatic Volgas were waiting. He tensed his muscles and held his breath, ready to lunge forward and shove Kosygin to the ground at the slightest noise. But there was no shot from a window, no shouts to take cover, and no explosion when Kosygin got into his car.

Knox watched the small Soviet motorcade pull away from the kerb and be quickly replaced by his Jaguar. He got into the passenger seat, and let Bennett tail the Russians all the way across the city to Kensington Palace Gardens, the wide street of mansions between Notting Hill and Kensington better known as Embassy Row, without incident.

'I don't like this,' Knox said, between bites of a sausage sandwich and gulps of weak coffee in a cafe on Notting Hill Gate, shortly after he and Bennett had watched Kosygin disappear behind the fence of the Soviet embassy.

'It could use some mustard,' Bennett said. 'And the coffee's so bad it's almost American.'

'But it gets the job done,' Knox replied with a grin, before adding, 'I meant having no idea when the KGB is going to strike.'

'I know,' Bennett said, as she gave up on her sandwich and pushed her plate away from her. 'At least we're on the same side again. And it's nice we can be pretty sure we aren't the bad guys.'

'There is that,' Knox said.

'But you're right. It'd be good to know for sure exactly who we're after – and how many of them there are. I'm not keen on being outnumbered and outgunned.'

'Are you thinking about the Wolf again?'

Bennett shrugged. 'We could be up against them, or they could just be a figment of my imagination.'

'Well, someone definitely put a bullet in Laing's leg and kidnapped you and Jack.'

'You say that like it's supposed to reassure me.'

'Things are so grey, I'll take a bit of black and white where I can get it.'

'Agreed,' Bennett said. 'Maybe we should just call their bluff. March up to the embassy and tell the ambassador and resident we know all about the plot and offer our help. Open the curtain wide enough to shove a peace offering through.'

'For all we know they're in on it. They could be killing Kosygin right now. Toasting him with poisoned vodka or serving up caviar sprinkled with cyanide.'

Bennett smiled. 'Maybe.'

Ten minutes later, Knox and Bennett were back in the Jaguar at the southern end of Embassy Row, where it met Kensington High Street, waiting for Kosygin to make his way to his big meeting with the prime minister, foreign secretary and president of the Board of Trade. This time Knox was in the driver's seat, and only two cars left the embassy. Kosygin, who was still very much alive, sat alone in the back of the second Volga.

The Russians didn't try to shake the Jaguar – the embassy's drivers were used to being followed wherever they went – and happily guided Knox and Bennett all the way to King Charles Street in Whitehall.

Under normal circumstances, the Foreign Office's mandarins would have baulked at a CIA agent being escorted through their hallowed doors without prior warning and clearance. With the prime minister about to meet another head of state on their turf, there was no way they'd let Bennett inside. So she was left again to keep watch on as many of the people coming and going through all the doors and arches that led in and out of the enormous building as she could.

Knox, however, was allowed in.

The courts and corridors of the Foreign Office were much grander than Congress House, full of gilt-painted arches, carved marble, and rich, dramatic frescos. They were also busier, full of furrow-browed civil servants rushing between meetings. Most of them, Knox imagined, about preventing another Ian Smith from seizing power in one of the coterie of other nations undergoing the delicate transition from colony to Commonwealth member. No one wanted Rhodesia to set the template for freedom.

But, those differences aside, the afternoon was a rerun of the morning. Kosygin was delivered to another room for another private conversation, and an hour later he was escorted to his car and driven back to Kensington.

There was no unexplained diversion, no attack, just slow-moving afternoon city traffic. And the longer nothing happened the more the tension coiled inside Knox and Bennett as they waited to spring into action.

They crawled along the south side of Hyde Park and Kensington Gardens, both of them constantly looking for cars or motorbikes jumping traffic lights, speeding out of turnings or swerving across the road. But none of that happened, and the Soviet motorcade safely turned into Embassy Row once more.

***

Shortly after Knox's Jaguar looped round Kensington Gardens Square and started heading back east towards Mayfair, the driver of Kosygin's Volga walked across the wide, tree-lined road from the Soviet embassy to the building site opposite it where the new Czechoslovakian embassy was being constructed.

The man was now dressed as a labourer – a light, worn sweater over his collarless shirt, a flat cap on his head, and a rucksack slung over his shoulders. The bag contained an empty lunchbox, a half-drunk flask of tea, and an old waxed jacket smeared with grime and oil. The Russians kept a variety of disguises like this one in the embassy garage, which they used from time to time to confuse the MI5 Watchers who had a habit of following their low-level staff. But Kosygin's driver was doubly camouflaged because, while officially he was merely one of the Soviet embassy's pool of chauffeurs, he also worked for Directorate S.

The man looked tired as he walked towards Notting Hill Gate tube station, shoulders sunk from a long imaginary shift pouring concrete. But he was in a rush.

He took the Central line to North Acton, then dashed over the Western Avenue, the wide arterial road that stretched out of the city, and into the semi-detached house on Cloister Road where he rented a room from an old woman who'd been widowed a long time ago and now offered cheap lodging for émigré workers with very few questions asked.

He went up to the first floor without announcing himself – he never did – locked his door behind him, and pulled the suitcase that contained an R-354 radio out from under his bed.

Sending a message burst from the house was dangerous, and a breach of standard protocols. But he'd been given explicit instructions barely eight hours earlier that if anything suspicious happened while he was transporting Kosygin round the city he had to get a message to the Lubyanka as fast as possible. And he'd decided that Richard Knox appearing at Congress House, the Foreign Office, and in his rear-view mirror as he drove between the two of them counted.

CHAPTER 47

As the illegal chauffeur-builder's message travelled east to Moscow, another was being sent west from the ZEVS broadcast station outside Murmansk to the depths of the North Atlantic. And Rykov was standing once more at the tall window next to his desk in his office, looking across the Moskva to the Kremlin.

He was thinking again about his encounter with Yegerova and Churkin. He'd let his anger and desire for revenge cool overnight, and was now content in the knowledge that Yegerova would have spent all day behind her small desk in her narrow little office, wondering about what retaliation he might be planning and terrified of the fate Churkin could hand down at any moment.

Rykov turned away from the window, and sat at his own desk. He resisted the urge to check his watch. There was no one in the room with him, but even alone he didn't want to give in to the nerves that were starting to probe the edges of his mind when it wasn't contemplating Yegerova's inevitable end.

He refused to fidget. But he did stare at his telephone.

He'd spent his day doing exactly what he'd promised Churkin – making sure Yegerova's meddling hadn't done any irreparable damage to either the Volk programme or Project Mykl. He'd been meticulous in his preparations, and he'd been just as forensic checking over them. He'd reviewed every scenario he'd planned out, every reaction they might provoke, and every psychological analysis of all his unsuspecting pawns. He was still confident each one of them would do what they were supposed to when the time came.

He hadn't gone stalking round secret laboratories, screaming at scientists who were kept locked up in a constant state of fear and exhaustion, because, despite the rumours about what happened in Line Z's headquarters – rumours he was more than happy to encourage – there were none. The security of the Volk programme and Project Mykl meant they were decentralised, distributed affairs. Staff and operations were both regularly moved, and some of them were in constant motion, their locations and destinations only known by Rykov himself.

Now, as evening was falling across Moscow, there was nothing else for him to do except will his telephone to ring. He was waiting for the call that would signal the start of the final stage of the stratagem he'd devoted so much to, and that would at last bring together his two great projects – hopefully to devastating effect.

No one but Rykov and Churkin knew how monumental the next few hours would be for the Soviet Union. Not the ZEVS engineers, not the crew of the *Yorsh*, not even the two operatives who were unaware that they were working in unison to bring Rykov's gambit to its explosive fruition.

Finally, the telephone started to trill. He picked up the receiver and listened to the two-word message the voice on the other end of the line delivered: 'Command sent.'

Rykov hung up, walked back to his window, looked again at the domes and spires over the river that were becoming shrouded in dark, and let out a long, contented sigh. His last set of orders had been given, and after several days spent holding position and doing nothing, he knew Captain Tokorev and his crew would jump to obey them.

Every piece was now in place, every wheel in motion. Soon it wouldn't just be deception that protected him. It would also be success.

***

But, as Rykov let himself fantasise about the victory that was almost within his grasp, another message was about to be sent west. One that he hadn't predicted.

The lights of the Lubyanka never went out, but deep in its bowels they did dim. Most of Directorate S's agent runners and clerical staff had already left for the night. Yegerova, however, had not. She hadn't moved from her desk since she'd slipped into her office just after six o'clock this morning. Over twelve hours later, she hadn't felt the hand of punishment yet, but she knew how the KGB worked, and that she wouldn't know it was choking her until it was wrapped tightly round her neck.

Her night had been sleepless, and her day had been spent barking at clerks to bring her unending stacks of files and reports that might help her comprehend why Churkin had acted so swiftly to defend Rykov when she'd confronted them outside the Palace of Congresses. Her search had been fruitless. She'd found nothing, and was on the verge of slinking back out of the Lubyanka when a messenger knocked on her door carrying a decrypted burst that had just been received from London.

The messenger stood awkwardly and silently while Yegerova processed the information he'd handed to her. She recognised the description of the CIA agent who'd been identified as Abey Bennett, and who yesterday had briefly been Directorate S's prisoner. And she knew who Richard Knox was. What she didn't understand was why they had both developed such a sudden interest in Kosygin when a day before they'd been so preoccupied with Jack Williams, the man she was convinced was a Line Z operative. Then a very troubling possibility occurred to her.

She'd believed Williams was a Line Z agent who had gone rogue then let himself get caught. And she'd dismissed the two apparent handovers in Regent's Park and on the Kent coast as a sign that MI5 and the CIA didn't know what to do with the gift they'd been given. But what if Knox and Bennett hadn't been bungling prisoner exchanges? What if they'd been removing Rykov's man from the

British capital, and she'd had him taken straight back there? It would explain why they'd spent today racing all over the city – looking for him, or looking to stop him from doing something.

Churkin had told Yegerova to let Bennett and Williams go, and had made it clear how much more she'd suffer if she didn't do it immediately. That suggested Williams might not be a rogue agent after all, that he was still working for Line Z, and under orders from the deputy head of the first chief directorate.

Yegerova had never sought favour from any of the troika that ruled over the Soviet Union. As far as she privately believed, even together Kosygin, Brezhnev, and Podgorny fell far short of what should be expected of them. But she, like the rest of the KGB, was an instrument of the state and so theirs to command. However, it was no secret that both Rykov and Churkin were favourites of Brezhnev, and that Kosygin was the only real force stopping him from reigning over Russia alone.

'Come with me,' she said to the messenger, squeezing past him and out into the corridor.

As she raced to the Lubyanka's radio control room with the messenger in tow, the sinister realisation sank in: Churkin and Rykov were planning to assassinate Kosygin.

The communications room was empty when they arrived, and it occurred to Yegerova that the messenger must be both errand boy and radio operator. She quickly scribbled down a short sentence on the piece of paper he'd brought her just a few minutes ago.

'Send this immediately,' she said, holding out the new message.

The man took it, looked at what she'd written, and stared at her, eyes wide in shock. She met his gaze with a look that made it clear she was serious and that he should consider himself sworn to absolute secrecy about what he'd just read. Then he nodded, took the paper to a control desk, and encrypted it.

CHAPTER 48

'You'll be glad to know I still don't think you're a Manchurian candidate,' White said.

'A what?' Williams asked.

'It's a book, and a film, about a Soviet–Chinese plot to brainwash an American soldier. Whipped up plenty of fear when it was released, but rather overstated how close Moscow and Beijing are, and both parties' ability to control minds.'

They were in the research and development department in Leconfield House. Williams was leaning against the side of one of the Atlas mainframe towers, which quietly hummed and beeped as it waited for someone to give it something to compute, and White was sitting at the table he'd spent most of the last week leaning over, and which had finally been cleared of its stacks of maps and reports about the disappeared ghost submarine. They'd spent the time Knox and Bennett had been following Kosygin around the city going over everything Williams could now remember.

'Then what happened to me?' Williams asked.

'Hypnosis is a cheap circus trick,' White replied. 'True mind control is a fantasy. But trauma is very real, and someone put you through the wringer.'

'The Russians.'

White gave a mix of a nod and a shrug. 'What you've described certainly fits their modus operandi. They like to keep their prisoners disoriented, shifting them round Russia and elsewhere while they pump them full of psychoactive drugs and try to extract whatever information or confession they can.'

'God knows what I might have told them.'

'Best to not focus on that now,' White said. He didn't want to add any more to the stress Williams was already under, plus he knew that at some point a very long debriefing process would eventually uncover whatever old secrets he might have divulged.

'But what if we could find out? Repeat what made me start remembering things?'

'For one, we wouldn't know how,' White said. 'We might stumble on the way to unlock more of your memories. Or we could end up driving you insane and shutting them all away forever.'

Williams looked like he was about to argue that it would be worth the risk, but instead he took a deep breath and asked, 'How's Richard?'

'You know him better than me,' White answered, surprise in his voice at the abrupt change in subject.

'Not recently,' Williams said. 'We've talked a little, but I can tell he's putting on a brave face. How was he after the *Surcouf*?'

'He survived.' White paused for a moment, then added, 'But possibly only because he never really let go of you.'

Williams nodded and opened his mouth to say something, but before he could a telephone attached to one of the small stretches of wall not hidden by an Atlas tower began to ring. It was Miss Albury, informing White that Holland was requesting their presence in his office.

***

Holland was waiting for them when White and Williams reached the fifth floor, along with Knox, Bennett, and Laing.

Knox watched both men as Williams walked over to the sofa Laing had already eased himself into with his left leg stretched out in front of him, and White hung back near the door. Neither of them looked thrilled or devastated with how their afternoons had gone, and Knox wished they were at least one of the two. After he and Bennett had seen nothing unusual while they'd been tailing Kosygin, he hoped White might have released something else locked away in Williams's mind that would confirm there was still a would-be killer out there and maybe, if they were very lucky, their identity.

'Laing discharged himself from Guy's and insisted on coming back to work,' Holland said.

'I won't be a lot of help,' Laing said, stroking the thick padding wrapped round his thigh. 'But I thought another head might be useful.'

Knox hadn't been surprised when Laing had appeared at Leconfield House on crutches twenty minutes earlier. Now the young officer was involved, Knox was sure he'd do whatever he could to stay that way.

'I've filled him in on what we think we know,' Holland said. 'Anything you want to add, Malcolm?'

'Only that I haven't changed my opinion,' White replied. 'I'm still inclined to believe Williams. Or at least believe that he believes something very serious is going on.'

Knox was buoyed by White's confidence in his best friend, but then realised that meant he would have to play devil's advocate.

'There was no sign of any plot in motion against Kosygin at the TUC or in Whitehall,' he said.

'But they weren't easy targets,' Laing replied. 'We've done what we can with the ballet, but the Royal Opera House is a public building. There'll be almost two thousand people in the audience tonight and we can't question them all as they walk through the doors.'

Knox was glad he'd chosen not to bring up that he'd warned Knox two days ago about the risk of this exact eventuality.

'We definitely can't cancel the performance?' Knox asked.

'I doubt the BBC would forgive us,' Holland replied. 'Or my wife.'

'I don't see why Kosygin's so determined to see Nureyev perform,' Laing said. 'I thought he was still a major embarrassment.'

'It's not about the dancing,' Bennett. 'It's about sending a message.'

'Asking him to come home?'

'Or telling him and everyone else who's made it through the Iron Curtain that they never really escaped. That wherever they go, Russia can still get to them.'

Everyone let that possibility sink in for a few moments, before Holland spoke again.

'Threats against one's life unfortunately come with high office,' he said. 'And ninety-nine times out of a hundred they're unsubstantiated, or made by people woefully incapable of carrying them out. But it's that one other occasion that concerns us, and sometimes the incredible trumps the credible.' He turned to Knox. 'I want you and Miss Bennett to go to the ballet. We'll watch from here. And I want you to go down to the quartermaster and have him issue you a sidearm.'

Knox nodded as Holland pre-empted the question forming on his lips.

'Pascal's wager,' the director general said. 'If Williams is wrong and we do something, we'll have egg on our face. But if he's right and we do nothing, the Russians might feel well within their rights to start launching missiles at us.'

'I don't have anything to wear,' Bennett said, half joking.

'That won't be a problem,' Holland replied as the door to his office opened and Sarah stepped inside, carrying two long quilted dress bags over her arm.

'This is for you,' Sarah said, handing one of them to Bennett.

'You're coming?' Knox asked, looking at the second bag, which Sarah had kept hold of.

'I wasn't going to miss this evening for the world,' she replied.

'And I couldn't stop her,' Holland added.

CHAPTER 49

Covent Garden was dark, cold, and wet. A brief spring shower had slicked the market's cobbles, driving away any last-minute customers but also saving the traders from having to wash them down as they closed their stalls.

Anna strode across the north side of the piazza.

She was wearing the deep-gold gown she'd bought on Bond Street after her early-morning trip to Shepherd's Bush. The dress looked like it had been fitted perfectly to her physique, the sleeveless, boat-neck bodice hugging her figure before flaring out at her waist. She'd picked it after wandering in and out of a succession of exclusive boutiques. Anna loved shopping for expensive clothes. It reminded her of all the wardrobes full of fine dresses she'd rifled through in the less damaged but still abandoned mansions of Dresden, and the hours she'd spent pretending they were her clothes and her palatial homes before her deeper urges forced her to skulk away to darker places.

Her only concession to the coolness of the evening was the black shawl draped over her elbows, which she'd bought along with her dress and a small emerald clutch that contained a bright scarlet Helena Rubinstein lipstick, and Elizabeth Arden powder compact, a few pound notes, and two welded-together metal tubes. She carried the clutch in her left hand, and held her invitation card between the immaculately French-manicured fingers of her right.

In Shepherd's Bush Anna hadn't wanted to be noticed, but in this market she was brazen, enjoying playing the part of the high-society woman on her way to the ballet.

She walked under the arches that lined the edge of Covent Garden, past the shut-up fruit and vegetable stands and beneath the covered path's old gas lamps, then turned off the market and strolled up Bow Street to the Royal Opera House.

Black cabs and limousines were disgorging a steady stream of people in front of the opera house. Anna joined them, and let them carry her through its columned entrance and past the line of people in ill-fitting uniforms who were discreetly checking everyone's invitations and tickets.

Anna thought the building matched its staff. It was ostentatious, and tired. She saw the cracks in the ceiling and the worn patches in the carpet.

The book that had been delivered to her at Durrants, along with her invitation and a set of blueprints for the Royal Opera House, had been full of pictures of its past glory, before its foundations had been shaken by the bombs of war.

She milled with the crowd, listening to old women pretend they were happy to see each other, gossip about who was and wasn't in attendance, and speculate on whether one of the royals might grace Nureyev with their presence. And she watched the poorly disguised security personnel in their cheap suits or borrowed dinner jackets hugging the walls and doorways that led deeper into the building. She was impressed by the number of them, but not concerned. They had no idea who she was, or what she was there to do. And, thanks to the architectural plans she'd spent the afternoon studying, she was confident she knew more about the opera house's deceptively labyrinthine corridors than any of them.

Anna was tempted to crash into one of the vapid conversations swirling round her and say something truly scandalous to a couple of well-to-do ladies, but instead she decided to take her seat before the rest of the audience began rushing into the auditorium at the last minute.

She walked through the double doors that led to the stalls and let an usher guide her to the seat that had been arranged for her at great expense, at the very end of the left-hand side of the second row, by a short exit staircase. She casually took in the three large BBC television cameras that had been installed around the edge of the stalls under the rim of the grand tier. One was on the far right, one was on the far left, and one faced the dead centre of the stage.

Anna thanked the usher, sat down, and stared straight ahead for ten minutes as the auditorium started to fill behind her all the way from the stalls up to the gods. Then, as the house lights began to fade and the orchestra tested their instruments, she got up and walked down the stairs next to her seat.

***

Knox and Bennett were nodded through the front doors of the opera house by a Watcher dressed as a ticket checker.

Knox had changed into a dark grey Henry Poole suit he kept in his office, and Bennett was wearing the simple black shift dress Sarah had given her. It fitted her, which, as she was almost a foot shorter than the director general's wife, suggested it had either been borrowed from a younger relative or bought specially for her. She liked the dress, but she didn't like the narrow-heeled patent-leather pumps that had also been produced for her – she'd been in them for less than an hour and they were already rubbing her feet.

'You ever been here before?' Bennett asked Knox as they scanned the audience festooned in fur and jewellery in the entrance hall.

'Once or twice,' Knox replied. 'But never to such a starry affair.'

His suit was expensive and well tailored, but surrounded by men in dinner jackets and bow ties he felt conspicuously underdressed.

Knox usually preferred to watch his ballet at Sadler's Wells in Clerkenwell. Its productions were more experimental, and its seats were cheaper. Ironically for Nureyev, the great ex-Soviet dancer had decided he wanted to come to London at the beginning of a revival of *Les Noces*, a traditional ballet about a Russian peasant wedding by Igor Stravinsky and Bronislava Nijinska. More ironically for Knox, it had been quickly agreed that Nureyev would instead perform in a one-night revival of *Card Game*, an abstract, playful work also scored by Stravinsky and choreographed by George Ballanchine that had been the opening dance in a mixed programme the Royal Opera House's ballet company had recently staged.

'Well,' Bennett said, lowering her voice as she kept looking round the crowd, 'none of these people look like assassins to me.'

'No,' Knox agreed, 'they don't.'

'So what do we do?'

'Trust the Watchers, the police, and Sarah to deal with the crowd while we look everywhere else.'

More and more people had arrived in the few minutes they'd been inside. Then a bell rang out over the sea of people and they all began to surge towards the doors and staircases that would lead them into the auditorium. Everyone apart from Knox, Bennett, and the other MI5 and police staff.

In a few minutes the entrance hall was almost empty. Knox looked towards a Met officer he recognised from Congress House, who shook his head at him.

'Maybe he's not coming after all,' Bennett said.

For a moment Knox entertained the possibility that Kosygin had, in fact, decided to spend the evening in the Soviet embassy, and he and Bennett could combine hunting for a soon-to-be frustrated assassin with watching at least a few minutes of Nureyev's performance. But then a set of the large glass front doors opened and Kosygin finally made his entrance, wearing a tuxedo and flanked by three other men. As he was guided up to the grand tier by an usher, any last drops of hope and levity instantly drained out of Knox.

'That's that, then,' he said, checking his watch.

If the assassin wanted to make the biggest impact and create the most terror, Knox was sure they'd strike when Nureyev was on stage and people all over the country were watching on the BBC. The curtain was due to go up in five minutes, and *Card Game* was twenty-five minutes long, which meant they had half an hour to stop a murder.

***

Sarah Holland never let her nerves get the better of her, but knowing she was very probably walking into the same building as a killer gave her arrival at the Royal Opera House a rather different tone to her usual evenings at the ballet. She maintained her composure as she mingled her way through the entrance hall, stopping to embrace acquaintance after acquaintance. But all she wanted to do was get to her box as quickly as possible.

She delicately excused herself from the last, old son of a banking dynasty who seemed to think that the sizeable donation Sarah had persuaded him to give to Great Ormond Street children's hospital a few months ago gave him permission to aggressively compliment her pink satin Christian Dior gown, and made her way up the wide staircase to the grand tier a few minutes before the warning bell rang. She felt a mix of hope and apprehension building inside her – hope for what might still simply be an evening of incredible human artistry and athleticism, and apprehension for what might turn it into something even more dramatic.

Sarah's seat was in the fifth box from the right-hand edge of the opera house's towering proscenium arch. It was her favourite spot to watch the ballet and opera from, as you could actually see the performances from it rather than just be seen by the rest of the audience during them.

'Darling,' a very loud voice said as she stepped inside. 'I was wondering when you were going to get here.'

Sarah had forgotten that one of the people she'd be sharing her evening with was Lady Jane Balcairn, another person she regularly charmed into giving significant amounts to good causes. Lady Balcairn was also an incorrigible gossip who only stopped talking when she was swallowing champagne or watching ballet.

'Good evening,' Sarah replied, a practised smile matching the calm tone of her voice.

Any other night Sarah would have found Lady Balcairn's company secretly tiresome, but this evening she was more than happy to sit next to her and give the occasional smile and nod as she talked and Sarah watched the auditorium fill with people. Sarah didn't even mind that Lady Balcairn had also taken her usual seat against the low wall shared with the next box, leaving Sarah to sit by the gap that split the box's two rows of padded velvet chairs in half.

Sarah considered herself a good observer of character, and she didn't see anyone acting suspiciously while Lady Balcairn monologued next to her. There were plenty of people in the grand tier and the better parts of the stalls who acted like they owned the place – and could probably afford to – and more in the higher levels and cheaper seats who looked a little nervous and unsure about how they were supposed to behave. But no one who looked like they might be a killer.

Excitement turned to anticipation that swirled around the audience as a thousand conversations rose and fell like waves. Sarah leaned forward, craning her neck over the stalls and twisting to look at the balconies above the box.

'Are you alright, my dear?' Lady Balcairn asked, finally realising Sarah's attention was not entirely devoted to her.

'Of course,' Sarah replied, sitting back in her chair and giving Lady Balcairn another practised smile. 'I just love a full house.'

Eventually the auditorium settled into silence. The house lights started to fade, and Sarah hoped again that the evening might pass without incident after all.

But then two things happened that told her she, Knox, and Bennett wouldn't be so fortunate.

First, there was a sudden shaft of light to her right as the door to a nearby box opened and she saw Aleksei Kosygin, half-silhouetted, take his seat.

And then, looking back towards the stage to wait for the curtain to rise, she noticed the faint glint of a reflection in the stalls as a lady in a gold dress at the far end of the second row stood up and walked down the staircase next to her seat. The staircase that Sarah happened to know led to one of the opera house's exits, and also to a service corridor that went all the way behind the stage.

CHAPTER 50

Sarah leaped out of her seat and into the corridor, surprising both Lady Balcairn and the police officers guarding the door to Kosygin's box. She rushed back down to the entrance hall, which was now deserted apart from a couple of men in Opera House uniforms. One of them, who was actually a Watcher, recognised her and stepped forward.

'Problem, ma'am?' he asked. His voice was gruff but deferential.

'Where's Knox?' she replied.

The Watcher pointed to a door. It led Sarah into another corridor that wrapped round the side of the building. Unfortunately it was on the same side of the auditorium as her box, which put it on the opposite side to the woman Sarah had seen slip out of her seat.

She could hear the orchestra switch from tuning to overture as she half-ran, half-skidded along the corridor's carpet. She turned a tight corner just in time to see Knox and Bennett disappear through another door.

'Wait!' she called out, stopping them in their tracks.

Then, when she reached them, she told them what she'd seen.

'Where does the staircase lead?' Knox asked when she was done.

'Outside, and backstage.'

A minute later Sarah was making her way back up to her box to apologise profusely to Lady Balcairn and pretend to enjoy the rest of the evening while also being sure someone was trying to kill a man seated less than twenty feet from her; Watchers and police were being despatched to every exit; and Knox and Bennett were sprinting round to the other side of the auditorium.

Knox thought again how Laing had made the right call about this evening, and he'd ignored him. He'd warned Knox the ballet would be an unmanageable security risk. Knox hadn't listened, and now here he was, racing to stop a foreign head of state being killed live on national television.

Then he felt something else. Something he'd almost forgotten about – a tingle in the old scar across the top of his head. It used to throb whenever he pushed himself too hard in the maelstrom of action. Now it reminded him how long it had been since he had, and he realised how much he missed it.

It was a sudden, sharp echo of the past. A painful sensation, but also vital, energising, and he didn't want to let it go. So, as well as chastising himself again for not paying attention to Laing, he decided that, whatever was about to happen, when it was all over he was going to talk to Holland about spending fewer hours sitting behind his desk or on planes and more time out in the field.

'You reckon she's our target?' Bennett asked as they shouldered open another set of doors that led into another stretch of corridor.

'It's the only lead we have,' Knox replied. 'And it's very clever. No one is supposed to know Kosygin's here, and it's not like we could strip search the whole audience.'

They finally reached the door they'd been told would take them backstage, but as Knox went to open it, Bennett put her hand over his, stopping him for a moment.

'I just had a really bad thought,' she said. 'The Wolf. I've never heard or read anything about them that didn't just assume they were a man. Even I did. What if they're real after all and it's her, and she's about to Abraham Lincoln Kosygin?'

'Then,' Knox said, feeling the Beretta in the shoulder holster under his jacket, 'we're about to face a Soviet super-soldier with one gun between us.'

***

Anna didn't understand why people paid so much money just to see what happened onstage at the ballet when the real performance was going on off it. She watched dancers limber up and flow effortlessly from light to darkness, seamstresses make frantic final checks and quick alterations to costumes, and technicians move huge sets and lighting rigs between them, all in near silence and perfect unison, as the music from the orchestra pit blared around them.

It was a smooth, professional production and everyone involved was too focused on what they were doing to notice Anna, wrapped in her black shawl, standing perfectly still in between a brick pillar and a gantry ladder next to one of the rear wing curtains. None of the dancers clad in their leotards covered with hearts, diamonds, clubs, and spades saw her as they dashed past her, and from her little nook she had a perfect, uninterrupted view of the stage itself, the BBC television camera on the far side of the stalls, and, directly above it, Kosygin's box.

She felt a change in the tone of the movement around her. It was small, as if the dancers and crew were all suddenly concentrating on their jobs just a little more intensely. Anna didn't know what had prompted this subtle shift, but then when a man dressed in a pink costume emblazoned with symbols from every card suit glided through the dark and stopped barely a foot in front of her in the empty wing she understood: Nureyev had arrived.

Anna was close enough to reach out and touch the great dancer's lithe, muscled body, and she almost did. But after a brief lull the music rose again and suddenly he was out under the glare of a spotlight, leaping impossibly high in the air as the orchestra reached a crescendo.

With the star delivered to his audience, backstage settled once more into its own quiet choreography, and Anna allowed herself a few more moments to appreciate it. But then she felt another change. Not a subtle elevation of the general tone, but an intrusion, an injection of commotion.

She shrank back further into her crevice as her eyes searched for the cause. Twenty feet from her, on the other side of a group of dancers and a large piece of plywood painted to look like a row of old chimneys, were two people who, like Anna, should not be there.

A man in a grey suit and a small woman in a plain dress were frantically looking round them, trying to work out what they had walked into and desperately searching for something. Instinctively, Anna knew that something was her.

Anna had come close to being caught more than once during her long career working for Line Z, and she knew how to spot an enemy. Unfortunately for whoever these people were and whoever they were working for, they were too late. And even if they weren't, Anna was sure she'd be able to handle both of them and complete her mission without much worry.

So she didn't try to hide or run. She reached into her clutch, pulled out the small double tube, took a step forward to the very edge of the wing, raised the weapon to her eye, sighted her target, and fired three times.

CHAPTER 51

White had left the fifth floor a few minutes after Knox, Bennett, and Sarah, leaving the director general, Williams and Laing to view proceedings at the Royal Opera House on the television Holland usually kept shut away in a cabinet in the corner of his office.

Williams and Laing were still on the sofa, but Holland hadn't joined them – he preferred to remain behind his desk for the duration.

In the middle of the preamble on the BBC, with none of them able to do anything other than watch events unfold and wait to hear from Knox, Holland had instructed Williams to open another cabinet and pour them all a large measure of Remy Martin XO cognac. Laing sipped on his tentatively, his free hand pressing on his good leg to stop its constant, nervous tremors. But Holland and Williams had almost finished theirs as the television screen showed the opera house's curtains start to rise.

'Which one's Nureyev?' Laing asked, a few minutes into the performance.

'None of them,' Williams replied immediately, to the slight surprise of all three men. 'The joker's the starring role in *Card Game.* That's Nureyev's part.'

After another five minutes of groups and duos of dancers showing the audience what they could do, Nureyev made his entrance. His first, giant leap caught the BBC's cameramen off guard and the top half of his torso sailed above the screen, but they were soon keeping pace with the Russian as he literally and effortlessly danced rings around everyone else on stage.

The three audience members in Leconfield House all unconsciously moved nearer the edge of their seats as they succumbed to the spectacle of Nureyev's preternatural talent. They sat in quiet awe as his body propelled him through the air, spinning and arcing over and over again, a childish, gleeful smile fixed on his face.

The screen cut to a side angle, showing the full depth of the stage and just how much ground Nureyev was covering with his *sautés* and *jetés*, then back to a face-on view, this time in a close-up just tight enough to show the beads of sweat that were trickling from his temples to the creases of his mouth, and then again to the opposite side of the stage. Whoever was editing the live broadcast knew what they were doing. The camera cuts of a particularly complex combination of *sissonne-jeté-assemblé-sauté* Nureyev moved through with ease were perfect, apart from a brief moment at the very top of Nureyev's *assemblé* when three bright flashes filled the screen, like flares set off in front of the nation's eyes.

Laing was halfway through asking what had caused the sudden interference when Williams knocked him out by slamming his forearm into his stomach, doubling Laing over and then smashing his face into his cognac glass and the coffee table it sat on.

A second later, Williams was behind Holland, his arm wrapping round the director general's neck in a chokehold. Williams's face was completely still and blank as Holland desperately tried to claw his way free, and then slowly started to lose consciousness. Then Williams dragged Holland's chair out from under his desk and, tapping even further into some hidden well of strength, tipped the older and much larger man over his shoulder and carried him out of his office.

The rest of the fifth floor was empty, so there was no one to stop Williams carrying Holland all the way to the lift and down to the underground car park to Holland's Bentley, the only car that was still in its space.

Its doors were unlocked. Williams eased Holland's body off his shoulder and propped him against the back seat. He removed the director general's tie, used it to bind his wrists together, then shoved him over onto his side. Finally, he walked round to the driver's door, got in, opened the glove compartment to retrieve the set of copied keys and the Makarov pistol that had been left inside for him, and drove up the exit ramp.

CHAPTER 52

'Stop!' Knox shouted as he saw the woman step out of the shadows towards the light of the stage.

She didn't.

She might not have heard him over the orchestra's rise and fall, but somehow Knox sensed that she had, and that she knew he was after her.

He clambered over the fake chimneys blocking his path to the stage with Bennett in tow.

Dancers and stagehands turned towards them, their irritation at the two sudden invaders replaced with fear as they saw Knox pull his Beretta from his holster and finally registered the woman who, until moments ago, had been completely invisible to them, as she stepped back from the edge of the wing, one side of her face and body caught in the edge of a spotlight. And then their fear turned into confusion as they watched the woman stride calmly towards the man pointing a gun at her.

'Stop,' Knox said again.

And again she didn't. Instead she started to move faster, unfurling the shawl she was wrapped in. In one fluid motion, she threw it over Knox's arm, twisting it tightly round the gun, as she also kicked Bennett in the stomach and sent her tumbling back over the plywood set. Then she used her shawl to pull Knox's gun arm behind his back, putting him in a half-nelson hold so she could ram him head-first into the metal gantry ladder.

Pain shot through Knox's head, and by the time he'd shaken it off and Bennett had pulled herself up from the floor, the woman was gone. Her attack had lasted less than ten seconds.

'We need to go after her,' Bennett said.

'No,' Knox said, turning towards the stage. 'We have to get to Kosygin.'

Bennett was right, but Knox needed to know if they really had been too late. He had to see if the Russian was now slumped lifeless in his chair, his forehead or chest stained with blood from a fatal shot.

He sprinted forward, and it wasn't until he was barely a foot from the stage that he realised the orchestra was still playing and there was no chorus of screams coming from the audience. He grabbed at one of the wing curtains to stop himself, looked out into the auditorium, and saw that everything was absolutely fine. Nureyev was still leaping from spotlight to spotlight, and Kosygin was still happily watching him from his box.

Bennett appeared next to Knox as he reholstered his Beretta, looking as confused as he was. She was holding the woman's shawl and something else – a small emerald clutch bag.

'She must have dropped it when she was whipping our asses,' Bennett said.

She opened the bag and checked what was inside – a compact, a lipstick, some money, and two stuck-together polished tubes.

'What do you think that is?' she asked, nudging it through the fabric of the bag.

'No idea,' Knox replied.

Bennett picked up the strange object, running her fingers along the weld and over the surface until she found the almost perfect edge of the trigger button. Then she held it away from her, aimed it at the wall next to the gantry ladder, and fired. There was no recoil, no propellant ignition, and no explosion of brick and mortar dust. There was just an intense, glowing red light where Bennett was pointing.

She wasn't holding some new sort of miniature gun dreamed up by Soviet engineers. The double tube was a very small and very powerful laser.

'What the hell does this mean?' she said.

Knox stared at the bright dot, his mind furiously trying to work out why the KGB would have gone to so much effort to get their agents a clear shot at Kosygin only to have them fire a beam of light instead of a bullet.

Then his brain broke his heart.

'It means,' he said, 'we need to get back to Leconfield House.'

CHAPTER 53

Anna had originally planned to leave through the opera house's front doors, making the ushers guess why someone would depart while Nureyev was still in the middle of his performance. But as she quickly exited backstage she decided instead to follow another route she'd memorised from the building's blueprints.

The Floral Hall next door had been built at the same time as the Royal Opera House, and had been home to Covent Garden's flower market until a fire had gutted it ten years ago. Its main entrance was on Bow Street, but it also connected to the north-eastern corner of Covent Garden Piazza. Its doors and passageways were shut up, but they were all still there, including one long-forgotten one that joined it to the opera house.

The hall was dark when Anna slipped into it from one of the opera house's quiet service corridors. She fumbled her way between piles of burnt wood and pools of stagnant rainfall let in through the holes in the roof, navigating using the dim light that crept round the edges of the heavy boards clumsily nailed across the hall's high, cracked windows.

It took her almost five minutes to find what she was looking for – the narrow, low door that opened onto the piazza. The old wood bent as she pressed against it, and flecks of paint come away on her palms. She felt a single padlocked panel holding the door shut, and she could tell its small screws would put up little resistance.

No one had followed her into the Floral Hall, but she still paused, listening in case the two people she'd briefly fought – or anyone else – were somehow waiting for her outside. But she couldn't hear anything and, when she shoved the door open, the piazza was empty.

The wet cobbles had started to dry and it only took Anna a few moments to skip over to the south side of the market. She was heading back to Durrants, but not directly.

It wasn't until she'd turned into Southampton Street, which led down a short hill to the Strand, that she saw another person – a tall man in a dark greatcoat – walking towards her. She stepped to the right, out of his way, and he stepped left, back into her path. She stepped left and he matched her again. She smiled at him, he smiled at her. Then they both stopped, six feet apart.

'Can I help you?' Anna asked, drawing out the syllables of the question.

She couldn't make out much of the man's features – he was lit from behind by the streetlamps on the Strand and his coat obscured the shape and size of his body – but she could see two very large ears poking out of his hair, and two even larger hands sticking out of his sleeves.

'No,' he replied, undoing the buttons of his coat so it hung off him, and twisting his body. He moved his right foot back and shifted his weight into a boxer's stance.

Anna didn't say anything else. She didn't cry out for help, or even pretend to look dismayed. She just matched the man's posture and waited for him to make the first move.

They stared at each other for a long, tense moment until the man lunged at her, his right hand balled into a fist. Anna easily deflected his cross-punch, but was surprised when he pivoted away from her instead of being carried forward by momentum, and her own jab missed his body and was lost in the folds of his coat.

She spun on the ball of her foot as they switched positions, him higher up the hill and her back to the Strand. The man now loomed over Anna, but she was happy to use that to her advantage and threw out another fist, aimed square at his stomach. Yet he managed to dodge her once more, floating left then right to avoid her punches.

The man smiled at her again. He seemed to be enjoying their little sparring session. Anna wasn't. She'd already had to deal with one surprise this evening; a second made her think that Line Z had got sloppy with its planning, and she didn't like sloppiness. At least this man, whoever he was, seemed to be a more worthy adversary.

She took a step away from him, putting more space and hill between them, and waited for him to leap at her again. When he didn't, Anna moved to the side, stepping out into the road. He still refused to attack, which was exactly what Anna wanted. She took another step, then another, curving round until they were on the same level of the slope. Then she feinted a left hook and, as he instinctively glided out of her fist's path, she turned and sprinted into one of the small, tight lanes that ran off Southampton Street.

Anna had decided she wouldn't be able to beat the man out in the open. She needed him pinned in close quarters where he couldn't get away from her so easily. She kept running, then, when she was sure he was following her, she ducked into an even narrower alleyway.

It was a short distance to the bright lights of the Strand, but Anna crouched in near total darkness as she held her breath and waited for the man to appear. After a few seconds she heard him panting quietly, but he was being careful, pausing just beyond the entrance to the alley and waiting for his eyes to adjust.

Anna waited too, and when he finally stepped into the black, she struck. She came up from the ground inches from his body, driving her knee into his crotch as her fist at last connected with him as she slammed an uppercut into his chin.

The man pitched backwards against the alley wall, stunned and groaning, as Anna's mind instantly went all the way back to her close-contact combat lessons at Bernau.

She held her hands out, stiff like blades, and jabbed at his sides and neck, hunting for the pressure points that would cause maximum pain. But as he came out of his daze, he wrapped his arms around Anna and drove her backwards, slamming them both into the opposite wall with enough force to add a few more cracks into its old tiles.

Anna winced in pain. However, worse than the sensation of her head bouncing off hard wall and having her lungs crushed, she felt the man starting to stab at her with his thick fingers and realised he was searching for the same spots on her body that she'd been trying to find on him.

She understood two things in very quick succession. First: they'd had the same training. And second: if she was going to win this fight she needed to improvise.

She made a couple of purposefully sloppy moves, flailing under his heavy grip, then, just as he tipped into overconfidence, she headbutted him, slipped down out of his arms, came up on the side of him, grabbed the back of his hair and open mouth, and gave his head a sharp, brutal twist that snapped his neck.

His body fell straight down, folding under him, and for a moment the man kneeled against the alley's tiles as if he'd suddenly turned to prayer. But then he slid sideways, hitting the pavement slab with a dull thud.

Anna glanced along the alley to the Strand. She felt a chill run through her and realised the night was turning colder – and that she had no money for a cab. So she turned the dead man over, checked his pockets, and pulled his wallet out of his trousers. There was some money inside, but nothing she could use to identify him. She rolled him onto his front, pulled his coat off, draped it over her shoulders, walked down to the Strand, and hailed a taxi.

She asked the driver to take her to the top of Marylebone High Street, and made the rest of her journey to Durrants on foot, pausing for a few minutes on the corner of George Street to see if anyone was watching the entrance to the hotel.

She'd spent the whole journey across central London thinking about the dead man and why he'd been able to predict her every move until she resorted to a lesson in how to kill she'd taught herself long before the Soviets had recruited her. She still didn't know who he'd been working for, but she didn't like the possibilities she'd narrowed it down to. Either Line Z had decided they no longer required her services and she'd become a loose end to tie up, or some other faction in the KGB had managed to identify her and wanted her eliminated.

Whichever the answer might be, Anna had little interest in facing it in London. In fact, she was happy not to face it at all. She had plenty of identities and bank accounts stashed around Europe, and she decided now would be a perfect time to use a fair amount of both to disappear for a while. If someone was after her she could wait them out, or take them on on her own terms. And if this was all just an unfortunate and fatal misunderstanding there would be ways for her to contact Line Z and come back in once things had blown over.

So, she went up to her room, which was still exactly as she'd left it, changed out of her gold gown, stuffed the rest of the money left over from buying it into the pocket of her new greatcoat, and left the hotel.

Back on Marylebone High Street she hailed another cab, which took her to King's Cross just in time for her to buy a ticket for the overnight train to Edinburgh.

CHAPTER 54

Captain Tokorev and Lieutenant Starikov stood next to each other on the *Yorsh*'s turret, leaning on the railing that ran all the way round the small oval of deck. The night was calm, there was no wind or rain, and it was warm enough that neither of them needed to fasten their coats against a chill. They were both looking in the same direction, towards a dark horizon pitted with specks of light: land.

'Have you ever been to France?' Starikov asked.

'Not the mainland,' Tokorev replied.

Starikov missed the allusion to some interesting tale in the old seafarer's past. Instead he took a deep breath of fresh air.

'It's so close,' he said, a sliver of wistfulness in his voice. 'Almost swimmable.'

'Perhaps we should invade,' Tokorev suggested.

Starikov straightened, and so did his voice. 'Those weren't our orders.'

Tokorev grinned. 'No, they weren't.'

The submarine captain had softened towards the KGB lieutenant, once he'd finally started to mellow and made impressive inroads into Tokorev's alcohol supply. But perhaps he hadn't got through to the younger man as much as he'd thought. Their long conversation in his quarters had ended up with them debating fanaticism, the kind so strong it becomes brittle, and how easy it was to be led astray by blind loyalty. But Starikov was still KGB, and still young, and now he had a mission again it seemed like he would follow his orders without question.

Tokorev's smile faded as he thought about the message the *Yorsh* had received from the ZEVS array two hours ago instructing the submarine to re-enter the Channel, hold position barely ten kilometres from the French coast, and surface and dive at twenty-minute intervals for three hours. Once the three hours were up, or before 'if new instructions were received', the submarine was to head straight for Murmansk at depth. No further details had been provided about what those new instructions might be, or who might give them.

Tokorev had been sanguine about his shakedown cruise being hijacked without explanation, but this latest set of commands worried him.

To get to the coordinates he'd been sent he'd had to plot a tight course between Jersey, Guernsey, and Sark, the islands off Normandy that were de facto British territory, and then sit in French waters with just a stubby peninsula between the *Yorsh* and the naval base at Cherbourg. Thankfully the sun had set before the submarine had surfaced for the first time, so anyone looking out to sea would be unlikely to spot the small turret poking out of the water in the distance. But if someone did, it would be hard to consider the sudden appearance of a Soviet submarine as anything other than a provocation and have a couple of destroyers sent to scare it off or sink it.

Starikov turned towards the open hatch. Tokorev was surprised he was ready to climb back into the submarine so soon after finally escaping it. They still had ten minutes before they were due to dive again.

'Heading down?' he asked.

'There's work to be done,' Starikov said, pausing briefly at the top of the ladder.

Tokorev watched him disappear into the hull, wondering what exactly the lieutenant thought they should be doing. Had he received some coded instructions in the ZEVS message, or was he just being eager?

Tokorev had also lectured Starikov about the value of patience over their glasses of vodka, but now his was wearing thin. He was confident that his crew, small though it was, could handle whatever might be thrown at them over the next three hours. But as he turned back towards the far-off shore, he found himself quietly asking why they should, or, more honestly, why he should.

His eyes landed on a small cluster of lights he guessed were raised up on a hill above the coast and his mind unfolded a whole new life in front of him in a split second. The lights belonged to a farm, his farm, that he lived on with a few chickens and cows. He was suddenly the quiet man who walked into the nearby village a couple of times a week to buy bread and exchange mumbled pleasantries with the locals, who didn't know where he'd come from, didn't ask, and didn't care. And the rest of the time, he was left to himself with his animals and his view of the sea to keep him company.

It was a peaceful fantasy, but it was also shocking and overwhelming, and Tokorev stumbled back from the rail he'd unconsciously been gripping. He knew of old sailors who one day found themselves craving the feel of dry land beneath their feet, but he'd never thought he'd be one of them. He was sure he'd be at sea until the day he keeled over or found himself on the receiving end of a torpedo. And yet he felt like he was moments away from hurling himself overboard, swimming to shore and finding a small, weather-beaten hut somewhere to call his.

Tokorev didn't want to defect, but he wondered if helping Starikov hold on to his faith had drained him of his. He felt tired, sick of the secret motives and unexplained commands he'd put up with for so long. He'd done everything that had been asked of him for decades, and he knew the only thing waiting for him back at Murmansk would be more orders. He also knew that if he announced that he wanted to retire the response from his superiors would be a swift no. He belonged to the navy and it would never let him go. Even if he was removed from active sea duty there would always be training to be given, lessons to be taught, and ceremonies to attend – all to help further the Soviet Union's global ambitions. And, on top of that, there would be the constant, quiet questioning about why, after so many years, he no longer wanted to serve the Motherland so devoutly.

His thoughts were disconcerting, disorienting. He felt uneven, like he'd lost his balance after years on sea legs. He forced himself to turn away from the coast and look out towards the Channel before something compelled him to disappear while he was alone and had the chance.

He told himself to follow Starikov back into the submarine, let his fantasy float away, and do his best to prepare for whatever was about to happen.

CHAPTER 55

Knox and Bennett burst out onto Bow Street as rapturous applause filled every cubic foot of the Royal Opera House. *Card Game* had finished, and Nureyev's ovations were beginning. Thirty seconds later, they were in Knox's Jaguar, heading north to Shaftesbury Avenue, then west, weaving through the traffic and jumping the red lights of Piccadilly Circus.

When they reached Leconfield House, Knox pulled into the underground car park and swung to an abrupt stop in his usual space. He noticed, grimly, that Holland's Bentley wasn't in the next bay.

In the director general's office they found Laing, propped up on the sofa holding a blood-stained bandage to his forehead, as White swept a smashed glass off the coffee table into a bin.

'What happened at the opera house?' Laing asked Knox.

'Not what we were expecting,' Knox replied as he looked round the room, in case he'd just missed Holland and Williams standing in a corner.

He told Laing and White about their hunt, finding the woman, and then losing her. Bennett handed the double-tube laser to White and showed him how to fire it, lighting up the centre of Holland's painting of the castle with a bright red glow.

'There were a couple of seconds in the middle of Nureyev's performance when the feed seemed to cut out,' Laing said. 'Three sudden bursts of static. Next thing my face was being smashed into my cognac and I was knocked out. When I woke up, Williams and the DG were gone.'

White fired the laser at the painting again.

'Impressive workmanship,' he mumbled to himself. Then, to the others, said, 'It was a message. A code, or an activation signal. I was wrong. Williams isn't on our side.'

Knox turned to White, angry that he'd voiced the same conclusion he'd reached but still, despite all the evidence to the contrary, didn't want to completely believe – that his best friend had been working for the KGB all along, and that he'd just kidnapped one of Britain's most valuable intelligence assets.

'And where were you?' he asked.

'Doing my job,' White replied evenly. 'Our ghost submarine reappeared just after you left and Naval Intelligence has got their knickers in a twist.'

'Jesus,' Knox said. 'When did we get so bad at our jobs? And when did the Russians get so bloody good?'

'If Williams is really working for the KGB, where would he take Holland?' Bennett asked.

Laing answered her question with another one. 'How did he get out of the building?'

'Holland's Bentley is gone,' Knox answered.

'Then we might be able to find him,' White replied. 'The car has a tracker. I can give you a remote receiver, but the range is limited.'

'How limited?' Knox asked.

'Ten miles.'

Knox sighed. 'So we need to be sure where they've gone before we chase after them.'

'And we have no idea if they've dumped the car and are lying low, or if they're already being spirited out of the country right now,' Bennett added.

White nodded, and Knox shook his head.

'We've got one chance to stop the Russians getting their hands on almost fifty years of our secrets,' he said.

'Would Holland talk?' Bennett asked.

'Not willingly,' Knox said. 'But they won't give him a choice.'

He thought for a moment, then said, 'We dismissed the plot against Kosygin when Williams first told us about it. It wasn't the real endgame but it was part of the bigger plan. What if it wasn't the only double-bluff?'

'What else is there?' Bennett asked.

'The submarine,' Knox and White said simultaneously.

'Where is it?'

'It's started popping up by Vauville every twenty minutes or so,' White replied.

'Where the hell is that?'

'Next to the Channel Islands, and just round the corner from Cherbourg.'

'That sounds like they're trying to goad the French, not you,' Bennett said.

'Except that the French don't know it's there and we haven't told them. They're waiting for something.'

'So do we get the navy to round up some boats before it makes a dash across to our coast?' Laing asked.

'No,' Knox replied. 'The submarine isn't coming for Williams. He's going to go to it. He's going to fly to France.'

'How do you know that?'

'Because I know Jack.'

CHAPTER 56

Holland came to somewhere outside London. Lying, hands tied, in the back of his Bentley, he guessed from how warm the leather seat felt under his face, along with the lack of streetlights and a glimpse of the corner of a motorway sign, that he was no longer in the city.

The car slowed momentarily and Holland saw Williams's shoulders rise in front of him as he turned the steering wheel through a junction. Holland didn't move his body, but he slowly angled his head up to try to see further into the front of the car.

'If you're wondering if I'm armed, I am,' Williams said.

'Actually, I was wondering where you're taking me,' Holland replied.

'I'm not going to tell you that.'

Holland shifted his elbow under his side and levered himself up into the seat diagonally behind Williams. It now looked like he was being chauffeured somewhere instead of abducted.

'I'd rather you didn't do that,' Williams said.

'I'm sure.'

Holland hadn't sat up to get a better idea of where they were going – the road they were now on was too dark to offer any clues – but to get a proper view of Williams. Holland had been surprised by how calm he sounded, and was equally shocked by how relaxed he seemed. Williams didn't look like someone who had lost their mind, or who was acting on instinct. He looked like someone carrying out a well-rehearsed set of actions.

Holland twisted and pulled against the tie round his wrists, but it was fastened tight. This wasn't how he'd imagined the end of his MI5 career – assaulted, abducted, and probably soon to face extremely unpleasant and invasive probing at the hand of, he assumed, the KGB. Not the retirement he'd expected, though he hadn't given much thought to what even a voluntary departure from Leconfield House might look like, should he ever have that luxury.

He knew all about the idle chatter among his junior officers, who seemed to think anyone over sixty was mere weeks away from digging an allotment or a grave. He'd also heard mutterings coming out of Whitehall that he'd only managed to fight the Cold War to a deadlock, and it might be time for a fresh perspective.

It was true that the last thing he wanted to do was hold the Service back, and that some of his most important contacts within the intelligence community were making way for their successors and their old, owed favours were evaporating before Holland had chance to call them in. But it was still his duty to protect Britain. And, if the man sitting in front of him who had managed to extract him so efficiently from Leconfield proved anything, it was that the intelligence fight with the Soviets was nowhere near a stalemate.

However, it was Holland himself that needed protecting now, and all he could do was hope that Knox or someone else from MI5 had noticed he was missing and was chasing close behind him.

Hope, and try to get through to Williams.

'Are you fully aware of what you're doing?' he asked.

'Yes,' Williams replied.

'Do you know why you're doing it?'

'I don't need to.'

'You never used to be the kind of soldier who followed orders blindly. You always wanted to know what you were going into battle for.'

'I'm not the person you knew.'

Williams slowed the car again and turned a near-invisible corner, confirming to Holland that he knew exactly where he was going.

'I think there's still some of the Jack Williams who used to work for me inside you,' Holland said. 'The Jack Williams who was a loyal officer for a decade and cared about his country, colleagues, and friends so much he'd willingly offer to sacrifice himself over and over to keep them safe.'

Holland felt the car accelerate sharply and saw the needle on the speedometer momentarily jump a few miles per hour.

'You can think that if you like,' Williams replied. 'But if you keep talking I'll shoot you.'

'Whoever is making you do this didn't go to so much effort just for you to kill me,' Holland said.

'I didn't say I'd kill you.'

***

Williams's mind was finally, mostly, at peace.

The slicing shards of confused memories had dulled, then faded away. He no longer tumbled or hung in a void, at the whim of forces that were determined to crush or pull him apart. And the maze he'd been so lost in was gone.

In its place was a single path, a line that stretched out in front of him and reached back behind him, through London and Haina to every barren room and wilderness where his psyche had been so carefully prepared for what lay ahead.

He saw with crystal clarity the intense training his body and brain had been put through, the tests he'd been set to prove himself, the murders he'd been ordered to commit, the blood his hands were soaked in. He remembered the feeling of being lost and then found, when he'd been pulled out the darkness and given the chance to become something new, powerful, and terrifying. But there was nothing further back, nothing beyond the darkness that might remind him of the man he'd once been before his rebirth.

Williams knew his purpose and his destination. Nothing else mattered, and nothing else could matter. His years of mental conditioning had been triggered, he could only do what it drove him to.

And now, in front of him he saw the last stage of the mission he'd been sent on. With all the camouflage of confusion finally stripped away, he remembered who he really was.

He was Project Mykl.

CHAPTER 57

'I hope you're right,' Bennett said as she stared at the tracker-receiver White had bolted onto the dashboard of Knox's Jaguar.

It was a deceptively simple-looking box with a couple of dials Bennett and Knox had been told not to fiddle with, and a round display divided by horizontal and vertical grid lines. It looked like a miniature radar system, but its screen wasn't lighting up with pings.

'So do I,' Knox replied, shifting gear to overtake a lumbering lorry in front of them.

Bennett had expected them to head back to Dungeness – she'd seen the same plane Laing had when they'd both been following Knox and Williams and not noticing the KGB hit squad on all their tails – but they hadn't. They'd sped south out of the city, passed through Epsom and Leatherhead, and were now just north of Horsham. So far, there had been no signs telling them they were headed in the right direction.

'Why do you think you know where they're going?' Bennett asked.

'Because Jack told me,' Knox replied, pulling back into his lane. 'When we were driving to Kent I thought I was helping him untangle everything in his mind, but he was trying to tell me what had been hidden in the mess. He talked about when he'd learned to fly at Shoreham Airport. It was the only thing he brought up that I hadn't prompted him about. That's where he's going.'

'That's a big gamble.'

'I don't think so.'

The road opened up in front of them and Knox pushed the Jaguar close to ninety miles an hour.

'The Russians must have been working on him for years,' he continued. 'Just waiting for the perfect opportunity to force him to do something like this. But he's always been fighting them, and I bet he's still trying to.'

Bennett frowned as Knox sped through a roundabout and the road started to curve, skirting the edge of Horsham.

'Kidnapping the head of a security service is a hell of a play,' Bennett said. 'Bigger than I thought even the KGB would try.'

'Apparently they're changing the rules of engagement,' Knox replied.

'But surely the fallout would be more dangerous than anything they could get out of Holland.'

'All bets would be off. It'd be total anarchy.'

Bennett stared at the display in front of her, willing it to light up. For another three fast miles there was nothing. Then, at last, a faint blip appeared on its edge.

'You were right after all,' she said. 'We've found them.'

'Thank God,' Knox replied, shifting once more into a higher gear. 'Now we can stop this and work out once and for all what those bastards have done to Jack.'

He smiled over at Bennett, but she was still frowning. She understood how desperate he was to save his best friend, and to believe he was only a victim. But with so much evidence to the contrary, she worried just how big a blind spot Williams was for Knox, and if that was exactly why he'd been sent to abduct the director general.

'Richard,' she said, 'I need to ask you something. If it's the only option, will you kill Williams to save Holland?'

'I'll do what I have to,' Knox said, keeping his eyes fixed on the edge of the Jaguar's headlight beams.

Bennett nodded. She wasn't happy with Knox's answer. But she didn't say anything else. She just looked at the blinking light that was starting to move little by little towards the centre of the tracker-receiver's screen.

CHAPTER 58

Holland spotted the glint of slow-flowing water in the clear moonlight. Wherever Williams was driving them, they were now following the course of a river.

After a few minutes, the water began to widen and they started passing the hulking shapes of sheds and warehouses lit by milky yellow lights that ran along narrow pavements. They'd reached the fringes of a town, but unfortunately for Holland there was no sign announcing where they'd arrived.

Williams kept driving in silence. Holland hadn't tried to get anything else out of him since he'd come to, but he had kept watching his kidnapper, looking to see if there were any signs of stress or cracks in his stony facade. There weren't.

The Bentley passed through a railway arch, and the buildings started to change. Holland could tell they were getting closer to the centre of town, but it was late and the place was extremely sleepy. Then Williams took an abrupt right turn and they crossed the river, which had suddenly widened again. Holland wondered if they were driving over an estuary and they'd travelled all the way to the coast.

Williams turned right again and steered the Bentley up an unlit access road that led to a row of large hangars. In the middle of it there was a kind of art deco castle – a two-storey white stucco complex with wide windows, curved sides, and a tower that added another couple of floors to its middle.

Williams steered round the small, circular lawn in front of the complex's jutting portico and parked neatly next to its oak and glass panelled entrance. He got out of the Bentley and gestured at Holland with his Makarov to do the same and follow him through the castle's unlocked double doors.

The few feet of salty air confirmed Holland's guess that they were near the sea, and the inside of the building told him that it was actually the terminal building of a small airport. It was dark, but he could make out photos and models of planes in the weak light coming in from the tall windows that stretched the height of the central, cavernous tower.

Williams, still silent, nudged him on by digging the pistol into his back. Almost as soon as they were in the terminal they were out of it again, through another set of doors on the opposite side.

Here there was only darkness, stretching out into nothingness. They were on the airfield. Holland couldn't see a runway or any planes, but soon enough Williams revealed both to him, guiding them to one of the hangars. They stopped briefly at its giant, gaping maw of an entrance as Williams opened a control box bolted to the steel-panelled wall and flicked two switches. The first lit up a single Cessna, parked in an angled line of other planes, its nose tilted up as if it was already eager to be up in the sky. The second turned on two parallel rows of lights on either side of the runway.

'Are you sure you don't want to wait until morning?' Holland asked. 'Night flights can be tricky.'

Williams didn't respond, he just grabbed the tie round Holland's wrists and dragged him over to the Cessna and into its cramped cockpit.

After Williams strapped him into his seat, Holland watched as he quickly inspected the two propeller blades sticking out at right angles to the plane's nose. He also noticed that the control wheel that should have been in front of him had been removed, leaving only the one for Williams, and a blunt spike pointing directly at his chest.

Williams climbed into the pilot's seat and started a short set of pre-flight checks. He was methodical and focused, but also distracted, giving Holland his only chance to stop them flying off to God knows where.

The older man lunged for the Makarov, managing to get his fingers on the barrel before Williams snatched it away, and drove its butt into his nose. Then, as blood trickled past Holland's lips, Williams reached over, twisted the director general away from the bank of dials and controls that filled the width of the cockpit, and fastened the end of his tie to the handle of the door next to him.

Williams's face had remained as passive during Holland's abortive attack as it had for almost the entire time since he'd put him in a chokehold in his office. And he stayed just as stoic as he turned the Cessna's engine over, pulled out of the hangar, and taxied towards the runway.

It was only when Williams had lined up the plane perfectly between the two rows of lights that ran down the airfield's longest, flattest stretch of grass that his expression changed. Because, just as he was getting ready to push the throttle stick in, the far end of the runway was suddenly lit up by the headlights of Knox's Jaguar careening across it.

'Oh good,' Holland said as another drop of blood fell from his nose and onto his shirt. 'The cavalry has arrived.'

CHAPTER 59

'Now what?' Bennett asked as the Jaguar and Cessna faced down each other from opposite ends of the runway.

She and Knox had followed the blip on the tracker-receiver display as they got nearer to the coast and their target inched closer to the middle of the screen. For a moment it had looked like they'd overshot it, but that was when Knox had known for certain that they were heading for Shoreham Airport. He'd taken the same path as Williams and Holland, passing the airport on the far side of the estuary, then crossing over and doubling back inland.

Bennett had already asked Knox what they were going to do when they'd turned into the approach road. Knox hadn't answered her, because he didn't really know. Then he'd seen the glow of take-off and landing lights beyond the terminal complex and row of hangars and realised it was too late to come up with a plan.

He'd floored the Jaguar's accelerator, but instead of turning towards the cluster of buildings at the end of the road he'd swung away from it, steering off the tarmac and onto grass. Almost instantly he'd had to swerve to avoid a ditch, sending both him and Bennett lurching in their seats, before they reached the airfield and saw the Cessna in the distance.

Now, as they stared at the plane through the Jaguar's windscreen, even in the half-light they could see the twin blades of its propeller starting to spin quicker. Bennett turned to look at Knox, and he turned to look at her.

There was a lot Knox had worked hard not to think about since they'd sped out of the car park under Leconfield House. He didn't want to entertain the idea that everything Williams had done following his miraculous return – his openness with Holland, his willingness to forgive Knox, his keenness to do whatever would bring him back into the fold – had been a trick. So he'd refused to.

But now, he had to face the possibility that it might all have been an incredibly cunningly orchestrated act of revenge and betrayal. And he had to do something. He had to stop his best friend from kidnapping his mentor.

Whatever was going to happen next, he couldn't let the Cessna take off. So he dipped the clutch, shifted into a low gear, took his foot off the brake, and slammed it once more onto the accelerator.

The Jaguar surged forward, leaping down the runway as Knox rapidly moved up through the gears to the car's top speed. In response, the Cessna's propeller blades became a blur, and it raced towards the Jaguar.

'This is your plan?' Bennett shouted as she braced herself against the passenger-side door and the armrest between her and Knox.

Knox didn't respond, or take his eyes off the Cessna. For five long seconds the car and the plane sped towards each other and it seemed like Knox and Williams were both going to lose the game of chicken they'd started. But then the Cessna began to tilt backwards and its three wheels lifted off the grass. The Jaguar was close enough for Knox and Bennett to see both Williams and Holland's faces as they rose up into the sky.

Knox kept his speed up, but drifted the Jaguar to the side, out of the plane's path. Then, just as it was about to pass them he held his breath, wrenched the handbrake on and heaved the steering wheel, skidding sideways under the plane. The car's roof smashed into the Cessna's wheel frame, shearing two of its struts clean off.

The Jaguar kept spinning off the smooth runway and onto the rougher grass. It hit a divot side-on and for a perilous instant almost flipped over before its horizontal momentum brought it bouncing back down to earth.

The Cessna rocked violently from side to side as it lost height and veered off course. Its wings tilted back and forth until one finally made contact with the ground, sending the plane into its own crashing spiral that snapped off the last wheel, broke a wing and the tail fin, and exploded the cockpit windows. It came to a shuddering halt thirty yards from the runway at the same time as the Jaguar finally stopped spinning on the other side of it.

Inside the car, Knox and Bennett both gulped for air as their hearts and lungs pounded inside their chests.

'I didn't know you knew how to do that,' Bennett said.

'Neither did I,' Knox replied between deep breaths.

He pulled the handle of his door, surprised that it still opened, climbed out of the car, and started sprinting towards the Cessna. He was already halfway to the runway before Bennett, who had kicked off her shoes after losing their heels in the airfield's soil, caught up with him. The coastal night was colder than London, and they were both underdressed in their ballet clothes, but the adrenaline pumping through their veins stopped them from feeling it.

The only sound coming from the broken plane was the slow grinding of the propellers, still trying to touch the sky. Then there was a louder bang of metal on metal as one of the cockpit doors was flung open against the fuselage and Williams climbed out, dragging Holland behind him. They both looked disoriented, their faces smeared with blood.

'Jack,' Knox shouted. 'Are you alright?'

'Richard,' Williams replied. His voice was quiet. 'What happened?'

'Don't worry,' Knox said. 'Everything's going to be okay.'

Knox stepped into the full light of the runway as something inside the Cessna exploded. He instinctively ducked, expecting the plane to go up in flames, but it didn't.

'You need to get away from there,' he shouted at Williams.

But when Knox looked at him he realised his friend's face had changed from confusion to a hard sneer, and he was staring down at the pistol in his hand.

Williams shifted Holland's semi-conscious body, holding him up with one arm and bringing the gun up to the side of his head.

Knox reluctantly reached for the Beretta, pulling it out of his shoulder holster but making a show of keeping it pointed at the ground.

'It's over, Jack,' he said.

Williams responded by pressing the Makarov into Holland's temple.

'No it isn't,' he said, his voice stronger and harder. 'I'm not finished.'

'What's your mission?' Bennett asked as she stepped into the light of the runway.

'Extract the director general of MI5,' Williams replied, almost robotically.

'We can't let you do that,' Bennett replied.

'You can't stop me.'

'You're cornered. There's no way out.'

Another explosion erupted behind Williams as the uncontrolled fire that had been growing inside the Cessna's mangled engine finally reached its fuel tanks. Chunks of fuselage and wing flew up into the air above Knox, Bennett, Williams, and Holland, and came crashing back down, miraculously missing all of them as the rest of the plane turned into a burning pyre.

The blast woke Holland and stunned Williams. He let the pistol fall to his side but didn't let go of it or his hostage. He shook his head, trying to clear it, then looked at Knox.

'Please, old man,' he cried out. His voice was now weak and plaintive. 'You have to end this.'

'You can,' Knox replied. 'Just drop the gun and we'll sort this all out.'

'I can't. They won't let me.'

'Why not?'

'I can't fight what they've put in my head.'

'You're stronger than you think you are,' Holland said, trying to pull away from Williams's tight grip.

There was another crack behind them as the tail section broke off the plane.

'I am,' Williams replied, his voice even again, and the Makarov back against Holland's head.

Bennett stepped closer to Knox.

'You have to stop him,' she said. 'Before he decides his only option is to murder Holland.'

Knox's mind was in almost as much turmoil as Williams's. He still couldn't answer Bennett's original question about if he'd choose to save Williams or Holland, because there was no way he could pick between them. They were his surrogate father and brother. He owed both of them his life and more.

He forced his arm to lift his Beretta, but the arm refused to aim it at either of the men in front of him.

'It's not too late,' Knox called out.

'Yes it is,' Williams replied.

'Shoot me, Richard,' Holland shouted. Then he winced as he felt the cold end of Williams's gun push further into his flesh.

Williams looked at Holland, and then at Knox. His finger curled round the Makarov's trigger.

'Now, Richard!' Bennett screamed.

But Knox was paralysed as he watched Williams turn his gun away from Holland and point it at him. He looked into Williams's eyes and saw the maelstrom of fear, anger, sadness, and chaos that swirled behind them. Knox had one chance, one shot to end it all, but he knew he couldn't take it.

Knox had told himself for so long that he'd trade places with Williams in a heartbeat, give his life so his best friend could have his back, and now, at last, he had the chance. It was twisted, as bent out of shape as the smouldering wreck of the plane, yet he still knew he'd sacrifice himself for Jack Williams.

But he wouldn't have to, because just as he loosened his grip on the Beretta, Bennett grabbed it from his hand and fired.

APRIL 1966

CHAPTER 60

Major Vadim Rykov had gone from visiting the Lubyanka very little to spending every waking and rarely sleeping moment in it.

After almost a month locked away in a succession of dark cells, he was now standing in the middle of one of its large conference rooms, wearing his dress uniform. It had been handed to him an hour ago after his first shower in weeks. Rykov had lost weight and it hung off his shoulders. He'd also been given a razor, which he'd used to remove his straggly beard under close watch from a guard in case he tried to cut something else with it, but he'd been left to use his overgrown fingernails to brush his hair, and been ignored when he'd asked for a toothbrush and some toothpaste.

Rykov faced a long table and five very senior KGB officers, who were all adorned with various combinations of braids and medal bars. Churkin was in the middle of the row. To his immediate left was Lieutenant General Dmitri Baranov, the head of Directorate S, chief of illegals, and Major General Yuri Sobel, the head of Directorate T, boss of the KGB's scientists. Rykov didn't know who the other two men were, but this only concerned him briefly, until his mind reminded him he had much bigger things to worry about.

'This tribunal has been called to review what we now know of the events that led to the attempted extraction of the head of a foreign intelligence service, namely James Holland of MI5, by agents of Line Z,' Churkin began. 'An unsanctioned and abortive operation that was carried out at great cost to life and resources, and risk to the security and safety of the Soviet Union.'

Ever since the *Yorsh* had arrived in Murmansk without two extra passengers on board and its captain had demanded to know who had commandeered his shakedown cruise, Rykov had been sure he'd eventually end up in this room, and that Churkin would be sitting on the other side of the table, pretending that he wasn't the one who had approved Rykov's plan to deploy Project Mykl in enemy territory.

Jack Williams had been a unique opportunity. He'd been captured by sheer fluke after his unconscious body had drifted into the path of a small yacht a KGB asset had taken out onto the Solent to get a look at the *Surcouf.* The operative had almost dismissed Williams as a lump of flotsam bumping against his hull, until he saw a stray fleck of starlight that had pierced a gap in the night's heavy clouds reflect off his cracked diving mask. He pulled him out of the water and checked him over. There were gashes in his wetsuit and skin where the straps of an air tank should be, but miraculously he was still breathing. Williams had then been transported back to Russia, where he'd been questioned, tortured, and forgotten in a cycle that lasted almost three years – until Rykov found out about him, and persuaded Churkin that there were better things the KGB could do with a highly trained foreign agent who had a personal relationship with the director general of MI5 than leave him rotting in an isolation cell.

For the last four years he'd been relentlessly experimented on in an effort to turn him. Eventually, Line Z had worked out how to do it without him even knowing. They used narcosynthesis, the scientific name for pumping someone so full of drugs that their brain's protective barriers broke down and their mind became exposed, malleable, and open to suggestion. But instead of using intravenous hypnotics to extract any last crumbs of information from him, they'd slowly hollowed out a tiny cave inside his mind and created a new Jack Williams inside it – a Jack Williams who existed only to serve Line Z. He became deception personified, and a perfect weapon.

Almost perfect.

Using Williams to snatch Holland was an audacious plot. It had taken months of planning and manoeuvring to create a bait so tempting and a narrative so compelling that both the Americans and the British wouldn't be able to resist getting caught by it. Kosygin's trip to London was the perfect final twist in the tale Rykov had written – the ultimate red herring that would make all his characters realise they'd never really been in charge of their stories.

If it had worked, Rykov would have been instantly promoted to colonel or higher and given even more power to wreak havoc around the world. But it hadn't. At the last second his troupe of players had rebelled and written their own endings, and he'd been grabbed from his apartment in the middle of the night and dragged to the Lubyanka, where he was now finally facing the consequences of his and Williams's failures.

'Thanks to the testimony of Major Yegerova, we are aware of the deaths of three Directorate S agents that we conclude were caused by the so-called Project Mykl, and four more operatives whose covers may have been compromised and who have been removed from Britain,' Churkin continued. 'While it is clear that Major Yegerova did not follow proper protocol in securing higher authority for acting against another department of the first chief directorate, we cannot fault the reasoning behind her actions or desire to protect Chairman Kosygin against a perceived, if entirely fictitious, threat to his life. This committee agrees with the recommendation of Major General Sobel that as reward for her devotion to the Soviet cause, Major Yegerova shall be stationed to the *residentura* in Buenos Aires to oversee Directorate S's operations in Argentina with immediate effect.'

So, Rykov thought, that was Yegerova's punishment for meddling with things she'd never truly understood – promoted to the South American front lines in the unending war with the West, and sent about as far away from Moscow as possible.

Churkin cleared his throat. 'It is now our responsibility to consider what should be done with Major Rykov.'

Rykov knew there would be no consideration – this kangaroo court wouldn't have been convened until he'd already been found guilty. The only question was, how guilty?

Rykov had stared straight ahead at a knot in one of the wooden wall panels behind Churkin since the colonel general had started talking, and he continued to as the charges against him were laid out.

'This committee has concluded that Major Rykov bears responsibility for the deaths of the three Directorate S operatives, the unapproved requisitioning of an experimental submarine that was exposed to foreign observation and potential interception, and the deployment of an unstable asset.'

Rykov noted that Churkin referred to only one asset. There was no mention of Anna, who he had also sent to Britain and who, Churkin had whispered to him at the end of an interrogation session a week earlier, had gone to ground. It seemed the colonel general was keen to keep the Volk programme in the realm of myth and secrets.

'Does the major have anything he would like to add by way of explanation for his actions?' Churkin asked, addressing Rykov directly for the first time.

Rykov lowered his eyes to meet Churkin's. The colonel general's face was inscrutable. Rykov didn't know if he expected him to apologise or beg, or if he'd damn himself if he did either.

After a long moment considering his limited options, he spoke. His voice was hoarse and contrite.

'I am sorry that the operation did not achieve its planned outcome,' he said. 'However, though it did not accomplish its ultimate goal, Project Mykl should not be considered a total failure.' He paused briefly as Churkin's eyes narrowed. 'Had it not been for the destabilisation of the Mykl asset by Major Yegerova's good intentions, I believe it would have been a success. It was not, but there is much that can be learned from the operation, and I would humbly ask this committee not to squander the possibilities Project Mykl represents.'

There was another pause as Churkin made a show of looking down the row of silent men to see if Rykov's defence had moved any of them to suddenly want to speak. It hadn't.

'Any one of the things you have admitted would be grounds for the severest disciplinary action,' Churkin said, turning again to Rykov. 'Together they are beyond reckless. Even absolute success would only have inflamed the threats the Soviet Union faces from foreign forces.'

Rykov held his breath, waiting for Churkin to deliver his predetermined sentence.

'However,' the colonel general said, 'the responsibility is not yours alone. This committee finds that Line Z has, since its inception, been given too much licence and, as a department, must be brought under stricter control. Therefore, it will be placed under the direct command of the office of the deputy head of the first chief directorate with immediate effect. In addition, all work connected to Project Mykl will be suspended pending a more thorough review, and you will be demoted to the rank of captain.'

So, Rykov hadn't been doomed. In fact, he'd been saved. Demoted, but not reassigned, court-martialled or sent to Siberia. And Churkin hadn't abandoned him, or Project Mykl – in fact, he wanted it for himself. It would be shut down for a few months, and then, once it and Rykov's supposed transgressions had been forgotten, it'd be quietly reactivated.

There was nothing else to say, except for Churkin to adjourn the tribunal. Rykov bowed his head, keeping his eyes cast down at the floor and a solemn look on his face. It lasted until Churkin and the four other men left the room.

CHAPTER 61

It was a sunny morning at Rabley Heath, and Richard Knox was leaning against the small kitchen counter in the gatehouse, waiting for the kettle to boil as he poured out a saucer of milk. The radio was on, but he wasn't listening to it. Since Wilson had been returned to Downing Street with a healthy majority, the country's broadcasters and commentators had quietened down. Times were still tricky at home and across the Commonwealth, but the news cycle was no longer constantly prophesying the collapse of Britain and her old dominions.

Abey Bennett had also moved on, to another far-flung adventure where Knox was sure she'd once more be the smartest person in whatever situation she found herself.

She'd stayed in London for a week after Kosygin's fateful visit, patching things up further with Knox and assisting MI5 with its hasty inquiry into what had happened – she had, after all, been the one who had stopped Williams by shooting him in the shoulder.

Hugh Hoffman, the CIA London COS, had been forced to bite his tongue and swallow his anger when it became clear his little victory over MI5 had been sacrificed for a much bigger one over Russia that would belong solely to her. And Knox had done nothing to hide his gratitude that she'd been able to do what he couldn't on the airfield at Shoreham Airport.

'That's what we do,' Bennett had said when Knox thanked her for the ninth or tenth time over their now-traditional farewell espressos in Bar Italia.

'The CIA?' he'd asked.

'Friends,' she'd replied.

When Knox had gone back to Kemp House an hour later, he'd found a parting gift from her waiting on his kitchen counter – a triangular glass jar with FOLGERS INSTANT COFFEE CRYSTALS printed on a red label, and a note next to it that read: For use in case of emergency.

Knox opened the window and looked out at Rabley Heath's sprawling grounds. Spring was being kind to them. Wild flowers were pushing their way through the lawns Knox had spent a couple of days the week before getting under control, and the thick, knotty hedges seemed more verdant than overgrown. It felt like life and order were returning to the place at long last.

Knox heard a distant, high drone and looked up into the blue sky just in time to see a tiny plane disappear behind an errant, fluffy cloud. It reminded him of the dream he'd had the night before. He'd been back at Shoreham, it was a long evening in mid-summer, and he was lying on the grass next to the terminal building watching a plane piloted by Williams climb, tumble, and loop through the sky. But instead of being filled with dread over his friend's aerial acrobatics, Knox was overwhelmed by a sense of calm contentment.

As the sound of a jangling bell replaced the plane's propellers, Knox's mind brought him back to reality.

'Stinky,' he called out.

A few moments later the caramel and white cat appeared on the sill, miaowing for a head-scratch and the saucer of milk. Knox gave him both, then poured the boiling water from the kettle into a cafetière of freshly ground coffee, put it on a tray with two mugs, and walked out into the garden.

He crossed the lawn, being careful to avoid the largest wild flowers, and paused in front of one of the big house's drawing-room windows, through which he saw the same sight that had been there every morning for the last week: Jack Williams in a cable-knit jumper, balancing on top of a ladder, repairing a few square inches of his ancestral home. This morning he was chipping away at a broken piece of cornice, the sling his right arm was supposed to be in tossed over the edge of the old sofa, and the bottom of his jumper riding up, revealing the scar tissue that spread across his side.

Knox still hadn't fully processed how it felt to have Williams back, alive, and home at Rabley Heath, and he wasn't sure he ever would. It was incredible, amazing. But, under his elation, worry rumbled.

A few days after an ambulance, fire engine, and several police cars had arrived at Shoreham Airport and Knox, Williams, Bennett, and Holland had been taken back to London, Knox had been sent a report from the doctor who had treated Williams for the bullet Bennett had put in his shoulder. It suggested that he'd been shot at least twice before, had had multiple bones broken and reset, and, at some point, had suffered severe frostbite. It was, in the doctor's opinion, a miracle that the man's body hadn't completely collapsed along with his mind.

The same afternoon Knox had received the doctor's report, he'd gone to see Holland and made several impassioned statements about returning to a more active form of duty, because it was clear that MI5 needed every able-bodied operative doing everything they could to defend the country against a seemingly unshackled KGB.

Holland had turned him down flat.

'You're not ready,' he'd said. 'And this isn't finished.'

Knox was a little affronted, but Holland was right.

The director general wanted to give Williams the rest he so badly needed, in the familiar surroundings of Rabley Heath, with Knox by his side. There were conditions, of course. The primary one being that Williams wouldn't be able to leave. He would be under house arrest, and Knox would be his jailer.

Knox wasn't sure if they'd be the last orders he'd receive from Holland as director general. Now things were calmer, he might be mulling over his retirement again – but Knox hadn't asked, just in case he was. For the same reason, he'd also never questioned whether Holland had been serious when he'd ordered Knox to kill him in Shoreham, or if he'd just been trying to stall Williams and buy some time.

Knox walked through the back door of the house, past its cavernous and non-functioning kitchen, and down a dark, creaking corridor to the drawing room.

'How's it going?' he asked as he stepped through the open door.

'Slowly, but surely,' Williams replied from the top of the ladder.

He looked healthier. His hair was neater and he had more meat on his fused bones, but Knox could still see the haunted shadows in his eyes.

'How's the shoulder?'

'Can't complain. Or at least shouldn't.'

'Coffee's ready.'

'That time already, old man?'

'Afraid so.'

Williams climbed down as Knox took the tray over to a desk next to a half-collapsed fireplace. Knox pushed the plunger on the cafetière and poured the hot, dark liquid into the two cups, then reached into the desk's top drawer and pulled out a leather-bound notepad and Dictaphone. He sat down, turned the machine on, opened the pad, and wrote the day's date at the top of a fresh sheet of paper.

'Where did we get to yesterday?' Williams asked as he picked up his cup and sat opposite Knox.

Knox checked the last page on the pad. 'Minsk.'

This was the other part of Knox's bargain with Holland. He was his best friend's carer, jailer, and interrogator.

For the first few weeks of Williams's incarceration, they'd had regular visits from White and a succession of psychologists who were desperate to work out what combination of drugs, terror, and coercion the KGB had subjected Williams to. White, faced with real, living evidence, had given up his belief that brainwashing was a fantasy and approached his new field of research with his usual zeal.

They'd even had a visit from Laing last week. He'd wanted to tell Knox in person about an old clockmaker who had been killed in his railway arch shop in Shepherd's Bush Market.

Laing had seen a note about the death in a case round-up the Met had sent to MI5 and felt a hunch. It turned out the man's bludgeoned body had been found in a workroom full of bizarre mechanical contraptions and technical drawings, including one of a gunsight and a laser welded together in two hollow tubes. Knox was fairly sure Laing would have earned his place back out in Britain's international domestic intelligence fray by the next time he went up to Leconfield House – whenever that might be.

Now, however, Knox and Williams were mostly left alone to tend to Rabley Heath's overgrown gardens and dilapidated walls in strange, quiet domesticity. And that, despite being what Knox had dreamed of for years, was the source of the concern that had accompanied him to bed every evening and waited for him every morning for the last month.

Williams had agreed to his confinement, and to let his friend pick his way through the ruins of his fractured psyche and broken memories for as long as he needed. But Knox knew there wouldn't be much he could do if Williams changed his mind and left in the dead of night, or if the KGB decided they wanted to stop him cooperating permanently.

Rabley Heath was a sanctuary, but it was also isolated and exposed, and it now felt too large for Knox to protect by himself.

Sometimes he wondered if that was why Holland had suggested this arrangement in the first place. The director general, like the rest of MI5, had started to take the idea of Soviet super-soldiers a lot more seriously, and Knox and Williams made tantalising targets.

Was there an army of Watchers hiding in the rustling bushes that surrounded the estate, keeping a constant eye on them and any unexpected visitors? Knox wasn't sure if that was wishful thinking or not. But, as he did each morning once he'd spied Williams hard at work restoring another small part of his family pile to some shadow of its former glory, he tried his best to shake such dark thoughts from his head so he could focus on helping his best friend with the ones locked up in his.

Both men took long sips of their coffee, savouring the warm bitterness for a calm, quiet moment.

'Where shall we start today?' Williams asked as he leaned back in his chair and cradled his cup in his lap.

'Wherever you want,' Knox replied.

HISTORICAL NOTE

There's a tendency to think of the Cold War as a battle of monoliths. Ideologies that rubbed and pushed against each other like tectonic plates along the Iron Curtain, causing the occasional, devastating earthquake.

Of course, it was actually a little more complicated than that, and sometimes those ideologies weren't so fixed or solid.

This is particularly true of the Soviet Union in the mid-sixties, when the troika of Brezhnev, Kosygin and Podgorny were trying to rule a population who had just experienced a decade of relative social and political openness while also fighting each other for absolute, Stalinistic power.

Things like this made a lot of people both inside and outside Russia very nervous. Paranoid even.

As with my previous novel, *Red Corona*, I've set *A Loyal Traitor* in a version of the real world, and created a story that captures its fears, along with the divided loyalties and grim determination of cold warriors who, at this point in the sixties, have been fighting side by side and against each other for a long time.

It's a story that might have happened. And perhaps one very similar to it really did. Though, I must confess that Nureyev's performance of *Card Game*, at least, is complete fiction.

ACKNOWLEDGEMENTS

Thank you first and always to Chris for being my greatest champion and most constant supporter.

Also to my family and friends for continuing to put up with my never-ending talk of spies and sporadic weekend disappearances.

To my agent, Gordon Wise, for his guidance and for so shrewdly suggesting the idea that became the germ of this story. And to Niall Harman and everyone else at Curtis Brown.

To my editor, Jenny Parrott, for her unwavering enthusiasm and alchemic expertise. And to Margot Weale, Mark Rusher, Molly Scull, Lucy Cooper and the whole team at Point Blank and Oneworld for all the incredible things you do. To Jacqui Lewis for keeping me on the straight and narrow.

Lastly, I'd like to thank all the readers, bloggers, reviewers, librarians and event organisers who reacted so positively to my first novel and made me feel a lot more confident about writing another one.